FUGLY

CLAIRE WALLER

carolrhoda LAB

MINNEAPOLIS

For all those who know their worth,
despite what others tell them

Carolrhoda Lab®
An imprint of Lerner Publishing Group, Inc.
241 First Avenue North
Minneapolis, MN 55401 USA

For reading levels and more information, look up this title at www.lernerbooks.com.

Image credits: 4691/Shutterstock.com (dot pattern); ikolaeva/Shutterstock.com (title lettering).

Main body text set in Janson Text LT Std 10.5/15.
Typeface provided by Linotype AG.

Library of Congress Cataloging-in-Publication Data

Names: Waller, Claire, author.
Title: Fugly / by Claire Waller.
Description: Minneapolis : Carolrhoda Lab, [2019] | Summary: Defined as nothing but fat in the real world, Beth Soames specializes in trolling beautiful girls online until two new friendships, one online and one offline, make her question her behavior.
Identifiers: LCCN 2018043550 (print) | LCCN 2018050561 (ebook) | ISBN 9781541561014 (eb pdf) | ISBN 9781541544994 (th : alk. paper)
Subjects: | CYAC: Overweight persons—Fiction. | Bullying—Fiction. | Online trolling—Fiction. | Conduct of life—Fiction. | Family problems—Fiction.
Classification: LCC PZ7.1.W356 (ebook) | LCC PZ7.1.W356 Fug 2019 (print) | DDC [Fic]—dc23

LC record available at https://lccn.loc.gov/2018043550

Manufactured in the United States of America
1-45463-39691-2/26/2019

ANOMIE:

Social instability resulting from a breakdown of standards and values. Also: personal unrest, alienation, and uncertainty that comes from a lack of purpose or ideals.

1: #THEBEAUTIFULPEOPLE

I'm in the library again. Not the university one, but the big one in town. I prefer this one. The uni one is newer and probably has more relevant texts, but it's full of students, and as a breed, students are pretty boring. All they tend to do is type, text and talk. In contrast, this place is a great place to people-watch. I have to do it surreptitiously, because no one likes to be stared at, but I do like to watch the other humans go about their day and imagine their thoughts: who's writing mental lists, who's imagining everyone without their clothes on, who's falling apart on the inside. The library assistant marches past me, shepherding a group of under-4s to a corner filled with beanbags. Their parents trail behind them with the hopeless expressions of the perpetually knackered. The library assistant is smiling brightly, but I bet she'd like to stove every single one of their little skulls in, the whining little brats. And their parents, too. Unless their parents end up being grateful to them. *Thanks for that, library lady. Little Johnny was doing my fucking head in, too.*

I turn the page of my book. Psychology is infinitely fascinating. There's Freud, who thought everything boiled down to you wanting to fuck your parents. Then there's Jung, who was all about the conscious and unconscious mind and how we're all egotistical dillholes. And Piaget, who developed that whole "stages of cognitive development" stuff. According to most of these guys, we're all barking. I like that. It's comforting, in a way. Doesn't matter what you look like, or what you dress like, you're still mad. Hear that, Jenna Thwaites? We're equal in that at least.

I twiddle my pen. Jenna Thwaites. Haven't thought about her in a long time. She was blonde, with shiny white teeth and a flat stomach. She did yoga. She wore a headband made of little cloth daisies and pretended to be vegan. Even I couldn't deny she was stunning. I remember watching her devour two chocolate frosted cupcakes one lunchtime, whilst I was eating a very limp salad. But no one glared at her. No one told her she'd regret it later. No, it's all perfectly acceptable when you've won the genetic lottery. It's all fine when you can walk it off just by strolling home.

Bitch.

I wonder what she's up to now. At a far better university than me, I bet, probably studying something arty. Or off on a gap year, somewhere exotic, filling Instagram with pictures of her looking impossibly beautiful in tiny bikinis where she is feeding orphans and building homeless shelters. Or maybe she's working in some supermarket where she isn't allowed to wear that stupid daisy headband, yeah, and she's already pregnant and getting fatter and fatter by the day, wondering where it all went wrong. Yeah, that's the one I like. That's the one—

"Hi! Uh, are you reading *Principles of Modern Psychology*?"

I look up. A girl my age smiles widely at me, to the point where her eyes crinkle a little at the corners, but she's probably just being polite. She's tall, with long dark hair pulled into one of those messy buns that are supposed to look deconstructed and carefree but actually take four fucking hours to perfect. Eyes accentuated by perfectly applied black liner, complete with perfect Cleopatra flicks. A kooky little dress and a pair of pink Mary Janes to complete the look. Anyone could see she's gorgeous. I hate her already.

"Yes," I say, slightly guarded.

"Oh, cool. The librarian said so." She lets out an awkward giggle. "Can I have it when you're finished?"

Bat bat bat with the stupid fake eyelashes. Why do some girls feel they have to wear them all the time? It makes them look like they've glued tarantulas to their faces. I spend a delicious moment picturing that, complete with facial devouring, but realize her smile is faltering because I'm probably giving her a weird thousand-yard-stare right now. I clear my throat.

"Oh, uh, yeah. Of course. I was just looking something up, but it's no biggie." I make a pantomime of scribbling down the last line. "There. You can have it."

"Really? You sure? That's sooo awesome of you!" Her smile transforms into a grin, and for a moment, it looks like it might be actually genuine. Maybe uni *is* different. Maybe people will see past the fat, past the ugly, past the whole concept of fugliness. I give her a little nod and a hesitant smile back, and hand the book over.

"Thanks! You're the best," she trills and bounces back to another table across the room. There's a whole gaggle of Beautiful People over there, and I instinctively hunch down in my seat. But hang on—wasn't I just wondering if uni might be different? I mean, she seemed nice. She said thanks. She didn't just take it and tell me to *fuck off, fatty*. I dare to glance over. She's talking in an animated way to her friends, who look over in my direction. One of them, a bloke who looks like he should be in some naff boy band, smirks and wrinkles his nose. And they all laugh.

I know they're laughing at me. Who else do you think they're laughing at? I'm fat, not stupid.

I grab my bag off the floor, but in my haste I've managed to grasp the bottom and I end up tipping its contents out all over the library floor. Bits of paper, old notebooks, pens, sanitary towels, and my emergency candy bar flood out for everyone to see. No one offers to help. They're all too busy staring while I paw at my possessions, stuffing them back into the Bag of Shame whilst my cheeks flame and my eyes burn. I don't bother looking back as I bustle out of the library.

I don't think I'll come here anymore.

♦♦♦

That's something you get used to when you're fugly. The minute a Beautiful Person drops something, others rush to their aid. When a fugly person does it, that's shameful. It's all their fault. It's happened to them because they deserve public humiliation. It's the only way they'll learn. If they're lucky, it might teach them a valuable lesson and they'll try harder *not* to be so fugly, because let's be clear on this: Fugliness is most definitely Your Own Fault, Eat Less Move More, Lifestyle Choice etc. etc. fucking etc.

I trudge down the road, my head tucked in, casting furtive little glances around so I don't accidentally bump into someone. The bus stop's not far, but I'm still breathing heavily. Must sound like a steam engine or an angry cow. But the more I try to control my breathing, the worse it gets until it feels like the air is lava, burning down into my lungs, setting my chest on fire. I need to stop, to sit down, but I can't because there are people here, people who could see, people who love to sneer and judge and hate, so I fight on, my thighs rubbing together, sweat running down my back.

I see it. The bus stop. My savior. Doesn't matter when the bus comes, because all I need is an excuse to sit down, to hide in the corner and gather myself, to—

Oh shit. It's her. The girl from the library. How the hell did she overtake me? What, Beautiful People have Star Trek transporters now? And she's sitting in the middle seat, so I can't perch on the end, pretending I haven't seen her. But I *need* to sit down. My legs are killing me. I pull out my phone: twenty minutes? *Twenty minutes* till the next bus? I can't stand that long. I just can't.

Keep your head down. That's the key. I stuff my earbuds in and crank up some tunes. Something nastily offensive— that always helps act as a repellent. Yeah, I know nobody else can hear it, but I think it helps me exude a *don't fuck with me* attitude. Plus, I can ignore people without looking like a total stuck-up bitch.

I approach the bus stop carefully. The girl is looking at her phone. Good. If she keeps doing that, I might just get away with this. I lean nonchalantly against the shelter and try to ignore the way it groans against my weight. To an outside observer, I'm concentrating on my phone, but I am an expert at covert surveillance; all my attention is on the girl, waiting for her to signal she has seen me. With any luck, she won't and I'll be able to sit down.

She looks up. Damn it! What was that, a minute? No, not even that. As if I needed more evidence that the universe despises me. She glances around herself, the way girls do, to make sure she's safe, or at least as safe as a girl sitting at a bus stop can be. Of course, she spots me.

And she smiles.

"Hey, you're from the library, right?"

Fuck. Can I pretend I haven't noticed her? A bit hard, as she's noticed I was looking at her. I pull one earbud out, and a gunshot crackle of drums floats out into the night.

"What was that?" I say.

"Oh, sorry, shouldn't talk to people on their phones, I know. But I can't help it. You get all your stuff? I hate it when things like that happen. I do it all the time—all my stuff, all over the floor. Mortifying, right? I so felt for you."

Oh, really? Was that after you'd stopped laughing?

She chatters on. "It was really nice of you to let me use that book. I put it on reserve ages ago, but it's always checked out. When they said it was in, I was so relieved. I can't afford to buy myself a copy right now, can you believe it's like eighty quid or something? Tried to get it online, but even those were selling for over thirty, and that was the older editions. I don't know why they make these books so expensive. I mean, we're students, right? How the fuck are we supposed to afford them? So I thought I'd try the library thing, but the uni one has only got, like, three copies or something, which is totes ridiculous, so I went to the town one, which only has one . . . ugh. It's almost enough to make you just bite the bullet and pay the eighty quid, right? So, uh, yeah. Thanks. You saved my ass. I can write the essay now. Yay!"

She gives me an expectant look, but I'm still stunned by her apparent ability to speak without having to breathe. Her smile falters a bit, and I plaster one on my face, remembering too late that smiling = chins.

"Um, it's okay. I've already written my essay."

"Oh, wow! You have? It's, like, seven thousand words long. How did you do it so quickly?"

"Uh, I'm a quick writer. Plus, I like to get things done and out of the way. Don't have to worry about them then."

"Oh, that's sooo good of you. I can't do that—I'm, like, procrastination central. There's always something more interesting to do . . ."

And off she goes again. It must be her superpower or something, because she never pauses, doesn't even check to see if I'm still listening. I reckon I could die right here, right now, and she'd still carry on talking. I'm kind of in awe of her, if I'm honest. But now she's looking at me expectantly again. Hell, did she ask me a question? Oh bugger, oh, fuck . . .

"Well? Where's your digs? I haven't seen you around . . ." She leaves the question trailing, and I have no choice but to answer.

"I don't have digs here," I say, cringing. Can I really admit that I'm living at home?

"Ah, you're still with your folks, right? Wise move. Rents are so ridiculous—my dad says that when he was a student, you could get digs for, like, twenty quid a week, but not anymore! So expensive. I totally don't blame you for living at home. Every penny helps, huh?"

"Uh, yeah." Well, what else am I supposed to say?

A distant chugging heralds the arrival of a bus. I try not to lift my eyes to the heavens in thanks and praise.

"Oh, it's the 21A—are you getting the 21A, too?"

I was going to, but not now.

"No. The 4," I say, and try to look disappointed.

"That's a shame. Well, I'll see you tomorrow."

"Tomorrow?"

"Yeah—tomorrow's lecture, silly. I'll look for you." She smiles again and her whole face lights up. She is ridiculously pretty, and unless all of this is some kind of weird, sadistic long-game thing, she's also very nice. I'm not used to nice. I offer her as bright a smile as I can manage, remembering the chins thing this time, and try not to screw my eyes up too much. Be brave, young Beth. Remember, this was the idea. New life. New friends. New you. Say yes instead of no and all that jazz.

"Yeah. Okay."

"I'm Amy, by the way. Amy Hardcastle."

"Um, Beth Soames."

Fuuuck. Why did I do that? At least give her a pseudonym so she can't look me up— No. Stop it. Outside life is not like Online life. People don't look you up and troll you in Outside life. Well, except when they do, but remember: Uni is a chance to do things differently. So, do things differently!

"Cool! Catch you later! Look me up online!" she calls as she jumps on the bus and flashes her pass at the driver, like something out of a perfume advert.

And then she's gone, leaving me very confused indeed.

2: #DESPICABLEME

Brat's not home when I get in. That's probably a good thing. He's been bunking off school again, but Mum still won't punish him. It drives me mental. I suffered at school, but she still made me go. When it comes to Bratley, though? Nah, he can do what he likes. Fucking favoritism.

"Mum?" I call.

Nothing.

I unzip my coat slowly. The house is cold. Mum can't afford to put the heating on unless it's absolutely freezing outside, and even then, it's only on in short bursts. Right now, it's jumpers and blankets weather.

I try again. "Mum?"

"I'm here," she says and lets out an almighty barrage of coughs. I close my eyes and count to ten.

"You all right?"

"Yeah, well, maybe. I could do with some help."

I dump my bag by the front door and trudge into the living room. Mum's sitting there on the sofa, wrapped up in an old crocheted blanket. Dark circles ring her eyes.

"Hey love," she says. "Good day? Get lots done?"

I nod and perch myself next to her. I'll stay for a bit, just to be polite. Oh, don't get me wrong, I do love my mum. But sometimes I could do without all *this*. The tired smiles and the aches and the pains and the *ooh, love, could you just*s. I know she needs looking after. I know she has issues. I respect that. But I have issues too, and all I ever get is "exercise is the best remedy!" Get outside. Don't eat cake. Think positive. Every. Single. Time.

She asks me about uni, and I give her a bare-bones reply. She's not really all that interested—the only thing she seems to be able to concentrate on nowadays is this pain she is supposed to be in, so she doesn't ask me to elaborate, which is fine by me. I don't tell Mum about Amy, but despite myself, I can't help but wonder if I'll see her again.

Mum mumbles about how the doctor's going to up her Amitriptyline prescription to help her sleep, to go on top of all the other medication she needs to help her function, oh, and could I be a dear and pick that up for her tomorrow, yes, it was done over the phone because she couldn't get out, too much pain.

Too much avoidance, more like. I sometimes wonder if this whole "phantom pain" thing is more about hiding something deeply psychologically broken within her. Maybe that's why I joined my course. To understand my own mother.

I just nod, like usual. She smiles weakly at me, a smile I know so well. I get up and make her a cup of tea. She acts surprised when I give it to her, like I've never done it before. Bit bloody rich, if you ask me.

I could stay longer, but I've got some unfinished business to attend to.

◆◆◆

My heart flutters painfully as I log in to my laptop and click my email. I dropped an absolute humdinger online this morning, and the anticipation of the backlash feels a bit like Christmas.

And there it is. Fifty-seven notifications, no doubt every one of them either hating my guts or worshipping me as a goddess. This is better than sex. Or so I think, not that I have any experience in that particular field. All I know is this makes me tingle all over in a mightily delicious way. I hover the cursor over the first message, drinking in the excitement.

You fucking bitch!

Oh yeah. That's the good stuff. Why yes, I do get off on it, thank you for obliging! I lap up every insult, every *lol!!*, every accusation of trolling.

THIS. IS. THE. LIFE.

3: #UNDERTHEBRIDGE

So just in case you were in any doubt: I am an internet troll.

Yes, I know what you're thinking. A troll? *Really?* After all your complaints about being judged? You spend most of your life seeking the approval of others, but you go online with the express intention of shaming people? And to that, I say yes, yes again, uh-huh, and I know it sounds mad but yes.

I am not alone. No one ever admits to trolling, despite it being everywhere. And don't get me wrong, if I was with a big group I'd deny it too, but here, I'll admit it freely. I am a troll. And despite the fact that I've only been at it a few months, I'm a good one, too. It's fun. I take an awful lot of pleasure smacking down people who, in real life, have everything. Y'see, I specialize in trolling those girls who like to take way too many selfies, in far too little clothing. I mean, what do they expect? Mass adoration? Stupid little tramps have it coming, if you ask me.

Oh, don't look like that. Wondering why I do it. Thinking I should show some empathy. No one shows me any empathy when they see me walking down the street. No one's kind to me when they realize I can't wear the latest fashions because they're all designed for rakes. No one gives me a free pass when they see me eating my lunch. Oh no, it's all *fat bitch* and *look at the state of it* and *it should be illegal to make me watch that*, right at me—not words on a screen, but speech, right into my ears, into my brain, scorching itself onto my very soul. I've been branded by that word. FAT. That's all I am now in the real world. No one cares that I like drawing, that I'm good with animals, that I have an eye for taking good photos. No one's interested in my strengths. Because the minute they have to see the whole person and not just the squishy, wobbly outer coverings, they're forced to realize that I'm just like them, with thoughts and feelings and hopes and dreams, and that the weight of their hatred is slowly crushing those things out of me.

So yeah, I like trolling. It's payback, baby.

On the internet, I can be anyone. At first, I joined a couple of art sites, tried posting my drawings, but I was largely ignored. I got four, maybe five likes if I was lucky—which, compared to the five hundred likes other artists got for bad sketches of scantily-clad anime characters, is pretty atrocious. But with trolling, people pay attention. I can sit in my room and play virtual dress-up to my heart's content. No one knows the real me. People ask, but I'll never tell. The minute I tell, the spell will be broken.

Right now, I'm about twelve different people. I've had to write all my alter egos down, just so I can keep track of them all. It's tremendous fun. I like the sense of control, the power that it brings. You can trap people, play with them the way a cat might with a cornered mouse. In real life, I'm the mouse, but in the digital world, I'm the cat, and woe betide anyone scurrying into my realm, because believe me, I have claws.

I'm currently tormenting a couple of wannabe starlets on YouTube. Since YouTube is already a cesspool of scum and villainy, it means I can really let rip. I'm tag-teaming myself right now, using sockpuppet accounts, and the page views are racking up. Those stupid bitches should be thanking me, if anything. Without me and my alter egos, they'd still be on three likes. Okay, so now they probably struggle to sleep after all the bile I've stirred up, but hell, that's a small price to pay for their coveted internet fame. If they didn't want to be told that their over-tanned asses looked like two oiled-up pigs trying to get out of a hammock, they shouldn't have pasted those stupid twerking videos in the first place—

My laptop pings. Oh, no. What's this? A DM? This is the only time I worry. Not a lot, because it's usually just someone telling me to lay off whatever bitch I'm savaging at the time— or someone trying to turn the tables on me. The delete button is my best friend in these situations—it's no fun to fight a *private* insult war. And engaging over DM would somehow feel more personal, make me more vulnerable. Even though I have twelve layers of armor (and counting) between me and the real world, I do harbor this little fear that one day, someone is going to pierce all of them and draw blood.

Hey

Yeah, they all start like that. Should I click? Or should I just delete? I should probably just delete. Mustn't tempt fate.

My finger hovers over the dustbin icon, but I don't press it. I don't really believe in premonitions or any of that new-agey bullshit, but something's telling me this one is different. I don't know why, or what it is. Call it curiosity.

I click the link.

Hey
Brutal takedown. Love it. You really have some claws.

Just thought you should know.
Ninjanoodle471

Right. Okay. That's . . . unexpected. I've had people agreeing with me before, but they usually do it on the thread, not in a DM. My spidey-senses are all over the place. Is this a trap? It feels like a trap. I kind of want to back out, but good old curiosity is getting the better of me. Who is this person? What do they want? Because everybody wants something. Altruism doesn't exist on Planet Internet. So what's Ninjanoodle471's angle? The downfall of MidnightBanshee? Should I tag-team them with one of my sockpuppet accounts? Or would that be showing too much of my hand? They might even realize it was a sockpuppet, and then they could out me in two seconds flat.

No. Leave it.

I know what you're thinking. When did I get this paranoid? Yeah, well, take away the armor and I'm just Fat Beth again. And I don't want to be Fat Beth here, the one place where I feel some measure of control, some iota of respect. I am a warrior here, chaotic evil to the bone.

I click out of the message without answering.

Downstairs, the front door slams, which means Brat's home. Oh, joy. Younger brothers are such dickheads.

Another clatter, this time from the kitchen. Mum must be trying to make dinner. An all-too-familiar queasiness twists my guts, one that makes me log out of my many and varied accounts. Online I may be a monster, but in real life, I can't watch my mother struggle.

I heave myself off my bed and try to tiptoe downstairs. Bratley's in his bedroom now, killing something in a video game. It's kind of all he does now.

As predicted, Mum's in the kitchen, wrestling with a tin opener. Her eyes are bright with unshed tears. I sigh. Same routine every day. Something out of a tin, Mum crying. It's times like this when I really despise my dad. He ditched Mum when he found a younger model, and now it's all sports cars and holidays for him while we—

No. I take in a deep, cleansing breath. Can't go there now. Getting angry about Dad won't do any good. Not when Mum needs my help. I gently take the tin opener and free the chopped plum tomatoes myself.

"What were you thinking of making?" I ask, mainly out of a need to say something.

Mum shrugs. "I'm—I'm not sure," she quavers. "There's tuna in the cupboard."

I hold in a sigh. There's *always* tuna in the cupboard—it's the one source of cheap protein that doesn't go off. Mum stumbles back to the living room, and I manage to turn the tuna and tomatoes into a pasta bake.

Carbs for the win.

4: #MIDNIGHTBANSHEE

After dinner I go back upstairs, feeling stuffed and loathsome. And yet, my secret stash is calling, so I help myself to a Mars bar. I love the way the wrapper splits, revealing that smooth chocolate underneath, and then beneath that, the fluffy, weird stuff that shouldn't work but IS OH SO GOOD, and the sticky caramel that coats my mouth with sweetness . . . oh yeah. I lick my fingers. Hello, sugar, my secret lover and my only friend.

Well, not quite my only friend. I crank up my laptop again—I don't dare look at my sockpuppets on my phone, as I'm not sure how the proxies I've set up would cope; the last thing I need is my identity being plastered all over a revenge subreddit.

There are only a few replies to my latest posts; I think I'll let them stew for a bit while I stalk around my favorite horror fiction site. It's kind of a halfway house for me; if the story is good, then I'm as happy to spend a half hour being weirded out as the next person. If it's crap, then I get to spend a half an hour smushing some hopeful's soul into dust. It's a win-win situation.

Another DM awaits me. My heart does that little flutter as I click on it.

It's Ninjanoodle471 again.

Awesome takedowns. So impressed. Inbox me?
Tori

Uh, excuse me? *Tori?* Complete amateur. No one gives their real name, not even in a DM. We Warriors of Internet Chaos are kind of like superheroes in a way—our secret identity must, at all cost, remain a secret, or we'll lose our powers because every fucker would block us and, if we're really unlucky, call the police to prosecute us for hate crimes. (I mean, seriously? Hate crimes? I said you looked like mutilated potato and I hope that something repeatedly runs you over. It's not as if I'm threatening to stalk your kids and gut them with a rusty hook, and even if I did, for fuck's sake, ever heard of something called hyperbole? I know it's a long word, but feel free to look it up, you self-obsessed moron.)

Unless Tori is a pseudonym. "Tori" could be using it to lure me into a sense of false security. That's what I would do. Okay, maybe I'm beginning to like the way this person thinks.

I gnaw on a nail. It still smells vaguely of chocolate. The message sits in my inbox, taunting me. Should I really respond? In the past, I've just deleted everything that came my way, but I dunno—this one feels different somehow. No insults, and more importantly, no gushing. You can always tell the ones who are fishing for info—they gush in the hopes you'll spill. Maybe I'll just give them a *thanks.* Either they'll go away or they'll reveal something. I'm pretty confident of that.

Thanks
MidnightBanshee

A few moments pass.

You're welcome.

You're vicious. I like that.

Tori

Hmm. Spidey-senses tingling again. Still feels like a trap. I delete the DM. Better to be safe than sorry.

Off to Instagram now to see what needs nudging. Interesting—one of the accounts I was working on has exploded. Someone calling themselves Teenytiny42 is not just agreeing with me, they're helping me build a massive empire of dirt, and they're dumping it all over one of those vegan health guru-types. It's actually quite glorious to behold this level of sophisticated shit-stirring. MidnightBanshee approves. Maybe SharkKrawler9 will also approve. Might stir the pot a bit and make FlounceyPouncey hate it all—you know, defend the vegans for a bit, just to really bring out the hate . . .

Another DM pops up.

I knew you'd like that.

Tori

Teenytiny42 is also Tori? Okay, that deserves a smile. This girl is *good*.

Lol

And that's all she's getting for now.

5: #D1CKLE55WONDER

Tori tries to engage me a few more times, but I'm not falling for it. She does seem pretty fun, though. We tag-team a bunch of morons on Reddit, and by the end, I'm actually crying with laughter. Yeah, it's cruel, but it feels so good, and to have someone on your side makes it all the sweeter. I haven't reached for a second Mars bar all evening, which is a first. Maybe having Tori around might be a good idea after all.

Around nine, I go downstairs to get a drink. Mum is mindlessly watching some crappy police procedural on TV. She gives me a sluggish smile when I enter the living room and doesn't even try to hide the glass. I try not to frown. She knows she shouldn't drink, given her medication. But, hey, who am I to judge? I shouldn't chain-eat chocolate, but I do. Whatever gets you through the day, right?

I sit with Mum until she starts dozing off. I take the glass from her hand, cover her with her blanket, and go into the kitchen. Dirty dishes festoon every surface.

"Brad!"

I pause.

"Bradley!"

No answer. Not even a grunt. I stomp to the bottom of the stairs.

"Bradley! Mum said you were supposed to do the dishwasher!"

As per usual, a "Fuck off!" floats out of Brat's room.

Every step I take up the stairs reverberates around the house. There's no lock on his bedroom door. Back in the day, Mum and Dad wouldn't have it—*In our house, we have an open door policy*, like we were a business rather than a family. I don't bother knocking, just burst into his room.

"Bradley, Mum said—oh for fuck's sake." I try to cover my eyes with my hands, but too late. "You know you shouldn't be watching that—"

"Beth! Fuck off! Just fuck off! Get the fuck out!"

He flings a stained pillow at me. I manage to duck just before it hits me.

"Yeah, well, I don't care. You've got to do the dishwasher. Mum said. Unless you want me to tell her you're too busy watching porn to help her?"

He gives me a really filthy look, the kind of look only a fourteen-year-old seems to be able to pull off. I know threatening to tell Mum is a low blow, especially given how unable she is to actually deal with the situation, but what choice do I have? I'm not going to wait on him hand and foot.

"You've got half an hour. If you don't, I'll text Dad and tell him, too."

Brat's face turns stony, and inside, I feel a little lift. Pulling out the big guns. Aww yeah.

Mum's the blackmail, but Dad's the real threat; despite his shitty parenting (or lack of parenting, to be more precise), Brat worships our father and I know exactly how to exploit that.

After he stomps off to the kitchen, I linger a moment. It feels weird, being in here. Years ago, Brat and I were always in and out of each other's rooms, half playing, half deliberately annoying each other. Not anymore. Now we're strangers living under the same roof.

I pick up his tablet and resume the clip he's been watching. It's pretty tame, to be honest. I've seen worse on 4Chan. Still fills me with revulsion, though. Revulsion . . . and something else, something pink and quivery. Were those girls coerced into doing that, I wonder? What would it be like to have that done to you? To do it to someone else? I shake my head, turn the clip off, and fling the tablet back on his bed. It stinks in here. Remind me to make him open his windows in the morning.

I don't bother going back downstairs to check on him. Doing that would just lead to an argument and blah, blah, blah, so I wander back to my room. I'm a bit ashamed to admit that I'm wondering if Tori's messaged me again. I mean, I know it's weird—I shouldn't care!—but it feels kind of good to have someone in your corner.

Yep. There she is. A DM is waiting for me, with one word in it.

D1ckle55wonder

Curious, I fire up Instagram and sure enough, there's D1ckle55wonder, causing absolute chaos. The handle makes people think it's an ironic name for a teenaged boy, and she's playing that persona to a tee. I'm amazed at how well she handles it—and I find myself feeling glad she's on my side. With it comes a little twinge of doubt. Maybe all of this is too good to be true. Am I being trolled? Maybe Tori is really good at this. Maybe she's better than I am—

Nope. I can't think like that. I am an undisputed queen

when it comes to this kind of shit. More like she's seen what I'm capable of and wants to be on my good side. Yeah. That makes much more sense. All Hail Queen MidnightBanshee. And Queen SharkKrawler9. And King FlounceyPouncey. And . . .

More pings. Another DM is waiting. The twinge has gone now; I think I'm actually excited to see what Tori has to say. She's praising me for how I set those morons up. I can feel her enthusiasm rolling off the screen. She's really enjoying herself, and it's all thanks to me.

I know it sounds weird, but that actually feels pretty good. I give her another lol, but that's it. Well, no point in being too eager, eh? If there's one thing porn has taught me, it's the importance of playing hard to get.

6: #YAY

I fall asleep halfway through a message. How fucked up is that? Luckily, I've programmed everything to auto–log out if I don't type for a length of time. Others might find that annoying, but for me it means I don't get my accounts mixed up, because that would quite literally be the end of the world for me.

I've slept through my alarm, so I don't have time to check in and see what havoc Tori has wrought in my illustrious name. Instead, I shower and get dressed as quickly as I can. Not only because it's cold, but because that way, I don't run the risk of seeing myself naked in the mirror. That's not a good way to start the day. I'm really hoping that one day soon, someone will invent a bot that can help you put your makeup on. Then I might not need to look in the mirror at all.

I grab a fiver from the pot Mum keeps for petty cash and buy some breakfast from the corner shop on my way to the bus stop. I scarf down the sausage roll and stuff the crisps and chocolate deep into my bag. I'll eat those later, probably in the loo, where no one can see me.

The bus is crowded with people avoiding each other's eyes, scared that someone might engage them in conversation, try to make some kind of human connection. Most of them pull out their phones and focus on those. Others stare mindlessly out the window. I choose my phone. Because my proxies are banished from my phone, I don't have much in the way of messages. Two notifications from that stupid self-help forum I joined in a moment of weakness. Some inevitable spam. Nothing else.

I delete all the messages, and my inbox is once again empty. Clean. Pure. Next I scroll through some trashy celebrity gossip site. I love it; these people are just as vicious as me, except they get paid to do it. I wonder if I should switch my course to gutter journalism. I'd be ace at it. I wouldn't need to stand in front of a camera—I'd be just another faceless jumble of letters and numbers on a screen, a professional troll saying whatever I liked and earning cold hard cash while doing so.

And people wonder why the internet has taken over the world.

Twenty to nine. Come on, hurry up. We've been caught up in roadworks, and now I am running dangerously close to late. I can't do late. Late means entering the lecture hall when everyone else has already sat down. Late means a sarcastic quip from the professor running the session. Late means everyone turns and stares.

Can't be too early, either. Got to be just right on time, that sweet spot when everyone is moving, worrying about themselves—can I get that seat I like, have I got my notebook, oh shit my favorite pen is running out, just three more hours and then I can drown my sorrows at the student union bar . . . No one has time to notice me. Even with my dumpiness, I am invisible, and it is wondrous.

At ten to nine, the bus slides into the stop. Luckily, the building my lecture is held in isn't too far away. I hike my bag higher up onto my shoulder, keep my head down, and power on. By the time I reach the end of the road, my heart is hammering and my face feels like it's going to explode. An uncomfortable trickle of sweat tracks its way down my back. I hate the winter. You have to wear a coat because it's cold, and there's the ever-present threat of rain, but when you're fugly, moving means you get hot real quick. Maybe I should get one of those blanket things to wrap myself up in. Or a poncho. They sell them in Primark, so they're quite socially acceptable now. Only problem, I fear I may look even more like a Weeble in one of those. Ahh, the cardinal sin of Making Yourself Look Bigger Than You Already Are. Believe me, it's easy to do, and as soon as the universe notices, it'll never let you forget that.

A bell chimes in the distance. Nine now, and I'm still a street away. Buggerbollocksballs, fuck, fuck, fuck. I need to pick up the pace, but I'm in danger of The Wheeze now, and my back feels like eels are crawling all over it. Stupid road-works! Ten minutes to get through them. Ten minutes!

No. Mustn't dwell. It's happened. Get to lectures. Just keep going. At last, the corner—and there, the stairs leading up to the building. Usually when people think of university build-ings, they think of great Baroque things, all crenulations and limestone slabs, with massive sets of sweeping stairs. The stairs here are three steps that lead to a nondescript pair of double doors. I could be entering a job center. Still, I'm grateful. Three steps are far more manageable than a sweeping staircase, espe-cially when you've been made to run for two whole blocks.

Still quite a few people milling around. Good. Good. If I can just tag myself on to the edge of the group—

"Oh my God! Beth? Hi! Remember me? I met you in the library yesterday!"

The sweat on my back turns cold. I turn around, slowly. Amy's standing there with a huge grin on her face, dressed like she fell into a Japanese comic book store display stand. The only thing she's missing is a flaming katana.

"Oh. Yeah. Amy, isn't it? Hi," I say weakly.

"I wondered if I might see you again. Normally I go in with the others, but today I thought I'd wait. And here you are. Yay!"

Yay? Seriously? What is she? Twelve? Still, I can't pretend I'm not flattered. Twice in two days, people have actually seemed genuinely pleased to see me; Amy, then Tori . . . maybe my luck *is* changing. Maybe things will be different now.

Someone shoves past me, tutting, giving me that particular filthy look reserved only for those of us who err on the side of Socially Unacceptable. No, nothing's changed. Tori wants to be my friend because she doesn't know the real me, and Amy is being nice because she's obviously suffered from some kind of brain injury, which leaves her permanently happy and with the temperament of an excited puppy.

"Come on! We'll be late!" she trills and skips up the steps. I galumph after her.

7: #LIFEINTHEBACKROW

This is where life gets difficult. You see, I'm a back row sitter. Not because I'm a rebel, but because I'm a hider. I can squirrel myself away, out of sight amongst the snoozers and the doodlers and the latecomers, safe in the shadows.

Amy, on the other hand, is a mingler. She's not in the front row as that's reserved for nerds and suckups, but somewhere in the middle, where the wannabes reside. Not the cool kids—no, they inhabit that elite section that isn't *quite* the middle, but also isn't *quite* the back, so they can participate in the lecture if they want to, or doss off if the mood takes them—but those who like to hover around the cool kids' edges in the hopes that they might be mistaken for one of them.

"Sit here! Sit here!"

Jesus Christ, she's like something out of a children's TV program; all bounce, bright colors, and cute voices. A couple of her friends look up and give her a slightly incredulous look. Yeah, I know. You and me both . . .

Clutching my bag strap, I shuffle nervously down the steps toward the middle. The rows look horribly tight down here. I'm going to have to ask some people to move so I can squeeze past. My irrational fear of breaking wind in someone's face floats to the surface of my mind. I mean, it's never happened, but what if it did? I can see the clickbait now. *Fat girl farted in my face when trying to squeeze past me! What happened next will shock you!*

"Sorry. Sorry. Sorry. Can I just . . . ? Oh, sorry. Sorry. I'm so sorry." I only have to move past two people, but I can't stop apologizing. Finally, I sit down next to Amy, who picks up a pen with a fluffy bauble on the end, because what else would she write with. In turn, I try to drag my notebook out of my bag without elbowing someone and fail miserably.

"Sorry," I whisper again. They shoot me another filthy look and snort.

What's that phrase? Oh, yeah. *Liberate tutemet ex inferis.* Save yourself from hell. Or something like that, anyway.

8: #BIGBUTTS

Another one of my irrational fears is that, with my ass being so big, I'm going to get stuck in a chair. It's why I never go on rides at theme parks. ("Madam, sorry, we're going to have to ask you to leave the ride as our safety belts do not go up to 'elephant.'")

Right now, that fear is running gleefully through me. It sprints down my spine to give my paranoia a good kicking and then off it goes again, trying to make my leg jiggle nervously. Dr. Grindle is droning on about the Seven Founding Principles, and whilst I am taking notes so I don't stand out, I already know all this due to the fact that I have done what I thought university students should do and actually read the recommended reading list over the summer.

Next to me, Amy's head is bent, her tongue poking out of her mouth as she scribbles down illegible notes. Her handwriting is exactly as I'd expect—all big loops and little hearts instead of dots above her i's and j's—and I realize there is something heartbreakingly adorable about her. She's a study all in herself, and I can't help but wonder why she's acknowledging my existence, let alone speaking to me. Before university, back at school, she would have been one of the airheads, all pink bubbles and pinup boy bands. Or maybe one of the anime kids, with her Hello Kitty earrings and her Totoro T-shirt. But here, she's sitting with me, and not only is she sitting with me, she *chose to do so*. Maybe this is it. Maybe this is the universe calling. Maybe she's the proof that life is now changing. Maybe I am a curvy diva rather than just another fat chick. Maybe—

My thoughts stop dead in their tracks as a horribly familiar sensation prickles over me. I glance past Amy and catch one of her pop diva friends looking at me, her top lip curled back into a sneer.

And that's when I realize that no, things aren't different. There might be the odd individual who could see past the flab, and even then that might be pushing it. For all I know, Amy is one of those girls who specializes in pity cases. The chances of her actually liking me for me are astronomically small, if you think about it. She doesn't even know me yet; how is she supposed to like me? Maybe I am nothing more than a project. Or is that just the paranoia talking? Well, whatever it is, I think it's on to something.

When the lecture finishes, I desperately want to dart off, but I can't because I'm trapped. My fear of getting stuck in a seat hasn't literally come to pass, but the two people I had to push past to sit down have to be the sloooowest people in the world when it comes to packing up, and so I'm stuck here, clutching my bag like a shield, hunkering down and hoping no one notices me. Amy, on the other hand, is sitting right up, gaily chucking stuff in her (can you guess?) pink backpack, chatting merrily with her other friends. Finally, the two slow coaches between me and sweet, sweet freedom leave, and I get into the aisle as quickly as I can, hoping Amy won't notice and I can sidle off.

No such luck.

"Hey, Beth?" Amy says. "We're going up to the union to grab an early lunch. You wanna come? They do fab chips there."

Right now, I'm not sure if she's being serious or taking the piss. Yes, I'm fat and therefore I must love fried potato strips. I get it. Ha ha. Judging by the way her two friends smirk, they get it too. I feel my cheeks heat up.

"Nah, it's okay. I have things to do," I mumble.

Yeah, like eat, the faces of her friends retort.

"Aww. That's a shame." Amy looks crestfallen and for a split second, I feel wretched, like I've kicked a puppy. "Are you sure you won't come? Nicki and Carla won't mind." She turns to Nicki and Carla. "You two don't mind, do you?"

Nicki and Carla share a look that says yes, they would mind, but it's obvious Amy doesn't see it. Instead, she looks hopefully at me.

"I'm sorry. I'd love to, but my mum's ill and I said I'd come home straight after lectures." Only a partial lie. "Sorry."

"Oh no! Your mum's ill? That sucks! Hope it's not too serious. My mum was ill recently, and that was no fun at all. She was in the hospital and everything—" She catches herself and grins nervously. "Look, give me your number." She whips out her phone before I have a chance to say anything.

I'm trapped. There's no excuse that doesn't make me look like a total snotty bitch, so I fumble my phone out of my bag and duly punch her number into my contacts while she does the same to mine. Her grin brightens, and we all say our goodbyes: Amy's enthusiastic, Nicki and Carla's relieved, mine suitably muted.

Before I reach the door, Amy yells out, "Beth? Friend me!" and my phone buzzes.

Amy Hardcastle. Find me online! ☺ *<3 xxxx*

Fucking hell.

9: #FAMILYCIRCLE

"Oi! Ever heard of Slimfast?"

As insults go, it's pretty tame. I still cringe, though. It's ingrained in me, and I wonder yet again why I bother venturing outside. Outside belongs to the Beautiful People. Any TV show will tell you that. It's a universal truth. Except I can't spend all my life in my house. I know how that turns out. People start asking awkward questions and make assumptions about your mental state. I wonder if it'll get easier once I get my driving license. Maybe that's like taking a little bit of lovely, safe Inside with you, like armor against the world. But having a driving license involves driving lessons, and the thought of those just makes me want to pull my duvet over my head and refuse to come out, which kind of defeats the whole damn object.

I wonder if Amy is enjoying herself with her friends, with their sour, scrunched-up faces, eating soggy student union chips. Yeah, I dodged a bullet there. Much better to go home and do some internet bashing. That's much nicer than dealing with real flesh-and-blood people.

Mum's in the living room again, huddled in her blanket, staring at the TV. Upstairs I hear the staccato of virtual guns— sounds like Brat is eschewing his education in favor of blasting his enemies to bits again.

"Hey, Mum," I say. Slowly, she looks up at me. Her eyes look red.

"Hello darling," she says. "Good lecture?"

"Yeah." I'll leave it at that. She doesn't need to know about Amy. It'll only get her hopes up. "Is Brad still at home?"

"Yes. He said he didn't feel well."

"Mum—"

"I know, I know. I just couldn't stand the arguments." Her voice thickens. "Don't start anything with him."

It takes everything I've got not to stomp upstairs and drag the little prick out of his festering hole and into school myself.

Ever since Dad left, it's been difficult. The last thing Mum needs is Brat playing the nightmare teenager card. I mean, I wasn't perfect, but he's taking the absolute piss. Sometimes I'd like to grab him by his badly shaved and spotty teenaged neck and just . . . squeeze. Squeeze all the bullshit out of him, all the spite, all the self-important crap until there's nothing left.

"You want a cup of tea?" I ask Mum.

"That would be nice, love." And she goes back to staring at the TV. I'm pretty sure she's seen this episode before. I know I have. Oh well. Whatever makes her happy.

As per usual, the kitchen is a mess. The least Brat could have done was wash up his breakfast bowl, but even that's too much of a chore for him. I squash down the urge to pick up the bowl so I can smash his face into it. Yeah, I know, I really should watch these violent thoughts, but I can't help it. Everything Brat does pushes those buttons right now.

Once the tea's made, I amble back to Mum. She's half dozing now. I'm sure it's the medication she takes, and not that she's simply lost the will to do anything since Dad left. I don't say anything to her as I set the mug down. Best leave her. Leave it.

Leave everything. It's the key to a happy life.

Back in my room, I close the curtains, making it all cozy and womb-like. I feel safe in here. Some of my best drawings adorn the wall, and on my shelf there are a couple of old My Little Ponies that I can't bear to part with for some reason. There's also a pile of dirty laundry in the corner, but I'll sort that out later.

I log into my various socks, and there are all the lovely messages of hatred and spite, lined up for me to shoot down at my leisure. My heart's going like the clappers, pumping lovely adrenaline around my body, lighting up my pleasure centers like a fireworks display. These people think they're punishing me, but they're wrong. They don't know me. They don't know that I tried the nice route, that I used to fawn over the Beautiful People—and that my only reward was to be ignored. It didn't take me long to realize the only real difference between these girls and me was their looks. In fact, most of them are as dumb as a bag of rocks, but who cares when you've got abs and boob implants? So much for your personality being the thing that counts.

Anyway, one day, I lost it. Called them all fake, dumb bitches—and I arrived. There it was: all the attention I've ever wanted. Sure, a lot of it was negative, and at first I felt awful, but it didn't take long for me to get over that and see that all the comments, both good and bad, were reactionary, and therefore *I could control them*. I could play my pipes and make the internet dance to any tune I wished. So I did. And it was *awesome*. Okay, I'm pretty sure this is how most supervillains start off, but I'm down with that. I'd rather be laughing with the Joker than righteous with Batman any day of the week.

There's another DM from Tori. Much to my surprise, my heart gives one big thump when I notice it and my hands go a bit shaky as I open it. Gosh, this is new. This feels different from the hate mail. This is . . . something else. Something unexpected.

Was I actually looking forward to her message?

Hey—been following your trail of destruction . . . you are the Mistress of Chaos! Anyway, I thought you might appreciate this. Cheered me up after the shit day I've had.

Interesting. Judging by that, she's in my time zone. That means she could be in the UK. I squirrel that bit of info away, more out of habit than anything else. You never know when you might need some ammo, and every little thing counts.

She's attached a short YouTube clip of various cats sitting on various Roombas. I've seen it before, but it's still cute. I wonder why she sent it to me.

Lol, flattery will get you everywhere.
Thanks for the vid. It's cute.
Soz to hear you've had a bad day.

I know it sounds naff, but I have no idea what else to say.

Flattery will get me everywhere, huh??
I might hold you to that one day!
Are you on Metachat? We could talk there.

Metachat is supposed to be this super-encrypted place, where people can talk about all manner of things without being kicked off. Heard really dodgy things about it. Not quite Dark Web, but getting there. I've never joined; I've never really had anyone to communicate with via it before.

But now I do. And I am very tempted.

Maybe I should just make an account and have a little wander around first? See how it works. Tori hasn't supplied a link and it won't turn up on any browser search, but I'm pretty confident I can find it. I'm not a hacker—Jesus Christ, no, those guys are way geekier than me—but I've flirted on the outskirts of the more forbidden parts of the net before. Just was ultimately too chicken to take the plunge.

Well, now I'm a few months older and a whole lot wiser than when I started trolling. Oh yeah. Rock 'n' roll. I can do this.

It takes me about half an hour to locate the Metachat server. You might think that "Metachat" is a bit of a naff name, but what else are they going to call it? Doillegalstuffhereyou don'twantpeopletofindoutabout.com? The whole point is that it's nondescript. A little part of me is grumbling about how I've spent valuable trolling time doing this and how I don't really know anything about this Tori person; they could be a fifty-year-old trucker called Trevor for all I know, but in a way, that just makes all of this more exciting. I'm taking a risk. My hands are shaking and I'm sweating like a pig, but I feel wonderful. I haven't felt this keyed up since I started my trolling campaigns. What a time to be alive, eh?

Well, I'm in, and the interface is disappointingly boring. No bells, no whistles, no emojis, just a panel to type into, a basic search bar, and a small discreet icon that will allow you to upload images. For the first time, I feel a bit uneasy when I think about the kinds of people who might use that image upload button. Is Tori that kind of person?

I shake my head. This is not the time to think like that.

There's no real way to create a proper profile—which is

sensible given how people always give away waaaay too much info on their profiles in a desperate attempt at sounding interesting. Just a random number-and-letter generator. Each time you log in, you get a new anonymous identity. You then tell the person you want to contact to type that into the search bar, et voila—you're connected.

That's good. And a bit scary. But mainly good.

I click out of Metachat and reply to Tori, telling her I've installed it. It's on one of my hidden partitions, so if anyone uses my laptop, they'd never find it.

It only takes her a few minutes to reply.

Yeah?
Cool! Hang on . . .

I wait.

4x729vWF14

I know exactly what that means.

God, this is exciting. I kind of feel like a spy. This whole anonymity thing is a massive turn-on. I wonder if Tori gets the same thrill. In I go again to Metachat, and type the code in. A little cursor appears in the conversation panel, blinking and waiting.

Hi

I'm breathless.

Hey. Tori?

Yeah. It's me. We can drop the act here. Feels good, huh?

Oh, she is *not* wrong.

I know you're MidnightBanshee and SharkKrawler9 and FlounceyPouncey, but you never gave me your real name?

Alarm bells. Can't be Beth here. Who can I be? Chances are she isn't Tori either. Need something that sounds plausible.

Amy.

Uh, okay. Not sure where that came from, but I'll roll with it. Lots of Amys in the world. Cool. Amy. Good.

So what you wanna chat about?
Lol, things that would get us banned on the boards, dumbass!
You know the admin can hack the DMs, right?
Yeah, course.
Why do you think I didn't say too much?
Cos you're a professional ;) . . . like me.

Oh, baby, where have you been all my life?

You can say that again.
We can use this to coordinate.
I know socks are fun, but eventually they always get caught.
You think I should stop using socks?
Nah, but we can sort out targets here.

Strategize. Cause as much havoc as possible.

                                                    That sounds cool

Yeah, I thought you'd like it.

I've been watching your trail of chaos for a while now.

You're sick. So good at taking down those tramps.

I'm not quite sure how to reply to this. I'm not good with compliments. I decide to ignore it.

                                    If they don't want ppl commenting,
                                    then they shouldn't preen over the web.

Ikr? They just want people to worship them. Ain't gonna happen, buttercup. And speaking of buttercups—have you seen Buttercup97 on Instagram? Was in the doldrums until she started posting those fucking stupid half-naked yoga pics and going on about fucking kimchi. Bitch needs to be taken down a peg. You in?

I'm not good with compliments. I decide to ignore it.

She seriously needs to ask?

10: #SUCKITUPBUTTERCUP

I have so much fun tag-teaming with Tori and her various socks that I completely forget to have lunch. She is delightfully vicious and is so adept at switching personas, I wonder if we might have actually attracted a few outsiders, like sharks at a frenzy. When Buttercup97, with her perfect ass and perfect eyebrows and perfect life, logs on she's in for a shock. Already, her fans are trying to fight through, telling us to leave Buttercup alone, stupid troll, why must u hate? Must be fat and ugly, fuck you, don't bother feeding the troll, u skank u whore u leave Buttercup be she's perfect we luv u Buttercup don't listen. Yeah, yeah, heard it all before, you bunch of amateurs. When my alarm goes off at two, I'm actually feeling pretty bouncy and I don't really want to leave the fun. Two of my socks have already been banned and I know three others have been reported and the chaos is just *delicious*, and Tori's on Metachat in the corner of my screen, laughing her ass off judging by the amount of "lols" she's typing to me.

But I can't stay and do this all day as I've got another lecture at three, so I say goodbye to Tori (who begs me to stay—boy, I've never felt so wanted! Maybe it's worth blowing the lecture off today after all!), and spend a good ten minutes diligently logging out of everything, clearing all my caches, and generally ensuring none of this afternoon's mayhem can be linked back to me and my IP address, before running out to grab the bus.

I meet Brat on the stairs. He's got a Coke in one hand and his phone in the other.

"What were you laughing about?" he sneers.

"Why aren't you at school?" I shoot back.

He glowers at me and pushes past. Ha. I win.

✦✦✦

I don't often win. I think that's one of the reasons why I'm interested in psychology. I spent most of my time at school deeply unhappy. Life isn't very kind to emergent fugly girls. Fugly boys (yes, they exist too) have it a little easier in that the patriarchy protects them a little, so fugly girls really are at the bottom of the pack, and I suppose I wanted to know why. What is it that makes us humans so obsessed with our appearance? With looking attractive? Why are the Beautiful People considered Beautiful anyway? What exactly *is* wrong with me, other than some deeply unfair social stereotyping? At first I read a load of bollocks about mindfulness and shit like that, but I wasn't looking to fix myself; I was looking to fix everyone else. So I turned to the scientific study of the mind.

Alas, today's lecture isn't particularly enlightening. Amy's sitting next to me again; like this morning, she'd waited for me and corralled me into The Middle, jabbering on about how it's so inconvenient to have two lectures at opposite sides of the day, don't they realize we have lives to live, I mean, come *on* . . .

I let her words wash over me, nodding occasionally so she thinks I'm listening. My mind is on other things. Like Tori. I doodle question marks surrounded by flowers over my notes.

What exactly is her angle? I do quite like her—she's funny and cruel and clever, all the things I want to be, but that only makes me suspicious. Doesn't mean I can't enjoy myself while I'm figuring her out, though. For once, this is a win-win situation.

The lecture's only an hour long (maybe Amy has a point about it being a waste of time), so it's not long before I'm back on the bus, and it's busy. I hate rush hour. No seats means I have to stand, and I'm so aware of my stomach and bum that I don't notice the guy standing behind me until I feel something brush my butt. I go to apologize for bumping into him and try to move, but between the girl with the enormous stroller and the old dears and their myriad walking aides, I'm stuck.

And the man isn't moving his hand.

I glance over my shoulder. He's not looking at me. He's gazing out the window. He's quite old, in his 40s, maybe 50s? I don't know, but he has graying hair and horrible sagging jowls with an uneven smattering of stubble. His nose is a bit bulbous and is covered in a network of broken capillaries.

I try to shift over, but I'm still stuck in a press of people, and now his hand has moved under my coat and he's running his finger down my butt crack.

I freeze.

I always thought that if someone felt me up, I'd kick the pervert in the bollocks. But then again, I never really expected this to happen to me, because why the hell would someone choose to grope me when the world is full of far more beautiful girls, with far prettier, perkier backsides?

So I stand there, my eyes wide, bile bubbling at the back of my throat. All around me, people are chattering, playing with their phones, getting on with their lives, not realizing that something so vile is taking place under their noses. I want to scream. I want to shout. But the fear that no one would believe me due to my fugliness—and the general ingrainedness of the old chestnut that nice girls don't make a scene—stops me. Hell, maybe I deserve this. I chose to wear leggings. Maybe this is it, the only attention I'll ever receive. Maybe this is how it's done? No—even I know this is fucked up, but I can't do anything about it. I'm paralyzed. People, help me, please. Someone, notice . . .

But they're all staring at their phones, lost in their own little worlds, while I am right there, trapped in this one.

His fingertips dig into my flesh and he clears his throat. I feel physically sick. Finally he leans over and presses the bell, and two seconds later, the bus slides into the bus stop and he murmurs "Excuse me" like nothing has happened, like he hasn't just spent the last five minutes feeling up my backside, humiliating me, stirring that already pretty massive pot of self-hatred up into a frenzy, and I know if I say or do anything now, I'll lose it and people will be questioning my sanity rather than his morals, so I let him slide past me and slink away to God knows where. I'm pretty sure he's smirking when I catch sight of him through the bus window.

There's still nowhere to sit, so I'm still forced to keep standing. I take advantage of the changeover to pull the back of my coat down. One of the old ladies looks up at me and smiles. It takes all I've got to smile back and not dissolve into tears right here.

No, that'll happen later, when I'm alone.

11: #METOO

When I get home I jump straight in the shower. I want to burn my leggings, but I can't afford a new pair, so instead I'll throw them into the wash.

The water is hot and good. It washes away all sin. I cry and cry and cry. Why am I so pathetic? I play the incident over and over in my head, each time my comebacks getting nastier and nastier until the sick fuck is cowering at my feet while I tower over him, my phone in hand, as he begs me not to post the video online, not to tell his wife, not to ruin his life. Doesn't make me feel any better, though, no matter how many times I scrub. If he'd been online, I would have destroyed him. In real life? I can't even tell a legit perv to fuck off.

After ten minutes, I get out. Yes, even now, I am aware of how much a long shower costs. Dad drilled that into me from a young age. Shut the door, were you born in a barn? Why are all the lights on, you trying to light up the street? What were you doing in there, washing an elephant? (Why, yes, I was: me. It takes time to make sure every nook and cranny in this over-inflated body is clean, thank you very much.)

The heating's not on yet—you never turn that on until six, on pain of death—so I wrap myself in a cold towel and run the gauntlet back to my room, praying that Mum or Brat don't see me wobbling down the hallway.

I'm in luck. Well, it's about time. I close my door and draw the curtains before flinging myself on my bed. The shame won't leave me. His hand is still there, and I think it will be for a long time yet. I dry myself off, telling myself sternly that crying never solved anything, and drag my pajamas on, even though it's only half past five.

Too late now. Best put it in a box and forget about it.

The vitriol flung at me online today tastes very sweet indeed, but also leaves me feeling a little bit hollow. Do the people I troll online feel the same way about themselves as I do right now? Was that guy simply trolling me in real life? I bite at the skin around my thumbnail until I taste copper.

No. It's not the same. All I was doing was standing on the bus. There was no invitation. Hell, *I'm* no invitation. Even if I was standing there in a bikini, wearing a sign saying *Get It Here*, people wouldn't see that as an invitation. I was a victim, pure and simple. Although—maybe I shouldn't have worn leggings. Okay, so they were under a long jumper that almost reaches my knees, but maybe some baggy jeans would have been better? He might have chosen someone else if I'd been wearing baggy jeans. Those girls on the internet, they wouldn't be seen dead in baggy jeans. Or leggings, really—just tight yoga pants. (What exactly are yoga pants, anyway? I've never really worked out how they differentiate from leggings, apart from you can pick up leggings for four pounds a pair at Primark, whereas you have to take out a fucking loan to buy a decent pair of yoga pants.) Or bikinis (SO many bikinis), or those stupidly tight dresses that'd show every lump and bump if they had lumps and bumps to show. Those girls are the ones asking for it.

Still, I don't reply to anyone. Not in the mood. I wrap my

dressing gown around me and run a brush through my damp hair. Doesn't smell like anyone's bothered to cook, so I creep downstairs. I don't really want to talk to anyone, but I'm hungry. I need to feed the beast.

Mum's not in the living room, so she must have gone to bed. Maybe I should make her something to eat. Not Brat, though. Brat can fuck off. Not that I know where he is, which is, admittedly, a bit weird. He usually beats even me in the dinnertime "I'm hungry" wailing. Maybe he's gone out and got himself a Macky D's. Hmm. I wish I'd thought of that. But that does rely on me entering a McDonalds and walking past all the people in it, with their horrible, judgy eyes. Sometimes the lure of the cheeseburger is too much and I brave it, but it never tastes as great as I want it to, because I bolt it down so quickly it doesn't touch the sides, because I'm just so mortified of people watching me, and *yes*, I do realize that to other people it looks like I'm so desperate for fatty crap that I shove the whole thing in my big gob as quickly as possible, oh my God, there should be a law against it, eat less move more, it's not hard . . .

I shake my head. Shame spiraling will not help. I open the fridge. It is depressingly empty. Half a carton of milk, a slightly squishy pepper, a jar of pickles from Christmas about three years ago, a jar of furry gooseberry jam. I ask you. Gooseberry jam. Who the fuck eats that?

I gallantly move the sad remnants of the fridge around, looking for some cheese (you never know, it might have been behind the pepper or in the drawer where vegetables go to die), but I come up empty. The tears well again.

"Mum!" I call out. No response. I pad to the bottom of the stairs. "Mum?"

Still nothing.

I listen for a bit. The house creaks around me. It's old and suddenly the weight of those years hits me. How many other people have lived here? How many have died? Are they still around, watching me in my dressing gown, shouting up the stairs, hoping I don't have to make the climb up?

"Mum!" There's a note of panic in my voice now. Oh no. Not again. Please—not today. I don't think I can cope with this today.

The bannister is cold under my hand. One foot up, onto the first step. I can feel the panic rise, like a little scrabbly animal in my belly, trying to claw its way out of my throat. More steps. Dammit, everything is just so quiet. The house is never this quiet. The only other time was when—

I take in a deep breath. Now is not the time to be thinking of things like that. Right now, I need to focus.

Up a few more steps. Feels like a mountain. My heart is thundering like a jackhammer as I crest the top of the staircase.

No lights on. Not even a bedroom one. I flick the switch, but the sudden harsh light is somehow worse. No place to hide now. Only stark truth to face.

"Mum?" I say. It comes out more like a whimper. Her door is the second one on the left, opposite mine. I tap my fingers on the door, but no one answers.

I enter her room.

Even by my standards, it's pretty rank in here. When Dad was around, this room always smelled of talcum powder and aftershave. Now it's unwashed sheets and menthol. I don't turn the light on, just let some spill in from the landing.

"Mum?" I whisper.

The lump on the bed doesn't stir.

I've made it this far, but I don't know if I have it in me to take it any farther. All I need to do is check on her. She's probably just asleep. She does that a lot now—between her various illnesses and her medication, she's often exhausted. Give her a little shake, just to make sure.

But I don't know if I can. Because there's always the reality that one day, she won't just be tired. That's inevitable.

We all die.

I just didn't think it would be now.

It *can't* be now. No, Mum, no . . . please be asleep. Please be asleep. Please . . .

I stretch out a hand and hesitate. If she is dead, then I'll be touching a corpse. A vicious shudder runs through me.

Come on, Beth—get it together. I shake the lump.

It doesn't move.

"Mum?"

I pull back the cover, just enough so I can see her face. She looks older than 52—much older, her once cheerful, open face now lined and pasty, with big black bags under her eyes.

She snorts, and I nearly hit the roof.

"Fuck!" I gasp.

Mum frowns. "I don't like you using that language, Bethany."

Jesus, of all the things to say . . .

"You okay, Mum?" I want to smooth her hair from her face, to hug her, for her to hug me, for her to tell me everything's okay, like she used to do when I was a child, but instead she only gives me a weak, kind of confused smile.

"Yeah, everything's fine. I was just tired. Is Bradley in?"

"No, not right now." Bradley. Always about Bradley.

She sighs heavily and lies back, limp. "Can you text him and ask him to come home? It's late now."

I squash down the urge to tell her to text her own damn son. But I know that would be cruel, given everything.

"Yeah, course I can."

"You're a good girl, Beth."

Yeah. The best. Go Beth.

"Why are you in your pajamas?" Mum continues. "Aren't you babysitting later?"

"No. It's Tuesday, Mum. Not Wednesday."

"It's Tuesday?"

"Yeah. I came up to see if there was anything to eat,"

"Oh, bugger. I forgot to put in the grocery order." She runs a trembling hand over her face. "I must've been asleep."

Oh, great.

"There's twenty in the mug," she says. "Get yourself and Bradley a pizza."

"And you?"

"I'm not hungry. Just tired."

She smiles, and her face takes on a cadaverous twist. She looks hungry. She looks like a skeleton. When was the last time I saw her eat a proper meal? Last night's pasta bake? She only picked at that. How long has it been since she really enjoyed food? Enjoyed eating? Enjoyed life? Too long.

I take in a breath and hold it.

Fuck you, Dad. Fuck you.

12: #HEAVEN

I enjoy food.

Actually, that's a bit simplistic. Food is everything. It's comfort. It's always there for you. It doesn't judge.

It is also the ultimate enemy. Tell a heroin addict they need to get clean, and all they need to do is wean themselves off the drug and never use it again. (Yeah, I know it's a *bit* more complicated than that, but that's the basic principle.) Doesn't work with food. Can't wean yourself off that. You wean yourself off food for too long and you're dead.

Why can't kale taste like chocolate? Life would be so much easier then. Everyone would be healthy. Sort it out, evolution.

I tried to give up carbs once, but Mum told me to stop being silly. This was before Dad decided he wanted a new and improved family, before Mum fell ill. She was far more no-nonsense in those days, but in many ways far, far easier to deal with. Anyway, I remember the time I left my mashed potatoes, declaring they were "bad for me." Everyone laughed, and Mum told me to clear my plate or I wouldn't get any dessert. Talk about not getting the point. Allegedly, there are plenty of starving children in the world who would love my mashed potatoes, so don't be so ungrateful and eat it up. It took all I had not to tell her to send the lot to that nebulous mass of starving children and instead shovel it into my mouth like a Good Girl. Because that's important. Being a Good Girl. Be home on time, clean your room, and ALWAYS finish your plate. I think Not Finishing Your Plate was one of Mum's cardinal sins before she stopped caring.

I kind of miss those days. At least dinner was always on time then.

After that, I tried to reduce my portion sizes. Mum was more on board with that. A few less chips, one less fish finger, maybe an extra bit of broccoli, because broccoli is good for you. It was a good plan.

Only issue is, eating less means I get hungry later.

I stare at the pizza menu. Old friend. Even older enemy. I tell myself I don't want anything on it, but my stomach growls as if to say *who do you think you're kidding?*

I could ignore it. The Hunger. Sometimes, I like it. I like to imagine that it's a monster living in my stomach, and each time it growls, it's actually eating away at my flab from the inside, and that one morning I'll wake up and emerge, like a butterfly from a cocoon, as a socially acceptable human being.

Other times, though, I just sneak downstairs and feed it biscuits.

Or, in this case, pizza.

Lovely pizza. How I loathe you.

Okay, I'm going to do it. I keep my promise to Mum and text Brat. I try to sound reasonable.

> Mum wants you to come home.
> Where are you?

My phone buzzes.

I don't even bother correcting his spelling.

Oh well, more pizza for me.

I get up and heave myself upstairs to grab my laptop. I don't usually like taking it out of my sanctuary, but there's a distinct lack of prying eyes downstairs, so I'm willing to risk it. I also grab my favorite blanket and a pillow, so I can make myself super-comfy. Might even watch a movie. It will be like a date night, only without a date. Well, they say you should spoil yourself.

What can I get for twenty quid?

Not *what do I fancy?* but *what will give me the maximum amount of food?* This isn't about quality, dear friend—this is all about quantity. You're talking to an expert, remember.

I can get a meal deal. £19.99 gives me two medium pizzas, potato wedges, garlic bread, and a Coke.

Pah. Amateur hour.

Okay—£24.99 will give me two large pizzas, potato wedges, garlic bread, and a Coke.

Now we're talking.

Getting another fiver shouldn't be an issue as there has to be at least thirty quid in loose change in the jar. Although it does feel a bit sleazy to be paying the pizza man with coppers, my need for comfort food far outweighs this, so I tip the jar out. Oo, there's a few 10 pence pieces in there, and a couple of 20ps, too. That'll help. I easily scrape together the £4.99 I need, ignoring the horrible scratchy feeling that I could put that money to much better use, like filling the fridge, or contributing toward the electricity bill. Not that I am 100 percent sure how the electricity bill works—Dad used to sort that out, which is why we've always had to watch our consumption. He used to get so twitchy, he'd yell at us, and then he'd yell even louder at Mum.

Nope—I need this. Today has been the day from hell. I deserve it. And everyone's allowed a cheat day, right?

I confirm the order and choose the "pay in cash" option. It tells me it'll take half an hour to arrive. This is the bit I hate. Oh, the waiting doesn't bother me (well, not much), it's more the fact that someone can knock on the door at any time, and I will have to answer it (in PJs, no less), and he will judge the hell out of me for the food mountain I've purchased. I mean, yes, technically he will be right—fat girl buys too much pizza—but I still hate that feeling. Thin girls buy pizza, too, and no one judges them. For all he knows, I'm hosting a slumber party. A really, really quiet one, where all the guests are hiding.

The clock ticks by. Still got twenty minutes. For a brief moment, I wonder where Brat is. It's now coming up on eight o'clock. Maybe I should text him again? Not for my benefit of course, but for Mum's.

Late now. Mum's worrying.

And a couple of minutes later.

I sed fuck of.

So good to see he's using his education wisely. Screw him. Fifteen minutes.

I settle myself down and log in. Normal accounts are as sparse as usual—only when I log in with my proxies do I get my fix.

The doorbell rings, and that familiar twang of panic twists

my guts. I grab the cash in two hands and make sure my dressing gown is properly closed.

"Hello! Pizza delivery!"

He's far too chirpy for a man on minimum wage. He starts piling boxes into my open arms, like a mother welcoming her newborn, and I dump the twenty quid note and the handfuls of change into his outstretched palm.

He looks at me properly. It isn't hard to read his thoughts. Yes, I am that desperate.

"Sorry," I say. "It is all there."

"Yeah," he says. I hope to God he doesn't insist on counting it all out. It's bloody freezing.

He makes a half-hearted attempt with the coins but then sighs heavily and stuffs the coins into his pockets whilst pizza grease soaks through the bottom of the box, warming my hands.

I close the door, trying not to feel bad.

I un-pause the film and spread the pizza boxes on the floor around me.

There's nothing quite like that first bite. I slowly push the piece of pizza into my mouth, savoring the salt of the pepperoni, the zing of the jalapeno, the sweetness of the red peppers, the creaminess of the cheese. I let out a long sigh as I chew, and slowly release the stress of the day, even if it's only while I'm eating. I imagine this is what meditation feels like, if you know how to do it properly, and don't secretly think the woman telling you to "imagine your negativity flowing away from you like a river with each breath" sounds like she's lost the new age plot.

Before I know it, half the pepperoni's gone, and I'm on the garlic bread and potato wedges. (Don't forget the sour cream and chives dip. Gotta be sour cream and chives. Anything else is just sacrilege.) Then I go back to the pizza, like a woman choosing from her many gorgeous lovers, and pick up a slice of the filthy, filthy Hawaiian. I know. Pineapple on pizza. I'm such a dirty girl.

I'm feeling pretty full now, but to my mind, that's just a challenge. How much can I stuff into my face before my brain catches up with my stomach? Screw the consequences. Screw the bellyache that I know will come; screw the indigestion; screw the inevitable squits I will suffer tomorrow morning. Right here, right now—that's what's important. That's what's *always* important.

I wipe my mouth. Grease coats my chin. I lean back against the sofa and cradle my stomach. Food baby. I have been impregnated with pizza. Maybe I should get pregnant for realsies. Then I can be fat and eat what I like, and no one would dare judge. Except then I'd be left with a screaming brat to look after. Plus, there's the obvious problem of finding a willing sperm donor. Nah. Right now, I have pizza love, and that's good enough for me. Oh, and Black Widow's leather-clad ass. Hello.

I watch for a bit, then slide my laptop closer. More messages of both hate and love have poured in. Brilliant. See? Here I'm not a loser. Here, I reign supreme. It doesn't matter what side of the fence you fall down on: lover, hater, you're still focused on me, talking about me, making me the topic of conversation. It's true what they say. You really shouldn't feed the trolls, because they fucking *love* it.

A little box pings up in the corner of my screen. Metachat.

LP479281X. Chat?

I smile. It can only be one person.

I click the OK button, and the box expands to reveal the chat panel.

Hey. It's Tori.

Yeah. I know. Hi.

Hi. What are you doing?

Watching a movie, eating pizza.

Oh, so, so much pizza.

Sounds good. Wish I was there.

Yeah. Me too.

You should send me a pic. ;)

Uhhh . . . no I shouldn't. Me eating pizza in my PJs is something no one wants to see.

Luckily, she replies before I can think of a suitable brush off.

You gave good hassle today on Reddit. #impressed

Hashtags, even though they don't work here? How very postmodern.

Was fun. Bit easy, tho.

Fish and barrels spring to mind.

I know what you mean. I tag-teamed you on Instagram.
Did you see?

Yeah. That was epic. Stupid bitch. She tried to block me.

Like that was going to work.

She's gone private now.
Wanna see if I can hack her?

. . . Okay. Trolling = good clean fun. I know the roaming IPs and proxies aren't exactly playing fair, but I've never stooped as low as hacking accounts.

You hack too?

Yeah. Hijacking accounts, posting sick shit—total chaos. Love it. Go on. You'll see. It's fun.

It's fun. Hmm. I've had little fun of late. Been groped by a vile pervert and thought my Mum might be dead, but not had much fun.

Okay. Why not?

I mean, what's the worst that can happen?

13: #MISCHIEF

Turns out, there's a whole 'nother level to internet mischief that has blithely passed me by. Controlling someone else's account is like holding their life in the palms of your hands, and then clapping. Loudly.

It doesn't take Tori long to take control of Freedomchick04's account. Oh, don't be so sniffy. She likes to pose in tiny shorts and cropped tops, holding large guns. She's basically asking for it.

Once she's in, Tori spends a gleeful half an hour posting all of her private pictures, including a veritable treasure trove of nude shots. Unsurprisingly, she's incredibly flexible. By the time Tori's finished with her, I'm laughing so much I'm kind of regretting my pizza binge, and all thoughts of perverts and dead mums have fled.

We finish the evening by creating a new Twitter account and shoving the pictures on there, which causes an absolute shitstorm. Freedomchick is going to have a hell of a time clearing up that mess.

That was fun!

I know, naff, but I can't help it.

I thought you'd like it. :) It's sooo much more fun when you're calling all the shots. All we have to do now is wait. Freedomtwat is going to shit when she sees what we've been up to!

Oh, she's an imp, that's for sure. I wonder what she looks like. I shake my head to stop those thoughts in their tracks. That's not how this works. I might consider her a friend, but staying faceless is staying safe when it comes to the internet. Hell, why do you think I called myself Amy? Though that particular name is a curious choice. After all, I barely know her—

The front door clicks as a key is turned in the lock, followed by a slam that reverberates through the house.

I glance at my laptop. Nearly ten. Brat knows the score. He might think he's a grown-up now, but staying out after nine is still a no-go. Eight o'clock was my latest curfew right up until I was sixteen, and I obeyed it. Okay, so I hardly had reason to challenge it, but that's not the point. If I had to obey the rules, then so does he. I psych myself up, taking in a deep breath and retying my dressing gown cord. I loom in the living room doorway, waiting for him to pass by.

"You're late," I say.

He narrows his eyes at me.

"Mum's worried."

"No she isn't. She's fucking drugged up to the eyeballs most of the time. If she cared, she'd be here, not you."

He's got a point.

"All the more reason for you to do as you're told," I volley back. "The last thing she needs to worry about is where you are. Oi! I'm talking to you!"

He saunters past me and up the stairs. "Fuck off. You're not the boss of me."

Again, he has a point. I mean, some people might argue that as a (technically) responsible adult, I am the one in charge. But I'm not. And I don't want to be.

Brat smirks, and I curl my lip at him. He knows it. He knows it all. This is to hurt me as much as Mum; he just wants to burn the world to see what might happen next, and I want to punch him for it, because deep down that's what *I* want to do, but I don't have the guts, so instead I just burn myself with food and spite.

"You're a selfish little asshole, you know that?" I hiss.

"Yeah, yeah, whatever." He slinks into his bedroom. Seconds later, there's an earth-shattering boom as he un-pauses his game. I close my eyes, my teeth grinding in unison with the rat-a-tat-tat of virtual guns.

◆◆◆

Everything ok?
You all right?
Amy? You there?

I can't help but feel touched by Tori's concern when I get back to my laptop. Unfortunately, what I found hilariously daring a moment ago now seems a bit cheap and, dare I say it, mean.

Yeah. Dickhead bro to deal with.

Ah. Younger?

You know it. Oh well.
We all have our crosses, huh?

Yeah . . . I know. You wanna talk?

Nah. Can't be bothered to waste time thinking about it,
tbh. Life's too short.

You're not wrong there, hun.

Still, if you need a shoulder, you know where I am, right?

Something involuntary catches in the back of my throat.

Yeah. Thanks, hun.

No problemo. That's what friends are for, after all.

Friends? I bite my bottom lip.

You're the best

I try. ;)

It's weird, seeing this side of Tori. From her public personas, you'd never guess she had it in her to be nice. We chat for a bit longer, trading cat videos mainly, until she announces she has to get up early for work tomorrow and should probably hit the hay.

I don't bother tidying away the pizza boxes. Fuck it. Let the scene of devastation fester for a bit. Instead I wrap myself in my favorite blanket and try to drown myself in mindless reality TV.

It's kind of wonderful. These people talk weird, they stand weird, and their hair is always weirdly shiny and it's great, like I'm David Attenborough studying a new species: *Here we see the Essexius vacuousi's mating ritual. Observe the male peacocking with many colorful tattoos, as his orange target preens to indicate her receptiveness. The intensity of the orange is directly proportional to the thickness of the eyebrows, and they relate to how easily the female will engage in the mating ritual. Mating grounds are often spontaneous and sometimes unsanitary, but the back of a car in a nightclub's car park is considered optimal.*

I snicker to myself and snuggle back. Mum sleeps here so often there's a really comfortable hollow, if you just shift this . . . and wiggle your butt cheek there . . . ahh. Life goals.

I let the drowsiness infect me. So nice. So—*yawn*—cozy. My eyelids droop, and I allow all the *do you know what I mean?*s lull me to sleep.

The next thing I know, there's a stamping on the stairs, followed by a whoosh of cool air as the living room door is flung open. I jerk my head up. I haven't a clue what's on the telly now—some kind of shopping channel trying to sell me some crappy gym-thing—so it must be the early hours of the morning. My neck's stiff, and I feel queasy. Ahh, the price you pay for Pizza Binge.

"I'm hungry," Bratley says and picks up a pizza box. "Just one slice? Did you fucking eat all of this?"

I try not to cringe and instead close my eyes.

"You fat bitch!" he snarls. "Two fucking pizzas? Fuck me."

"If you'd got home at a sensible time, then I would've shared—"

"But instead I didn't, so rather than sticking one in the fridge, you fucking *ate* it? Fuck. Hey fatty boom boom, no wonder no one fucking wants you."

"Will you stop swearing," I say through gritted teeth.

"Fuck off. Will you get your fat ass off the fucking sofa for once?"

He's doing this to rile me up. I know it. And the sad thing is, it's working. Shame reeks out of my every pore.

He makes those piggy noises I hate so much, and the urge to punch him becomes unbearable.

"Stop it," I hiss.

"Little Miss Rotunda. Biiiig Beth! Ten ton Bethy! Will do anything for a Mars bar." He makes a wanking gesture at his crotch. "Nosh on that—"

"Fuck off!" I scream.

He laughs and waves his phone at me. On the screen is a picture of me, asleep, surrounded by pizza boxes. "You wait until I tell my mates about this."

I turn cold. Because some of his mates are the younger brothers of Tormentors of Schoolmas past. Will I ever escape? He gives me a vicious smile. He's none too skinny himself, but no one questions him. He's quite tall, and his flab makes him look intimidating rather than just plain fat. He can get away with it, because he's a boy. I can't, because I'm not.

"Ta-ta, Fatty!" He wiggles his fingers at me in the parody of a wave and saunters back out of the room, knowing full well he's won.

14: #SOHOTRIGHTNOW

I can't sleep. My guts are churning after all that dairy, but all I can think about is food. I do know this is ridiculous. I do know I'm going to be sick. But I can't help it. I cannot fight this demon. I don't know how.

There are no more Mars bars left in my secret stash now. I've eaten them all. Wrappers litter my bed. And I'm lying back, burping and farting, trying to psych myself up to do the inevitable.

♣♣♣

Let's just get this out there. I don't *like* being sick. I don't think anyone does. I'm not full-on bulimic—those girls are hard-core, 'cause that means throwing up every single day, and I simply couldn't face that—but it's another string to my bow when things get too much. Eating is a pleasure. Digesting? Not so much.

Maybe I'm lactose intolerant. They say you crave the things you shouldn't have. It would explain why I always want choco-late and cheese. Well, okay, that and they taste absolutely *amaz-ing*, but I always feel terrible after eating them. All bloated and gassy. Maybe I should give them up. Okay, so the carb thing

was a no-go, but now that Mum doesn't give a fuck about anything any of us do, maybe it would be easier.

Maybe.

I slump over the toilet. Urgh. My throat feels sore, and
pizza and chocolate do not taste as nice coming back up as they
do doing down. My face feels hot and puffy, and my eyes sting.
I blow my nose. A chunk of pepper flies out.

This is pretty low.

I've got to do something. Sort myself out. Sort *everything*
out. Stop worrying about other people's opinions. Make a
change. Fuck the haters. They can kiss my fat ass, for all I care.

Ha. Watch it, you're beginning to sound like those Ins-
tagrammers you loathe so much. Next thing you know, you'll
be setting up an "inspiration" account, posting how far you've
run and taking pictures of your boringly healthy meals, complete with hashtags like #soblessed and #lovinglife. And then
some poor sap will come along and troll you until you snap and
trough down a whole family-sized candy bar so fast, the Guin-
ness Book of Records will come knocking.

Nah. I'm not that desperate. Not yet.

Not ever.

15: #ANOTHERDAY

Today is a full uni day. I'm not sure I'm up to it, but hell, it beats sitting around here, with the pizza boxes of shame lurking in the bin. I check on Mum, who is still asleep, and ignore Brat completely. Fuck it. I don't care. Not anymore. If he doesn't want to go to school, then let him deal with the consequences. In a way, that makes me much stronger than him, because I had a far harder time but I didn't bunk off. Well, not *that* much.

I take some time to check up on the havoc Tori and I wreaked last night, and I am not disappointed. Freedomchick04 has pulled her Instagram account, but the Twitter one is still going strong. People are still talking about it, and the secret pictures of her are still circulating. This lifts my mood immeasurably.

I decide to listen to something a little more upbeat this morning, so I can hold on to the lovely, bubbly feeling that destroying Freedomchick04 has sparked within me. I'm not a monster. I'm a loveable rogue. I should wear a black cat suit and have a mask. There she goes! The Anarchist. She doesn't care; she thrives on chaos.

The bus is on time. I flash my pass, and in a fit of daring, take the back seat. I was never allowed to do this at school. The back seat was for the cool kids. Now look at me. Bus Queen. At the back, no one can grab me; Bus Pervert will have to get his kicks off someone else.

"Hey! Hi!"

A squeak breaks through my musing. The bus has stopped to let in the next batch of wage slaves and coffin dodgers. Amongst them is Amy. Shit. I forgot she got this bus.

Without waiting to be asked, she plonks herself next to me. Today, her hair is up in pigtails, and she's wearing pink hot-pants over green and black stripy tights.

"Why didn't you friend me?" she asks, her kohl-rimmed eyes huge.

"Uh, sorry. I was busy last night. Like I said, my mum wasn't well, and—"

"Oh, God, yeah, I'm sorry. I feel bad now. I should have remembered. Is she okay? Must be a massive strain on you. But you have to look after yourself, too. You can't neglect yourself. I know, why don't we do it now?" She pulls her phone out, and since refusing her would be like kicking a puppy squarely in the face, I fish mine out too and tap the Facebook app.

"Yay!" she says, in a way that would make even the most hardened Manic Pixie Dream Girl cringe. "Now, this is me—isn't my avatar cute? And yeah, hang on, hang on—ooh! Beth Soames! There you are. And . . . friendship request accepted! Now we can stay in touch! Isn't that great? We can arrange to meet outside of lectures and everything now!"

She speaks as if this is the most exciting, revolutionary development ever, leaving me to wonder just how pathetic the rest of her life is. Before I can say anything, my phone buzzes and a bunch of nonsensical emojis flood my screen. Amy laughs. Of course they're from her.

"Online party! Let's celebrate. Come on!" She wiggle-dances

in her seat next to me.

Good lord.

I spend the rest of the bus journey listening to Amy chatter on while my phone almost vibrates itself to pieces. Even though she's here, talking to me, she's still sending me stuff online, mainly cute pictures of cute animals being cute. There's no edge to Amy at all; she's like a ball of candyfloss caught in the mind of a five-year-old, wrapped up in the body of a supermodel, and I find myself both liking her because she's so obviously harmless but also hating her because she's so, well, *fluffy*.

Tori would have a field day with her online.

So would I, if I'm honest.

"Oh my GOD! Look at this one!" she moans, and yep, that's my phone again. I bring up the video—a sphynx cat trying to warm up on a larger, fluffier cat. It is undoubtedly cute.

"Aww. He's cold," I say. I mean, what else is there to say?

"I would huggle him so much if he was mine," she says in a voice people usually reserve for toddlers.

"I do quite like those sphynx cats," I say. "They always look kind of angry. And how can you not love something that deliberately ugly?"

"I know!" Amy nods enthusiastically and pantomimes stroking her phone. "With their grumpy little faces . . . ooooh! Look at this one!"

I have a feeling I am going to get a lot of these videos now.

The next stop is ours, and when we get off, Amy waves at the bus driver, who has the good grace to scowl back at her.

"So, did you finish your assignment?" she continues. "I did. It was soooo hard, though. I had to spend over an hour looking up half the stuff online, and even then I don't think I really got it, not properly, anyway. I bet you did okay, though. Did you do okay?"

"Yeah," I say. "I mean, it's probably crap, but it's done."

She beams at me, but I can't help but notice there's a fragility to it. In fact, everything about her has a brittle quality. That whole manic pixie girl thing she has going on, the talking a mile a minute, the deliberate cuteness, the pigtails—it's all too much, a bit too contrived, and I am left wondering if it's all an act. If this is her armor against the world. If instead of black and chocolate and online trolling, she's chosen to become the living embodiment of an anime character.

She clutches her folder tightly to her chest as we walk. She giggles a lot. I don't have to say much, which is kind of perfect. Maybe this might work? Maybe we could be—no, I can't bring myself to say it. Because saying it would jinx it, and as much as I would never admit it, I don't want to jinx it. Not yet, anyway.

She waves and says hi to everyone. Only about half do the same back. That's probably the me factor.

By the time we get to our lecture hall and Amy starts leading me toward the middle rows, my post-trolling euphoria has completely worn off, and my stomach is hurting. There are too many people in here today. Usually I can cope with it because I'm at the back, but now that I'm in the thick of it, my heart is racing and my palms are sweaty. I turn around and bump into someone. They glare at me and I mutter "sorry," carefully avoiding their angry eyes.

I turn again and someone brushes past me. The sensation extends farther than the actual touch, down my back, toward my buttocks, and I am there again, on the bus, with that guy feeling me up. My head swells as my pulse builds. This is what happens when you bury stuff in food and cruelty. It gets hidden, sure, but it doesn't get dealt with, which means it runs the risk of popping up again in all manner of inappropriate places.

Amy's shuffled into a row and is beckoning at me to join her, but the gap now looks tiny, like you'd have to be a pixie to get through it, and that's fine for Amy because we've already established that she *is* a pixie, but I'm a troll, a massive, galumphing troll, and I am never, ever going to be able to squeeze in there, especially with all the people around, God it's hot in here, but I can't take my coat off because then I will have to carry it and that makes me bigger and I'm going to end up knocking someone out and then they'll all turn and laugh and laugh and laugh . . .

My head's spinning now; my tongue is dry, like a big, fat slug, no, not a slug, slugs aren't dry, they're wet, so what is it like? Too big, too dry, too big too big too big—

"Beth!" Amy trills. "Sit down, honey!"

She's staring up at me, her eyes huge. She reaches out and gives my arm a little tug, and I collapse onto the chair next to her.

"Oh my God, you're, like, shaking—are you okay?"

I give her a jerky nod as the chair tightens around me, cutting into me, until I feel like it's going to crush me. She gives me a concerned look and rummages in her bag.

"Do you want a bonbon?"

What the *fuck*? I'm suffocating here. I glance to one side; people are talking amongst themselves, but I know they're talking about me, whispering as usual, look at the state of it, thinks it's normal, thinks it has a right to be here with the Beautiful People, out in the open, lock it in a box, never let it out, shouldn't have to suffer its presence—

Amy jiggles the bag at me. "Go on. The sugar will make you feel better."

I feel the laugh build within me, but I know I can't let it out, because if I do, that's it: game over, man, game over. She really doesn't have a clue, does she? Of course sugar will make me feel better. It's my best friend. We just have a bit of a toxic relationship. I love it, it hates me. If people see me taking a bonbon, then they'll know that I'm a cheater, I'm one of the lazy ones, eat less, move more, eat paleo, no grains, no carbs, definitely no sugar, no sugar, sugar, sugar, sugar, sweet, sweet, sugar . . .

I give her a jerky nod and take one. It's dusty with icing sugar. I haven't had one of these since I was a kid. I wonder where she found them. Probably in some elitist hipster shop in a trendy part of town I don't know of, despite living here all my life.

She grins at me and pops one in her mouth.

"Strawberry. My favorite." Her voice sounds full—well, of course it's full, she has a bonbon in her mouth, you fucking *idiot*—

I shove the bonbon in my mouth and hope the sugar will shut the voice up. And it works. Sort of.

Bonbons are hard to chew at first, so I concentrate on sucking. My mouth is flooded with a chemical-sweet synthetic strawberry flavor. Then the outside begins to soften and I probe it with my tongue. Hmm. Time to chew soon. But not yet. Chewing makes them go away and I want to savor this. I roll it around my mouth. Hmm. Sweet. *Sweeeet.*

Slowly, my hands stop trembling, and I find I am able to move. I'm actually right at the end of the row, so I can take my coat off without running the risk of punching someone in the face. My bag nestles comfortably beside me. All because of sugar. Lovely, lovely sugar.

"There. Better now?"

Amy's voice has taken on a soothing edge. I like that. It's nice. Amy is nice. Maybe we could be—cross fingers to ward off the jinx—friends? Or is that just the sugar talking?

"Yeah," I say. "Thanks."

She leans over to me, giving me a conspiratorial look. "I know what it's like. Crowded places? Ugh. Hate them." She does a little mock shudder to prove her point.

I look at her perfect legs, and her flat stomach, her high cheekbones and her small, perky breasts.

Yeah, of course you know what it's like, sweetheart, of course you do.

16: #ASSHOLESTUDENTS

I'm still feeling a bit jumpy. Someone's phone goes off halfway through the lecture, and the professor goes apeshit, yelling at them to get the hell out of his lecture hall. At one point, I wonder if he's going to storm out, or grab the phone and throw it away, or both. I kind of like how these professors operate. Unlike school—which was all *please* and *thank you* and *don't damage their fragile little egos even if they are bullying little shitheads who give other kids nightmares*—university is much more brutal. You step out of line? You get bawled out, simple as that. Forget safe spaces. You're here to learn.

Amy gives me a fake worried look, and I dare to smile before the professor carries on. Today's lecture is about Jung—not one of my favorites, but interesting nonetheless. Some people might complain about lectures, but I like them. I like the focus. Concentrate on this. No need to interact with the rest of the world. It's good.

Afterward, I wait until nearly everyone has filed out before I scuttle toward the door, my head down, my arms full of folders. I'm still not used to being this visible, and I wonder if I ever will be. Maybe I should speak to Amy about it—ask her if we can sit at the back, where I feel safer? Or would she totally, like, laugh at that?

Whatever she'd do, she has followed me out and is looking at me expectantly. I have no idea what to say to her.

"Uh, good lecture?"

"Oh, yeah!" she replies. "Listen, do you want to come back to mine for some lunch? We could look at those references together. Are you in digs or halls? Oh, no, you live at home, right? I remember, your mum's sick. Is she okay? Do you need to get home, or can you come round? I mean, if your mum needs you, then of course, go do that, but if not, you could come back to mine. I know there's another lecture at one, and I'm not that far away, I mean, we could go to the library, of course, but then we can't eat, and if I don't eat I go all weird and wobbly, like properly hangry, so, uh, yeah?"

Oh God. This is good, right? This is what I wanted? Uni was a new start, a new opportunity, and here I am being offered that opportunity—the opportunity to make a real friend and not one that is just strings of zeros and ones, one made of flesh, not of data. I was just planning to hang around the library, but okay, this is something else, something new, something . . . good?

"Uh, okay," I say, hoping my voice doesn't crack. "Whatever you want. Are you in halls?"

"Yeah, I am. The nice ones, not like, you know, Bateson. Do you know they still have shared rooms there? It's like the fucking stone age! Luckily I got into Watson. It's a bit more expensive, but I get my own room and bathroom. Nothing worse than having to pull someone else's hair out of the plughole, right? It's just disgusting. So when I applied, Mum and Dad said that they'd help me pay for the nicer halls as long as I kept my grades up, God, you'd think that was all that mattered, fucking grades, don't they realize the *experience* of uni is the important thing?"

She seems to expect a response so I say, "Uh, yeah, absolutely. Get out there, in the real world. Try to figure out who you are." Not that I have a clue.

"I know, right? I tried to tell them, but they think everything has to be tied to what job you can get, how much you can earn, like money is everything . . ."

I try not to gawp as she carries on talking. It's a gift. Or a curse. She can witter on about anything. No need to worry about uncomfortable silences with Amy around. It's kind of adorable. And annoying.

"Oh, look! Squirrels!" she squeals as we walk past the park. "Oh, I love the way they scamper about, holding things in their little paws. They are so *cute*!"

I don't have the heart to tell her I saw three of them mug a couple of old ladies of their sandwiches not that long ago.

We grab the bus, and from there it doesn't take us long to reach her residence halls, but I'm still breathing pretty hard when we get there. I'm trying to disguise it, which is only making matters worse, but I can't let on that a simple stroll has knackered me quite this much.

She lives on the third floor, and I suffer a moment of panic when I think I might have to climb three flights of stairs, but it's okay—there's a lift. Thank the Lord for small mercies, I suppose.

Her halls aren't quite like I'd imagined university accommodations to be. In my head, it's all very much filthy bathrooms and greasy kitchens, cigarette butts, and pyramids of beer cans all over the place. This looks more like a Travelodge. Okay, so there's washing-up piled in the sink and about a million takeaway menus covering the table, but on the whole, it's pretty civilized. Nicer than home, anyway. At least someone vacuums here. They probably have a cleaner who comes in, or something.

Amy bounces off and opens one of the doors.

"This is my room!" she says, and wow, yes it is. It looks like there was an explosion in a glitter factory. Fairy lights twinkle around the mirror, and there are posters for various anime movies on the wall. And, Jesus, is that tinsel? It's not Christmas! But it does sparkle, and Amy's obviously a magpie, so why not?

I sit on the edge of her bed and she throws herself down next to me.

"So, this is my home at the moment," she says. "I mean, it's small, I know, but it's homey, isn't it?"

I glance around myself, trying not to be blinded by all the sparkling. Is she . . . seeking my approval?

"Uh, yeah. It's really nice. Really . . . glittery."

"Yeah, I like glitter. It's really important to make your living space yours, otherwise I don't think you could ever really relax there. Mum didn't like me having the lights up, said they were a fire hazard, and she thought that sparkly things made the room look cheap, but fuck it, she's not here, is she?"

The sudden viciousness in her voice shocks me.

"Anyway, I decided I was going to craft my dream room when I was at uni." And just like that, the viciousness is gone. "So I did! I love it. It's my haven. My sanctuary. Shall we go and get something to eat?"

And she's up again, bouncing to the door. If this is such a sanctuary, then why does she seem so keen to get out of it? But then again, that's not really my business, is it? I eat family meal deals' worth of pizza to escape my issues. We all have our quirks.

The kitchen is the only shared space, but there's no one else in at the moment, so I don't feel too uncomfortable. Amy puts the kettle on and goes to the fridge, where she rummages for a bit and then surfaces, empty-handed.

"Those jokers," she says. "No milk. Again. We're supposed to get all our own stuff, but they keep borrowing mine." She rolls her eyes in a dramatic way, as if it's all just a big joke, but I can see it bothers her. "Good thing I've got some Coffee-Mate. Are you okay with coffee?"

"I'm fine with coffee," I say.

"Sugar?"

Three.

"No, thanks. I'm trying to avoid added sugar as much as possible at the moment."

"Oh, you're so good! Not like me, I'm hopelessly addicted." She adds two teaspoons of the white stuff into a mug.

Look, I know. I know, okay? You don't need to say anything. I have to pretend I'm avoiding. It makes it look like I'm trying, and I've learned that people are more willing to give the overweight the benefit of the doubt if we piously restrict ourselves in public. It's an unwritten law: never add sugar, always stick to the salad option even if the lasagna looks reeeally good, and never, never, NEVER order a dessert, no matter what. People will then tell you you're so good, oh, it's so unfair for you, you try so hard, and for a fleeting moment, you are allowed to believe them and it's okay to feel, if not good about yourself, then maybe a smidgen less self-loathing.

Anyway, you can always stop off at Tesco on the way home, buy a family-sized chocolate trifle for a fraction of the price of the tiny slice of cake you've just refused to eat, and trough the lot, preferably while lying on your bed in your underwear. It's a win-win situation. Well worth suffering a cup of bitter coffee. "Oh, I don't know where I'd be without coffee," Amy says. "Half asleep, propped up in the library somewhere, I expect. I reckon the whole university industry is probably run on coffee. I must go through a good jar of it a week." She lowers her voice a bit. "Then again, I do think some of the jokers here might help themselves sometimes, I mean, I know I'm a coffee addict, but I don't think my habit is *that* bad."

"Maybe you should just keep it in your room?" I say. "Lock it up so nobody else could get it. You could get a mini-fridge, too, stop people from nicking your milk."

"Uh, wow, yeah. That's such a good idea." She beams at me, but I can hear the doubt in her voice, and I wonder why she doesn't want to protect her stuff.

"How many people live on this floor, anyway?" I ask, hoping to change the subject just subtly enough so she doesn't realize that's what I'm doing. I don't know what it is about her, but she stokes my maternal instinct; she has this wobbly-legged-fawn-born-next-to-a-motorway quality to her, and I can't help but want to protect her, even if it's just from herself.

"There's five, including me. Indigo, Dizzy, Patrick, and Richard. They're great. Really great. I really like all of them. Really."

Really?

"That's good," I say, and take a sip of my coffee. It's not a bad brand, not like the cheap shit we get at home, but it still takes everything I've got to not pucker my mouth and reach for the sugar bowl. "I can't imagine how bad it would be if you didn't get along."

For a second, Amy stares out the window, sipping on her coffee. "Yeah. I know. Some people are having a really tough time, you know, homesick, not really getting on with anyone, just struggling in general. I'm so lucky." She gives me a brittle smile.

Okay, so this isn't one of the most awkward conversations I've ever had . . .

"Where are you from?" I ask, hoping it's innocent enough and isn't the thing that finally breaks her.

"Buckinghamshire. I know, *ooh arr*, I sound like a farmer. Mum and Dad wanted me to go to Oxford, like my brother Rob, but I wasn't having that. So much pressure, you know? So I, like, decided I was going to a *real* university. Experience real, proper life, not the weird stuff Rob does. He's a member of a really bizarre society, and quite frankly, I didn't want anything to do with that, so I said 'Fuck no, I'm going to forge my own destiny,' you know what I mean? And so I'm here now, and it's sooo much better than I expected, it's sooo real, so nice to be with authentic people, not the fakes I had to put up with at home, because I think it's far more important to be authentic, don't you? So many people are just, like, so fake nowadays, it's all 'what car do you drive' and 'who does your dad work for,' but there's more to life than that, isn't there?"

"Uh, yeah. Of course there is," I say, wondering what the name of her childhood pony was and how much longer her membership to the local tennis club has before it runs out. Then I feel a bit bad, because that's MidnightBanshee kind of thinking. So Amy's trying to reinvent herself. I can't judge her for that. I'm doing exactly the same thing. Let her do whatever she has to do to make herself feel better. Live and let live, and all that jazz.

The main door bangs, and Amy flinches. I frown into my mug. Heavy footfalls echo up the corridor. A handsome, if heavyset, young man strides into the room, and I instinctively lean back, as if I might be able to press myself into the wall and disappear. He grins at both of us.

"All right, chicks? Hey, Tinks, mind if I steal some coffee? I'm mucho parched, and I've run out." Before she can answer, he turns to me. "Heyyy, Big Bird! I'm Patrick, but everyone calls me Bear. You know, because of Paddington and everything. It's a rugger thing. Can't help it, everyone has to have a nickname. You okay, Tinks? You look a bit tired. Okay with the coffee, yeah?" He doesn't wait for her to answer, just helps himself to a cup. "Anyway, you seen Diz? She was supposed to meet me for lunch but never showed. Stupid thing, no wonder everyone calls her Dizzy. If you see her, tell her I stayed for a bit, but I'm not hanging around."

He takes a huge gulp from his mug. "Right then, I'm going to have a shit, a shower, and a shave, smoke a boom batty, and then I'm off. Catch you later, Tinks. You too, Big Bird. Have fun."

And he leaves.

I don't quite know what to say.

"That was Patrick," Amy says. "He's funny."

"Yeah, he comes across that way," I say dryly. "Why does he call you Tinks?"

"Tinkerbell." She almost whispers it. "He says it's because I'm away with the fairies. You shouldn't be offended by his silly nicknames. He plays rugby, went to a posh school."

Like that makes it somehow okay to be a prick to everyone.

"What's his surname?" I ask.

"Uh, Dalgleish, I think. Why?"

"No reason," I say.

17: #SECRETSANDLIES

After coffee, Amy offers me a mug of soup with some pasta in it. It's like she's read a how-to-be-a-student handbook and needs to prove that she knows all the tricks. I accept the pitiful rations she offers me and try to eat slowly. My usual portion would have covered hers as well, but I don't want her to know that. Halfway through the soup the room shakes as Patrick turns his music on—no headphones for the Bear, and even Amy can't help but roll her eyes. A few minutes later, I hear a bang on his door and Patrick booming, "Dickie! What? Turn it down? Why? This track's *banging*!" I can't help but sympathize with the poor sod who wants the Bear to shut the fuck up.

By the time we head to our lecture, Amy's a bit subdued, and I don't really like that. On the plus side, though, she's quite happy to sit at the back with me, so I don't have to suffer another public meltdown trying to find a seat. This lecture is a two hour-er, and about forty minutes in I'm struggling to keep my eyes open. The Powerpoints blur, and my mind starts wandering. Judging by the way Amy is surreptitiously fiddling with her phone under the bench in front of her, I'm not the only one struggling to pay attention.

I start to doodle, nothing specific at first, but then the lines come together to form one of my favorite computer game characters, and before I know it, I'm bent over my page, hatching, shading, sweeping lines in blue ink—

"What's that?" Amy whispers, gesturing to my page.

I hastily try to cover up the doodle with one hand. "N-nothing."

"It's good. I didn't know you could draw."

"I can't. Not really. Just a silly hobby. I don't take it seriously."

"You should. You're good! He's gorgeous. Who is it?"

"Just a game character I like," I mutter.

"A game? I like games. Maybe you could show me it sometime?"

"Um, yeah, if you like."

Amy says something in reply, but I'm not really listening because I'm too busy thinking *Not on your fucking life*. These are mine and mine alone—unless I'm posting them up anonymously, and even then . . . yeah. It's complicated. I'm constantly caught between wanting to share and the fear of making myself that vulnerable. Needless to say, I haven't posted anything since I started trolling. All it takes is someone to realize the person tearing them apart also fancies herself as a bit of an artist, and my carefully constructed house of cards comes crashing down.

But, at the same time, I can't quite bring myself to delete my page . . .

"Oh, Fisher's looking twitchy. Better shut up."

I glance up, and indeed, Dr. Fisher is glaring in our direction.

Good old Dr. Fisher. I think I like him.

♣♣♣

At the end of the lecture, Amy wants me to go back to halls with her, but I make my excuses and head home. Tonight is Wednesday night, and I babysit the kids down the road on Wednesdays so their mum, Mrs. Olgive, can go to her night class. This is one of the up-sides of being fugly: whereas people your own age generally shun and belittle you, older people, especially mothers, tend to trust you over your skinnier peers. Maybe they think you're less likely to organize an orgy while they're out. It's not much, but it means I get a bit of money each week to myself. Enough to maintain my stash of secret chocolate, anyway.

And speaking of secret chocolate, it's time to go and replenish the stash. Luckily there are three mini-marts, a Tesco Local, and a small Sainsbury's all within a ten minute walk, so I can buy a couple of £1.00 four-packs in each without the cashier giving me funny looks. Yes, I know this is the behavior of someone with a problem, but fuck it. If I've got to put Natalie and Jordan to bed tonight, I'm going to need something to keep my strength up.

As it happens, Natalie and Jordan are pretty much the cutest kids ever. And I feel for them. I know what it's like, to have your dad decide you're not good enough. At least they're young enough that they might not remember what it was like to even have a dad, unlike me.

Half an hour after Mrs. Olgive leaves for her class, they're scampering up to bed. I read them *Hoot Owl*, and after one request for a drink of water and one subsequent bathroom visit, they're both fast asleep, so I retrieve my four-pack of Bounties from my backpack (a quid for four chocolate bars! What a time to be alive), get my laptop out, and log into Mrs. Olgive's Wi-Fi.

The flutter's there when I sort my proxies out, and boy, there's a real smorgasbord of treats on the menu tonight.

Freedomchick04's roasting has taken on a life of its own, and I can't help but wonder just how many other people like me are out there—people who are completely alienated by these so-called perfect specimens and just want a good excuse to take them down a notch.

Metachat pops up, asking me if I want to accept a password. Is it really Tori? If so, she's quick. I've only just had a chance to check on a couple of profiles. She probably realized I was online when the infamous SharkKrawler9 logged in to check on Freedomchick. Still, I'm not sure if I should be flattered that she's waiting for me, or weirded out that she's monitoring me.

Hey!

she says as soon as I accept her chat request.

All right?
No. Shit day. Fucking numbskulls everywhere.
Yeah—know what you mean. You ok?
Will be once we've destroyed the fucker.
Absolute dickhead. Name's John Corlen. Wanna join in?

Well, how is a girl supposed to turn down such a lovely invitation?

Who is he?
Sub-level boss. Such a cockmuncher.
Wish I could push him under a train, but I can do the next best thing.
Mrs. Corlen, say hello to Alexandra, John's "mistress."
Wow—you found that out?

What? No, fuck off. Alexandra doesn't exist.
But Mrs. Corlen doesn't know that.
Getting into his account should be a piece of piss—just
need to lay the breadcrumbs, expose him, et voila!

She's my dream. She's my nightmare.

Turns out, the kind of plot Tori's cooked up is as much fun as straightforward trolling. I realize now that I'm really just an amateur with a gift for acidic comments. I can whip up a crowd and make them dance to my tune, but I've never had the guts to actually hack accounts to orchestrate the outcome I want. That's a whole new level for me, a whole new learning curve. And it's steep. Yeah, I know how to craft an online persona, but most of mine are as 2D as possible, so no one can trace me. When you're hacking to set someone up, you need to be able to wear your victim's skin so no one will realize it isn't them. Any doubts, and the whole thing comes crashing down.

This time, Tori wants me involved. She's going to be Corlen, and I'm Alexandra. We've nabbed some pictures off some dodgy Russian dating website—she's gorgeous, whoever she is, with long dark hair and big blue eyes—but not so gorgeous people won't believe. I soon discover it's fun being someone else. Tori-as-Corlen flirts with "Alexandra" over chat. We exchange photos. Nowadays it seems like everyone has a dick pic somewhere, and as predicted, Creepy Corlen has one buried in his cloud account. Alexandra gets that and obliges with a couple of fingers rammed up her fanny. I am laughing so much at this point that I worry I'm going to wake up the kids, but it's okay. They're dead to the world when I go and check up on them, oblivious to the utter devastation that is being wreaked.

I've had so much fun, I've only eaten one of the Bounties

and I haven't touched the penguin bar and can of Coke she left out for me. Hey, maybe this is the secret—do something fun and you forget to eat. No wonder skinny people always look so damn happy.

I've decided Alexandra is going to stick around. I quite like her. She's a sexy, confident woman who knows what she wants and goes for it, even if it's a balding man in his late-forties with a mid-level job in a boring insurance firm, a wife, and two kids.

I do feel a bit of a pang when I find out about the wife and kids. Of course I knew he was married, but when the wife starts virtual sobbing over "Alexandra," and the real John Corlen starts trying to deny it all and save his relationship, and she declares she's taking the kids to her mother's and she doesn't know when she'll be back, I do feel bad.

I wonder what he did to piss Tori off so much. It must have been serious for her to want to ruin his life.

Still, I stand by my assertion that Alexandra is fun. I do wonder if that makes me a bad person.

At ten thirty Mrs. Olgive gets home and pays me, telling me she doesn't know what she'd do without me, so good, hope the kids weren't too much hassle. I smile that weird, fake smile you give to parents when you tell them they were fine, to hide the fact that the minute they were in bed, all thoughts of their precious moppets flew out of your mind. Honestly, those kids could've been planning a riot up there, and I wouldn't know.

I feel a bit of a pang for her, though. I know she struggles. Women tend to. I wonder why we're so horrible to each other, then? You'd think we'd stick together a bit more, what with this being "a man's world" and all, but we don't. We'd rather gossip and fat shame and sneer and steal each other's men. I wonder if life's easier if you're a lesbian. Do they have Alexandras to contend with? I suppose so. It's all human nature, isn't it? Life is so complicated sometimes, I do wonder why we bother at all.

I nip back home—Mum's slumped in front of the TV watching generic US crime drama No. 6734. I think Brat's in, judging by the heavy atmosphere. When I check in on Mum she nods at me and calls me a "good girl." Heh. If only she knew.

Back upstairs, I secrete my three remaining Bounties away and feel oddly up on the deal. Then I plug my laptop in and go back to Tori, who is gleefully crowing about her takedown of the now infamous John Corlen.

Didn't take long, did it?

Long for what?

For his wife to find out?

Oh, she's had her suspicions for a while.
I needed you to play the other side so it looked authentic.
You were a star. I don't think I've ever met anyone else
quite like you, you know.

An odd feeling stirs in my belly. I feel full, yet hungry. Butterflies flutter in my chest, a weird trembling sensation that makes it hard to type. I have felt this before, but it led to a place of hate and shame, and I promised myself I'd never go there again. I can't help it though. This is completely involuntary. I haven't even seen a picture of Tori, but I don't need to. Attraction is more than just physical looks. Go ask anyone.

You're welcome. I guess the scumbag had it coming.

Oh, he sure did. Fucking dickhead.

What did he do?

She pauses.

Just shit at work. Fucking bully. Takes advantage of his
position.

I get the feeling Tori is dancing round the edge of the real
reason. If she is alluding to what I think she is alluding to, I
wish Alexandra had done more. I don't feel bad about his wife
and kids anymore. If anything, I now feel they're well out of it.

You did what you had to.
Yeah. I did. Couldn't have done it without you, tho. :) <3
It was nothing. Anything for you.
Same here. You name it, it's yours.
I've never had so much fun or been able to sort out my
shitty life before I met you.
So glad you replied to me and didn't just block me.

I bite my lip. Wow. My fingers twitch as I dust them over
my keyboard. How do I respond? Is this how friends talk to
each other? I don't really know. I've never really had what you
might call a proper friend, not since primary school. Is this
BFF stuff, or is it something more?
Do I want it to be something more?
I manage to type:

Come on :P. Let's go make some more mischief.
^_^ I thought you'd never ask!

18: #REAPWHATYOUSOW

You know when you fall asleep and your hand goes numb because you've been lying on it, and then it comes back to life and it feels like a million wasps are buzzing inside your skin? That's what the rain outside my window makes my head feel like.

I peek outside. It's still dark, but I can see it bounce off the tarmac, sheets of near vertical water sweeping up the road like marching soldiers.

I don't think I'm going to go to uni today. Okay, so I know I should, but fuck it. I'm not getting soaked just so I can sit in a lecture hall for an hour and a half going through something I can read in a book.

I snuggle back into my covers, relishing the thought of not getting up. Maybe I could spend the entire day in my pajamas. Maybe Tori will be in all day, too, and we'll go play in all of our favorite playgrounds, doing the online equivalent of pushing kids off swings and then punching them in their virtual faces so they stay down.

I wonder what Tori looks like. I don't know why, but I think she might look a bit like old-school Lara Croft, all Sloanie yet brassy, with a knowing smile and a pistol at each hip. Or maybe she's a deadly redhead, like Black Widow. Or a blonde, all shimmer and ice like January Jones. In any case, she's an assassin, and I adore her for it.

I wonder if she thinks the same things about me?

My phone shrieks at me. Bugger. Forgot to switch off the alarm. Shit shit shit. And like Pavlov's dog, there goes my bladder. Hear the alarm—oh, need a wee! It's inevitable. Suppose I'll have to get up.

The house is quiet. After using the loo, I pad downstairs to get a drink. I could make a hot chocolate and take it back up to bed. Now that *would* be decadent. Back to bed with my laptop, and by proxy, Tori.

I shake my head. Got to watch this. Last thing I need is to develop another obsession.

I fill the kettle and flick it on. There's one sachet of Galaxy hot chocolate left. Should I leave it for someone else? Should I balls. Sorry, you snooze, you lose in this house. This is *my* hot chocolate now. I wish we had some squirty cream to go on top of it, like they do in all the coffee shops, but let's face it—unless it's Christmas or you're planning some kinky shenanigans, who has squirty cream in their fridge? Click! Pour. The familiar aroma of chocolate swirls around me, lovely and comforting. Delicious.

Hot chocolate in hand, I'm about to head back upstairs, but this time the murmur of the TV catches my attention. I peer through the partially opened door. Mum's still on the sofa, asleep.

I could leave her. I don't want my hot chocolate to get cold. But what kind of daughter would that make me? I dither for a second, and then set my drink down on the little table in the hall. I'll just make sure she's okay, then go back upstairs.

No pill packets nearby. A cold, half-drunk cup of tea on

the floor next to her. No booze. That's a good sign. I smile and smooth her hair down. She stirs like a child, and sighs in her sleep. I hope she's happier there than she is here. She deserves that at least.

A sudden lump swells in my throat. I swallow hard and blink furiously. It's so unfair. So unfair for all of us.

Before my mind can delve deep into this pit of emotion, I squash it down, force the beast back into its box, and sit on the lid so it can't wriggle out again. At least I can do this now. At least I can wrestle with it. Sometimes, I even beat it. Mostly I'm just restraining it. But at least I don't cower from it anymore. Well, not much, anyway.

Back upstairs, to my room. My haven. My sanctuary. Back under the covers, where nothing can hurt me and fantasy rules. I go straight for my laptop. Tori may not be awake yet, but I can still go through our conversations, relive our past glories.

The internet's a weird place when it comes to time. It never really sleeps, and not in an insomniac way. It's like an all-devouring beast, containing worlds within worlds, yet none of them exist, not really. In reality, they're lines of data, GO TO commands, binary strings of ones and zeros that mean nothing to most people, yet through this, those same people create their lives, their loves—measure their whole self-worth. Whole communities have sprung up around people's bizarre obsessions, that need to know that no matter what, they are not alone and they are accepted. It takes a very strong person to deny that pull. No wonder people go to virtual war when those communities are threatened. It's fascinating to watch.

The rain continues to pound against my window as the dawn lightens the day to a dull gray, and I continue to survey my Empire of Hate. It is *magnificent*. I've been blocked so many times now, it's unreal. So many accounts suspended, never to darken our doors again. I suppose I'll be found out one day, exposed, pilloried. Hell, I might even get arrested; ever since they made trolling a hate crime, I've been waiting for the knock on the door: "Hello, are you Bethany Soames, also known as, amongst others, MidnightBanshee? Can you come with us, please?"

But that just makes it so much more exciting. When you've spent most of your life living in fear, bearing the brunt of others' cruelty, terrified of putting a foot wrong just in case anyone notices . . . it's a release. It's like sticking a red-hot needle in a festering boil and drawing the pus.

It's fucking salvation.

19: #FIENDS #IMEANFRIENDS

I must've fallen asleep, because the next time I look at my clock, it's nearly ten in the morning. The remnants of my hot chocolate are congealing in the mug, and my mouth's got that horrible, furry quality to it. I feel a brief burst of irrational panic as I wake my laptop up, despite knowing my protocols would've logged me out automatically. Yes, I know I was just philosophizing about how the fear of getting caught only adds to the thrill, but I'm not always up for that.

I decide to be Beth for a bit and check my regular accounts on my phone. Unlike my alter egos, Beth doesn't get much attention. If I'm lucky, I might have a couple of notifications, maybe a like if I've posted something containing cats. But this morning I've got loads of messages. All from Amy.

She's tagged me into almost everything. Things she finds funny, little psychology jokes, in the comment section of things she thinks I might like. Curious, I check her profile. She has hundreds of friends (compared to my eighty-six, with a good half of them being various family members and friends of my mum), but it all seems a bit, I don't know, superficial. Cautiously, I like a few of the things she has tagged me into, and give her a lol and a ❤ on things she has posted on my timeline. It's kind of cute, in a way. I wonder if this is how normal people use social media.

It doesn't take long before a Messenger box pops up.

Heya!!! Where r u? r u ill? Missed u this morning!!!

Gosh. That's a lot of exclamatory enthusiasm for just ten in the morning.

> Hi. Yeah, not feeling great. Headache.
> Might be migraine.
> Think it's the weather. Always makes me feel bad.

Awww!!!! Poor u!!!!
I have the notes—will give them to u when I see u next.
Hope u feel better soon!!!

> Me too. Head is banging.

☹ That's not good.
I was going to ask if u were free on Friday nite?
Me and a few of the others were going to go to the union, and then maybe out to a club? Thought u could come too!!!

An icy trickle tracks down my back.

Out?

For the evening?

On a Friday night?

To a club?

Immediately, I'm scrambling for every excuse under the sun. My mum's ill. I'm ill. The dog's ill. She doesn't even need to know the dog was put down over a year ago. I've broken something. Bradley's broken something. Fucking hell—say something, anything! This is not a drill!

> I dunno. I don't have a union card atm.

Shit. Is that the best I can come up with? I stare at my

fingers in horrified disappointment.

No union card? Why? Did u lose it?

No, I didn't lose it. I never picked one up, because I never went to Freshers' week, because I had no intention of ever going to the Union, despite university being my big excuse to reinvent myself and maybe meet new people who might not hate me on sight because I wear larger clothes than they do, and YES I am aware of how contradictory all that sounds, and YES I know it's stupid, but fuck it, you want to judge me, come live in my head for five minutes and see how you cope.

Yeah. I'm always losing stuff.

Oh, FOR FUCK'S SAKE! Give me a pseudonym, and I can lie and lie and lie without a hint of conscience. Talk to someone I know and who knows me? It's nothing but guilt. Stupid brain.

That's ok, we can apply for another one! And we can go somewhere else tonight, like Sanford's. Say ull come! Itll be fun!!!

I now feel physically sick. This is it. In my more fevered moments, this is exactly what I'd dreamed of—an invitation from (sort of) normal people for a (sort of) normal night out, doing all the (sort of) normal things normal people my age do. But, at the same time, the thought of entering a crowded bar makes me want to flee in the opposite direction and never, ever come back.

I dunno . . .

Aww, B!!! Please? Ur, like, my BFF here!! I'll be lonely if u don't!!

BFF?

Surely she's taking the piss. We've only known each other for a couple of days. Been to a few lectures together. I only went to her halls because I really didn't have much else to do. But she thinks I'm her BFF?

This is a trap. It has to be. Some kind of prank. A cruel trick.

Disgustingly, my eyes well up. Fucking hell, I am MidnightBanshee, Destroyer of Online Worlds. I hunt down pretty girls like Amy for breakfast and pick my teeth with the bones of their Instagram accounts.

And here I am, crying, because someone has called me their friend. I type with shaking fingers . . .

Ok, I'll come. If I'm better, of course.

SQUEEEEE!!!! Of course! But ull be better. U have to be, cos were gonna tear up the town! Watch out TOWN, because Beth and Amy are gonna be in the house! Woop woop!!!!

Well, I can always say I still feel horrible.

20: #SOGGYCHIPS

The rain doesn't ease up. Tori's nowhere to be seen, but that's understandable, given that most proper grown-ups are at work right now. I get out my sketchbook and try to lose myself in that, but my heart isn't into it, so I decide to switch to terrorizing a Q&A board. People ask such stupid things, it's like shooting fish in a barrel.

I potter downstairs to find some lunch, but the cupboards are basically bare.

In the living room, Mum's watching TV again. The screen is reflected in her glasses, making it look like her eyes are flickering.

"Mum?" I say.

"Hmm?" She doesn't look at me, just keeps staring at the TV. I purse my lips and swallow. She hasn't been this bad since Dad left. I suppose it is coming up on a year, and everyone says anniversaries are the hardest things to deal with.

"Have you sorted the food delivery?"

"Hmm?"

"The Tesco delivery. Have you sorted it? We're getting low on stuff."

She slowly drags her attention from the screen and blinks once, twice, three times, like a lizard.

"I don't know. I think so?"

"Shall I have a look?"

"That would be good." She stretches her hand out to me, beckoning me to join her on the sofa. It smells faintly rank in the living room, and I am ashamed to admit that I hesitate before sitting next to her. She drapes her arm around my shoulders and pulls me close, cradling my head against her chest like she used to when I was small, and starts to rock me. I swallow again, harder this time; it's all I can do to stop myself from breaking down.

"My little Bethany," she croons. "So grown up now. I remember when you were little. You used to climb into my lap and beg me for cuddles. You don't do that anymore. Too big now. Too old."

Her voice hitches and I squeeze my eyes shut. Mum desperately needs to take a shower and change her clothes, but nothing could drag me away from her right now. I wrap my arms around her neck as she cries, piteously, and I cry too, a mixture of grief and anger; grief at my lost mother and my lost father, and anger that the two of them allowed us to get to this point.

Slowly, times slips by and Mum's tears subside. I sniff, and the ugly sound echoes through the room. Mum slumps back, spent.

"There's cash in the tin," she whispers. "Go get some chips for lunch, love."

Yay. Chips.

More carbs.

◆◆◆

I guess I kind of saw it coming. Dad leaving, that is. I don't think Mum did, though. Despite the arguing and all the "meetings" that meant he had to "work late" yet again, *I know, I know, but if you want food on the table* yadda yadda yadda . . . I think Mum was too close to the signs to read them accurately. Either that or she ignored them, hoping they'd go away. I think that's why it hit her so hard.

Sometimes, I'm a bit ashamed of her. I mean, come on, she should be out every night, guzzling prosecco straight out of the bottle, celebrating her freedom. But Mum's not like that. She's too fragile, like a bird who actually liked the safety of her cage. I can't help but wonder if she's always been like this but did a better job of hiding it when Dad was around. I remember, when I was little, how she "liked a lie-in." As a kid, I took that at face value—Mum liked to sleep, simple as that. Same with her never working full-time. She said it was so she could be there for us. Maybe it was actually because she couldn't cope. I don't know. I doubt I ever will.

The chips are soggy, but they still taste good. I love the way the acid of the vinegar catches in the back of my throat, offsetting the fluffy greasiness of the potato in quite a lovely way. Mum doesn't eat much, so I polish off her leftovers, too. Well, waste not, want not.

She assures me she's rebooked the Tesco delivery, but I check, just in case. I also add a few essentials to the list—hey, she'll never remember, and it's not much; just a pack of biscuits here, a couple of cheapo multipacks of chocolate there. Doesn't even amount to a fiver—what's happiness compared to a fiver? Not sure what we're going to have for tea tonight. If I can't scrape something together from the remnants in the freezer, well, there's always takeaway.

I make Mum a cup of tea and then slope back off upstairs. I know it's a long shot given it's just past one, but I log into

Metachat anyway to see if Tori's around; she's not, and I swallow down a little bubble of disappointment and switch to my favorite hunting grounds.

It doesn't take long for me to get my fix. I'm flying high. No one can touch me up here. I have wings made of lies; I am carried aloft by the scorching thermals of their collective hatred.

And I feel alive.

Here, I am nothing. I have no flesh. No bones. No blood to shed. I am a binary figure, an abstract force, zeros and ones, data strings, Boolean scripts.

I am whatever I want to be, and you can't stop me, no matter how hard you try.

When you're nothing, you're indestructible.

Freedomchick04's back. Stupid bitch. She's full of *oh, I was hacked* and *evil trolls* and *pity me, for they are trying to destroy me!* I laugh. You think that's it? Give me a break.

Time to try on some new faces.

Of course, my old accounts have been blocked or suspended, which might work for the peasants, but for those of us who stalk the dark side, it's par for the course. It takes less than a quarter of an hour to set up four new accounts, each with their own email accounts and IP addresses, and I'm ready to go hunting again.

I'm not just after Freedomchick today. A couple of my old targets have been lulled into a false sense of security and need taking down a peg. Plus, there's a new girl, some stupid slapper who seems to think the world wants to see snaps of her sandy ass as she poses on various beaches. Stupid thing is, the number of followers she's managed to accrue in a short space of time bears her confidence out. Sometimes I despair.

The new girl has already managed to gather a pretty hardcore group of worshippers, who go on the defensive straight away, calling me stupid, just jealous, and probably fat and ugly in real life, but I simply don't care, because no one can say anything for certain; I'm an internet shadow, a ghost, out to haunt you and your idiotic so-called friends. Oh, she loves them all, does she? Yeah, right, even the spotty ones and the fat ones and the creepy ones and the ones who smell funny and the ones with weird hair—yeah, she'd toootally give them the time of day if she met them on one of her oh-so-perfect beaches and wouldn't look at them like they were pieces of crap she'd just scraped off the bottom of her designer flip-flops.

I only have to switch accounts a couple of times before a band of vultures swoops in. Good old vultures. They make my life so much more fun. I sit back and watch them tear into the carcass that was a stupidly self-congratulatory Instagram account. Bumgirl is trying to delete stuff now, but once you get a few snowballs rolling, they quickly turn into an avalanche, and it isn't long before she is buried.

Oh, when will the Beautiful People learn? We fuglies outnumber you. We may not have your glitzy life, but we do have numbers on our side, along with the rage stoked by years of being sidelined and belittled.

Do not underestimate us, or we will destroy you.

21: #PSYCHOBITCHEX

It's just before three when a Metachat key pops up in my inbox, and I smile properly for what feels like the first time in weeks. Tori! Tori's here!

I copy the code down and key it in carefully, the unmistakable fizz of excitement bubbling away inside me. I'm not quite sure when I went from "suspicious conspiracy theorist" to "actively looking forward to communicating with this person," but a switch has most definitely been flicked. My only problem now is I've got to hide it until I've figured out if Tori feels the same way. No one likes an overexcited fat chick, after all.

> Hey. You're home early. Or has work finished where you are?

I know. Shameless digging, but can you blame me? I can't just ask her outright where she lives. That would be weird.

Left work early. Not having a good day. Feel like someone's attached jumper cables to my spine. Freaked out.

> Oh no! Is it the weather?
> It's shit here and that always makes me feel jumpy and weird.

No, not the weather.

Something happened this morning . . .

not sure if it's what I think it is, but it's freaked me out.

OK . . . you can tell me, if you want. No pressure. But I
might be able to help?

The seconds tick by. Still no reply. Oh, crap, what if I've overstepped the mark, what if she thinks I'm taking liberties, but then why bring it up if she didn't want me to ask about it? Gah, I hate this, it's like when people do those horrible ambiguous "some people are shit" or "you are terrible—you know who you are" posts, except I *don't* know and I automatically assume it's me. It's why I ended up abandoning my first attempts at social media and opening new accounts, to wipe the slate clean. Well, that and the insufferable bullying and the fact that I simply don't give a shit about what anyone I went to school with is doing—

I dunno if I'm right, but I think I saw my psychobitch ex this morning. I was grabbing a coffee, and I saw her walk past the window. I nearly had to hide in the fucking loo so she wouldn't see me. If it is her, it can't be a coincidence, can it? I moved away to get away from that bitch! And now she's here, in my town, strutting around like she owns it? I can't deal with that. But I can't move again, I've got a job here and everything now. I'm sorry to dump all of this on you, you don't deserve it, but I need to tell someone or I'm going to explode . . . arrrrggghhhhh!!!!!!!!!!! *rage*

Wow, that's . . . dramatic. Might explain a bit about her,

though. Looks like she's trying to claw back as much control of her life as she can. And I can't help the little smug smile that tugs at the corners of my mouth. She has a psychobitch ex—and she's telling me about it. Not her work friends, not her followers, but *me*. Shame I don't really have much experience (okay, none whatsoever) in the whole ex department.

> Yikes

Dumb, I know, but I can't just launch in with *omg, I'm so chuffed you're trusting me with this, and I want to help you in any way I can.*

> What was she doing?

I dunno. Just walking, I guess. It wasn't so much what she was doing, more that she was even here. I live in a backwater shithole! Nothing ever happens here. Why would she even move here, if it's not to find me and torture me again? Oh, Amy, what do I do?

Amy. That bursts my bubble. I'd forgotten I'd called myself that. Major regrets now. Why couldn't I just be honest in the first place? Well done, Beth, way to go in the Making Life Difficult For Yourself stakes again. Big round of applause.

> First off, I'm no expert . . . but maybe you could check her online? Stalk her for a bit? See if she's changed her location anywhere or if she posts any photos with places you recognize . . . with any luck, this is just her

doppelganger and you have nothing
to worry about.

And my name isn't Amy, but maybe we'll tackle that after I've (hopefully) done something right for a change.

Omg that's actually genius. Why didn't I think of that? Fuck me . . . hang on . . . brb . . .

Why am I holding my breath?

You're right!! No evidence of moving. Location as it was before. No photos of here. Unless she's literally arrived today. And even then, she'd tell everyone cos she literally documents everything she ever does online. Omg, I think I might actually cry, I'm so relieved. All that worrying for nothing? I am such a fucking moron. Thank you so much, hun. You're the best! Xxx

I'm the best. See, it's up there in black and white. AND three kisses. Maybe today isn't such a write-off after all. Now all I have to do is own up to not being an Amy.

That's it. Just type *Sorry, but my name is actually Beth.* Easy-peasy.

. . . fuck.

As if on cue, my phone pings; it's the real Amy, and she's been busy. On Facebook she's sharing dumb listicles with me, mainly ones about life at uni and cats. So far, so cliché. She's also messaged me, asking for my email as she couldn't find it in the uni database. I almost say that she was probably looking under Beth rather than Bethany, but instead I just give her my home email since that's easier for me to use.

I'm trying to construct a confessional to Tori when a new email notification pops up. In it are all of today's notes, neatly typed up.

Had nothing better to do this afternoon, she replies when I ask her about it. *U better get better soon or I'll turn into one of those weirdos who do nothing but study all the time!!*

This kind of leaves me speechless. I keep trying to turn her around in my head, but no matter what I try, she just doesn't fit. She's pretty. She's sparkly. She certainly isn't fugly. So why on earth does she want to be my friend? She must have some kind of defect (apart from a terminal case of over-perkiness) that she's hiding from me. That's all I can come up with.

Tori's back on track, sending me links to a new target. Okay, how am I going to do this? Quick and to the point, like ripping off a Band-Aid, or slow and gentle, like a breakup?

Yeah, I think I just answered my own question there.

Tori, can I tell you something?

Course. You can tell me anything :)

Oh, you say that now.

I just have something to admit. My name isn't amy. I told you it was amy cos the internet and all that but I feel really bad about that now. Just wanted u to know.
Pls don't be too mad . . . :(

I wince, my fingers crossed on my left hand while my right goes off groping in my bedside cabinet for a candy bar. Tori's reply comes through just as I manage to grasp one.

Lol! You're so funny. I guessed it wasn't your real name.
I mean who gives their real name straight away? I could
have been anyone! Don't sweat it, chick. I get it.

I pause, mid unwrap, and set the chocolate down without
taking a bite.

You sure? You're really ok with that?
Yeah! It's not like you've shot my dog or robbed me or
anything. Fuck, half the people I've slept with don't know
my real name. Who needs that hassle, amirite? :P
Seriously, though—don't worry about it. I mean it.

I can't believe she's being so cool about this.

Really? I've been worrying about this for
a while cos its plain you're not a freakshow
or anything. should have told you ages ago
but the time was never right . . .
I know how it is. You've got to do what you've got to
do to keep yourself safe. Like I said, I get it. Although I'm
not so sure about the freakshow thing . . . ;)
Oh really?!
Hey, why do you think I have a psychobitch ex?!
Once you go Tori, nothing else compares! ^_^

She ain't wrong.

Oh, but one thing . . .
Yeah?

What IS your name?! You still haven't told me!

Oh god i'm such an idiot! It's Beth.

Beth? I like that. Much better than Amy. Amy's a
bit basic bitch, you know what I mean? Beth,
though—yeah, that's much better. Like the chick
on The Walking Dead.

Lol! Wish I was called Carol now, cos she's hardcore.

Beth was a bit whiney. Cute ass, tho.

Lol, you know it! And she got to eat snakes with Daryl.
That's pretty hardcore . . .

And that's that. I am seemingly forgiven. I scan each of her
posts for any hint that she might be playing me a line, for anything that could be construed as a barb, but nope, she's clean.
It may be raining out there, but it's beaming bloody sunshine
in here.

22: #SUGARRUSH

After that, Tori and I spend some time just chatting. Nothing big—no plans of attack, no discussion of future targets, no "where do we go from here"—just talking about what we do, who we are. As suspected, she does work in the tech industry (she describes herself as an "IT grunt on the frontline of customer stupidity"), working for a big company. I admit I'm a student and that I've never really had a job, apart from some babysitting on a Wednesday evening, which gives me just enough to keep me in the essentials.

Lol. Maybe, when you're a rich psychologist with a string of letters after your name and we're living in a massive mansion, we'll look back at this time fondly, eh?

Haha with our millions of cats around us

Damn straight. I want an army of cats.

Imagine it—no one would be spared our wrath!

I can't help but smile—a deep, secret smile that I don't think I've ever shared with anyone before.

Man, we would lay waste to the world.
Tremble before us, humanity, for we march

with our cats and our devastating wit.
You know it!

By now I've munched through two Bounties and a Mars bar, but it isn't the same as having a proper tea. I don't really want to stop our momentum, but my stomach is growling in a most threatening way, so I tell her I'll brb and grab some toast. The sugar from the chocolate buzzes through me, and before I go back up to my haven, I pop my head round the living room door.

"Hey, Mum. You want some toast? You know you should eat when you take your meds."

She smiles slowly, like a stoner after a particularly potent bong hit. "Yeah. That would be nice. Some toast."

I offer her a slice.

She takes a mechanical bite, her attention fixed back on the TV.

I hover for a second, but no, that's all, folks. Good night, and God bless.

♦♦♦

Back upstairs, Tori is waiting for me.

She's gone back to picking out new victims for us to torment. At the bottom of the thread, there's a link to a Facebook profile. We don't usually bother with Facebook—there's not much point in baiting a bunch of middle-aged Pinterest fanciers who think a meme is the height of mindfulness—so it's a surprise that she's sinking that low.

I munch on my toast and click the link, and then almost choke when I realize whose profile it is.

Tori Heidegger

It's hers. It's Tori's.

She trusts me enough to share her Facebook profile with me.

I know it sounds silly—pathetic, even, but tears spring to my eyes.

This is literally the best thing ever.

She trusts me. Even though I lied to her about my name.

She trusts me.

◆◆◆

I feast on photos. I literally gorge myself on them. There aren't many of Tori herself—she's a bit like me in stuffing her photo albums with things she likes and finds funny, rather than selfies, but from the few that I do find, she's everything I expected. Everything I *wanted*.

I can't click the "add friend" button quickly enough.

It doesn't take long for me to get a response.

Messenger chimes, and it's her, really her, in the flesh.

You found me then?

Yup! I love that pic of you with that cute cat.

Oh, that's Kiki.

She's my soulmate.

She might look cute, but she is a hellbeast in disguise. ;)

. . . Tori is typing . . .

. . . Tori is typing . . .

. . . Tori is typing . . .

Hard to talk here. MC?

Oh, fuck, yes.

I log back in to Metachat and send Tori my key—she's there within milliseconds.

That's better.

Feels so exposed otherwise.

Feds looking over our shoulders, you know?

I know what you mean. They record
every conversation.

And they follow you around the web.

All those targeted ads.

Ha—one word for you my friend: encryption!

Lol—you serious? You think I've got this far
without some kickass encryption?

Ahh, touche. I'm just teasing you.

And off we go. We talk about encryption programs and alter egos and the latest edition of *The Banshee and Midnight Jim* (I mean, come on! I didn't think I'd ever meet anyone else who liked The Banshee outside of the community! Whenever I mentioned it at school, I'd just get blank looks—BUT SHE KNOWS! She's read it from the start!) and Aeon Valhalla and how cute Sable is (although she says she prefers Tirra, which I can totally see, as she's a ninja babe) and TV and life and the universe and everything, like we've know each other for years.

Every now and again, I flip open her Facebook page and look at her picture. She has amazingly dark shiny hair and these gorgeous hazel eyes. She's a little on the chubby side, but I like that, because to outsiders, she's just like me. Obviously *I* don't think she's fugly, I think she's the opposite, but some people just can't get past the sight of an ample bottom or a wobbly upper arm.

But then again, it's that kind of crap that has driven us together. Without that, would I have even met her? Doubtful.

I wonder if it would be weird to nick one of her photos and save it on my hard drive. Yeah, that would be weird, wouldn't it? Without her knowing? No, mustn't be weird. Is she thinking the same about me? Shit. What if she's looking through my profile and she sees those awful pictures Auntie Sadie tagged me into when I was her bridesmaid three years ago? Fuck, I begged her to take those down, but she just laughed and told me they're lovely, you look really cute. I don't want to look cute, I want to look cool, which is why the only pictures of me that I have personally posted involved either a) only my eyes up or b) me hiding behind things that obscure most of me, and even then I bury them amongst stupid pictures of things that make me laugh. Which is also exactly what Tori does. Oh my God. We're so compatible. Same sense of humor and everything. I have a funny feeling that if we met in real life, the world would probably explode due to our combined awesomeness.

I never believed in soulmates before.

I do now.

♠ ♠ ♠

Omg! Have you seen this? It's so cool! Who thought to draw fan art of Sable and the Banshee together? I think the internet is trying to break me! ❤ ❤

She sends me the picture, and I blush, because it's one of mine. She's found it. Talk about cosmic coincidences. Do I tell her? Or just leave it? But I can't gush over my own work. And she must really like it, because she has no idea that I actually drew it. Fuck. I don't think this has ever actually happened before.

> Uh, me, actually.
> I drew that, like, a year and a half ago.

Get the fuck out of town!
You're TheBanshee99?
Fucking *seriously*??????

> In the flesh. *sheepish grin*
> I used to do shit like that all the time.
> Haven't drawn much recently, tho.
> Here, I'll send you the initial sketch.
> I colored it in photoshop.

I search through my all-but-forgotten art files and find the scan. To me it looks pretty amateurish, but if Tori likes it . . . I attach it to the message and send.

Whoa!
I mean, I believed you before, but now no one can deny it.
That kicks ass! You've totally got Banshee down to a tee.
I'm really impressed!

I can't help but smile. No one has ever complimented me this way, and it feels weird and awkward, but mainly good, so good I have to hold myself back from sending her the entire folder of vaguely embarrassing sketches.

We continue chatting until past midnight. In that time, we also identify some new targets and plan the virtual assassination of some older ones. By the time I log off, my whole body is thrumming.

Tori.

She's the best thing that has ever happened to me. While I am talking to her, I'm not worrying about food, or Mum, or what Brat's up to, or how I'm going to finish my next assignment. It's just us, in our own little world. No one can touch us.

I don't think I can sleep. My head's all over the place, and it's a real challenge not to log back in to Facebook and spend the rest of the night going through Tori's page again. Does that sound a bit obsessive? Probably. I need to sleep. I need to sleep. I need . . .

I wake up with a start. My arms feel tingly and I'm a bit cold. Judging by the gray light filtering through my blinds, it's still early. I check my phone. 6:12 a.m. Ugh. Five hours of sleep, if that. Today is going to be hell.

Or maybe not. I glance at my laptop and smile. Because after lectures, I can log in and get lost in my happy place. I grin to myself as I check my messages. Any from Tori? Of course not. She would have gone to bed too. She has work today, but she'll be back by six, she said so—

Hey, Beth! Hope to see u tomoz. Got tix for u just in case. Hope thats ok! Axxxxx

Crap, I'd forgotten about Amy. I'd forgotten she'd asked me if I'd like to go out for the evening. Can I blow her off? I could. There's no rule that says I can't. But I would feel a bit bad bailing on her. She's even bought me a ticket. I can't let her down. Can I? As I dither, a little thrill runs through me. I've never been so in demand before.

I don't text Amy back. Not yet, anyway. Texting back at a quarter past six in the morning smacks of desperation. Anyway, I'll see her later today, won't I?

I pick out some leggings (black) and dig out one of my

oversized jumpers (also black). I don't fret too much about what I'm going to wear. Why bother? No one who matters is going to see me. Plus, I like black. It's a safe color. First lecture is at nine, so I wolf down some toast, check on Mum, yell at Brat to get up (yeah, I know, like that's going to happen), and rush out to get my bus. My head's so full of imagined conversations that I don't even feel the familiar twinge of dread that usually comes from squeezing down the bus aisle to find a seat. Bottom-fondlers are forgotten. Nothing is going to get me down.

I space-walk off the bus and down the road toward uni. Outside, I hear a squeak; it's Amy, waiting for me. She waves furiously, grinning from ear to ear. I grin back, which is a first for me. Usually, I wouldn't dare for fear of The Chins, but today I genuinely don't care.

"Here you go!" Amy flourishes a badly printed piece of card at me. I take it from her.

"Disaster Zone. Interesting name for a club," I say.

"I know, cool, right?"

There's an awkward pause. I haven't actually confirmed whether I'm going or not yet, but now that she's given me the ticket, I kind of feel trapped. Some of the warm, fuzzy feeling leaks away, making room for the more normal buzz of dread.

"How much do I owe you?" I ask, trying to keep the reluctance out of my voice.

"Aw, don't worry about that." Amy flaps a hand at me. "It wasn't much."

I really don't know how to proceed from here. These really are uncharted waters. If she won't let me pay, then I really don't have an excuse not to go.

She ignores me and jabbers on about how much fun we're going to have, so much fun, fun fun fun, as if she's trying to convince herself. I just nod helplessly and stuff the ticket into my purse, vowing that I'll give it an hour and then make my excuses.

After lectures we go back to Amy's for lunch. Patrick the Bear is thankfully out. I don't think I'm up to dealing with him right now, and I'm too scared to ask Amy if he's coming to Disaster Zone tonight. A very pretty, very skinny student saunters into the kitchen to make herself a coffee at one point; Amy welcomes her with her trademark enthusiasm, introducing her as Dizzy. She offers Amy a smile that may as well be a sneer and completely ignores me.

"Oh, and Amy," she says in a slightly plummy accent. "Don't forget the milk next time you buy groceries."

Amy blinks and nods tightly. "Oh, yeah, of course."

"Hate relying on Coffee-Mate. Feel like I've been to a fucking food bank. And don't get the crap supermarket stuff. God knows what they pump into that. Makes me break out. Organic." She takes a sip of her coffee and pulls a face, as if that makes her point.

"Oh. All right," Amy says, and I feel my insides scrunch up as I try not to scowl at Dizzy. Who does she think she is? Actually, I know *exactly* who she thinks she is. Posh bitch, used to getting her own way, but not bright enough (and Daddy not quite rich enough) to get into one of the better universities, so she's slumming it here. Then it's off to whatever internship Daddy can secure her, but before that, it's all snooty glances and pushing around the little people to get what she wants, not because she's trying to be nasty but simply because that entitlement has been bred into her. My palms itch. Well, love, there's one great leveler . . .

"What's her full name?" I ask Amy.

"Uh, Denise Reitman. She's from Guildford, I think. I haven't really talked to her much, but she's kind of like our floor's den mother, always reminding us to make sure we clear up after ourselves, or to get the milk—"

"Whilst never doing any of those things herself, I bet," I can't help interjecting.

"Uh, well, you know, she's not that messy, and . . ." She trails off, her fingers clenching and unclenching from around her mug.

"Yeah. Whatever. You do know you don't have to listen to her, right?"

"Yeah, I know, but, you know, for an easy life and everything."

It's weird how angry this makes me. Dizzy has clearly picked up on Amy's *I don't care what you do—just love me!* vibe and is exploiting it up to the hilt. I doubt she talks to the rugby twat like that.

It's a shame I'm not the kind of person who's good at standing up for other people. But since I'm not, I can do the next best thing.

Denise Reitman, beware the infamous MidnightBanshee and all of her various heads. She's a fucking hydra, and if you don't tread carefully she is going to eat you alive.

23: #REALLIFE

I feel a bit bad exploiting Amy's trusting nature, but a few leading questions and she's shown me Denise "Dizzy" Reitman's social media accounts. As predicted, she goes by Dizzygirl on one and Dizzybabe00 on the other, and I have to hold in a cruel chuckle. I'm not going to target her straight away, mainly because I don't want to run the slightest risk of her connecting me (and, by proxy, Amy) to the carnage that is about to rain down on her profiles, but that's fine. Half the fun's in the anticipation. Plus, this means I can key Tori in and we can plot. Dizzy will never talk to Amy like she's a piece of shit again.

After grabbing a baguette (tuna mayo and cucumber—well, it's *kind* of healthy, especially compared to Amy's cheese and bacon monstrosity), Amy and I head to the library to do some studying. And, dare I say it, it's kind of fun. We don't do a lot of work. Amy can literally turn any topic into a conversation, and I find myself lurching from *Bake Off* to *Stranger Things* by way of the Neon Seven's new album. Her sense of fun is infectious, and so we end up giggling a lot. I even sketch out a quick series of stickmen on the edge of her notebook and flip the pages, making the little stickman dance. Amy claps gleefully, which earns us a disapproving look from the librarian. We exchange guilty looks and then burst out into snorting laughter. It's stupid, it's childish, but it's also glorious, and a little remote part of me watches everything with wary eyes, wondering if this is what it's like to have a proper friend and predicting when it's all going to come crashing down around my ears. But I squash that miserable bitch down and try, for once, to just live in the moment.

At four, it's starting to get dark, and so I wander over to grab my bus, but not before Amy throws her arms around my neck and says, "See you later! Remember, eight at Sanford's, okay?" and I can't help but be struck by the note of desperation in her voice. For a moment, I let my arms hang by my sides— I've never been one for hugging, mainly because I was never initiated into the Circle of Friendship that involved hugging— before I eventually cave in and do this weird half-pat, half-rub on her back that might be a hug but might also be a plea to let me go. When she does, she grins at me and jiggles on the spot.

She's actually excited. I can see it twinkling like a little star above all the other fake twinkly stuff she projects.

Oh *fuck*.

❦ ❦ ❦

I spend most of the bus journey home hoping the thing will crash and get me out of this evening. No such luck. Could I step out in front of a car? That certainly would sort the issue out.

But before I know it, I'm sticking my key in the front door, completely unscathed.

The house actually smells of cooking. Mum only cooks on her good days. Maybe I should take that as a sign. The club might be called Disaster Zone, but the omens aren't all that bad. If I find Brat sitting at the table doing his homework, I'm going to start wondering if I've fallen through a dimensional hole and am in a completely new reality.

In the kitchen, Mum's sitting at the table, reading a magazine. In the oven, what looks like a sausage casserole is cooking. Okay, so it came out of a packet, but it's definitely better than nothing. It looks like the cupboards actually have food in them, meaning the Tesco delivery's finally come. For a moment, I can almost kid myself that everything's back to the way it was. Maybe Dad's on his way home from work. Maybe the Cosmic Overlords have decided to load an earlier saved game, and everything's going to be okay from now on. I have to admit, I like the sound of that. Sure, things weren't perfect then; I was still a struggling chubster, but at least home was stable.

Brat storms downstairs, barges past me, and starts yelling about internet connections lagging and how Mum is fucking trying to fucking ruin his fucking life, and her eyes well up, and we're back in reality.

Mum's all but cowering in front of Brat, and I'm paralyzed. I want to go over and stop him, to break his teeth, to tell him that's *not* okay you little shitbag, but none of it happens. Finally, Brat storms back off. The house shakes with his every footstep. I stare helplessly at Mum, who is still weeping. The smell of the casserole, once so promising and wholesome, now seems cloying and rank.

I want to go to her. I want to comfort her. But I don't know how. I've just stood to one side and watched her other child abuse her, and I did nothing. Something hot bubbles up within me, something horribly familiar: shame.

"Mum . . . ," I manage.

She shakes her head. "No. No!" She raises one hand at me

as I take a step toward her, but she doesn't look at me. "Check on the casserole. I don't want it to burn."

So that's what I do. That's *all* I do. And I hate myself for it, every step of the way.

24: #RULESANDREGULATIONS

The problems that one might face when going clubbing when you never go clubbing because you are basically the dictionary definition of fugly are myriad and hideous. Allow me to outline them for you:

1. What should I wear? Can you get away with jeans? Do clubs even let you in if you're wearing jeans? Why am I worrying about wearing jeans, anyway? I never wear bloody jeans! But what else is there? Can't really go down the old faithful route of leggings and oversized top, can I? Which leads to . . .

2. What *can* I wear? I don't have much of a wardrobe, because most shops don't cater to my "unique" shape, and those that do are usually aimed at fifty-year-old women called Beryl. I have found some gems on the internet, but you do rather run the *what size is it really?* gamut with online purchases. Spin the dial to see if it's eight sizes too big and makes you look like someone is trying to drown you in cloth, or eight sizes too small so you look like a badly stuffed sausage. Send us all your financial details to find out! In the end, I settle for the black 50s-style swing dress with the applique skulls on the hem I bought for my prom (which, of course, I didn't go to), but then that only leads to . . .

3. What kind of place is it? According to Google, it's "banging." Right. Is it mainstream? Alternative? Get your head kicked

in if you look like you might have, at some point in your life, flirted with emo? Watch your best friend snort drugs off the toilet seat whilst someone else is doing it doggy-style in the stall next to yours? "Banging" does not give me sufficient information! I could rock up in my skull dress and spend the rest of the night shuffling to Little Mix. Which would be hell, and leads me to . . .

4. Music. I will admit that my taste is somewhat eclectic, and I've managed to cultivate a taste for stuff that sounds like someone beating R2D2 to death with a guitar. This is fine when you're feeling angry and alienated, but how does that work in a clubbing scenario? Will I be forced to listen to Chart Shite for the whole evening? Which nicely dovetails into . . .

5. Club etiquette. As in, I do not know it. Get smashed and dance ironically? Cool indifference whilst sipping on a bottle of something I've carefully purchased and nursed? (I don't know why I'm paranoid about date rape drugs. It's not as if anyone is going to be clamoring to drag my fat, drugged-up ass home. You'd think, anyway.) Do we buy rounds? Shots? Pints? I JUST DON'T KNOW!

6. Coats. It's fucking freezing out there. Do I take one? Will I need to queue for a cloakroom? Or will I just sit in the corner all night, clutching mine? Or should I just risk it and wear a cardigan and hope it doesn't rain?

7. Forget cloakrooms—what about simply arriving? Amy said to meet at Sanford's first. What, inside, outside, in the beer garden, by the bar—where?! I can't just wander in there on my own. Everyone will look and judge and give me those looks that say "Jeeeesus," and then I'll have to run away, which might be a good thing, because then I won't have to deal with . . .

8. How the holy fuck do I get home? I'm not walking—it's,

like, four miles into town. No buses at that time of night. Uber? Taxi? But that means getting into a car, with a stranger, on my own. Even the thought is enough to make me feel violently ill—how would I cope with the reality?

I think it is safe to say that I did not think this through when I agreed to go out, and now that I have thought it through, I have come to the conclusion that it's literally the worst idea anyone has ever had in the world, ever. Yes, I know, countless people manage to do this quite happily every week, but I am not one of those people. Those people are well adjusted, non-paranoid, and normal.

I want to cry.

✦✦✦

When I tell Mum I'm going out for the night, she looks surprised. Well, I suppose it's better than the usual slack-jawed zombie expression.

"You're going out?" she says.

"Yeah. With some friends" (yeah, okay, *a* friend) "from uni."

"Oh. Oh, that's good. That's what you should be doing. You have your phone on you, don't you?"

"Yes, Mum, I have my phone." I wave it in front of her.

"Good. So, if you get into any problems—"

"I'll call. I know." The fact that you'll probably be in a medication and wine induced coma by eight thirty won't interfere with your availability, of course.

"Right. Well. Have fun."

She smiles at me. I think she's going for bright but it has come out more brittle. I can't help but glance toward the stairs.

"I don't have to go—"

"Yes, you do," Mum interrupts, with more force than I thought she could ever muster. "This is the kind of thing you *should* be doing. I did it at your age, and so should you." It's the first bit of spark I've seen in her in a while now.

"As long as you're sure," I mumble.

"I am sure. He isn't your problem."

Of course, that's where she's wrong.

◆◆◆

I don't like getting the bus at night. Okay, so *at night* encompasses everything after 4:30 p.m. in the UK in winter, but you know what I mean.

I try to make myself comfortable and fight the urge to rub my eyes, aware of how much makeup I've plastered on myself. I feel like a fucking rodeo clown. And this dress feels weird. I don't usually wear dresses. What does one do with one's legs when wearing a dress? I tug the hem down in a futile attempt at covering my knees. Tights are not the same as leggings. God, I wish I'd worn leggings—

I catch a glimpse of the little rotating info sign. My stop is next. Bollocks. I nearly missed it. Maybe I should take that as a sign and just go home?

But I don't. Instead, I smooth my skirt down, sling my bag over my head so it crosses my chest like some kind of shield, and grit my teeth.

Time to go get this godforsaken night over and done with.

The bus grinds to a halt and a stream of underdressed people gets off. The night is cold, the air damp. I wish I'd decided to bring my coat and not just my cardigan. Oh well. Too late now. Time to add frizzy hair to tonight's inevitable list of disasters. If this is the worst thing that happens to me, I guess I'm lucky.

Sanford's is two streets away. I'm out of my usual Doc Martens (fashionable, comfortable, and above all, *wide*) and in a ridiculously tottery pair of heels that pinch my toes. I wonder if it's too early to change into the ballet flats I've secreted in my bag. I mean, who am I kidding? I look like I'm walking on ice.

All around me, music blares and signs flicker. The town has transformed from a homogenous shopping blob to a kind of low-rent Vegas. I spy Sanford's up ahead, and my stomach flips. Come on, girl, you've managed to make it this far without completely freaking out. Just a little farther. You can do this.

What if Amy's late? What if I go in alone and have to sit there, waiting? What if all of this has been a hoax and she's invited me just to leave me sitting in there while they all stand outside and take photos of me, laughing at how trusting I am, at how easy it is to fool me—

No. Fuck this. I am not going to be made to look like an idiot. Why the hell didn't Amy say meet her in halls? That's where she lives—she can't stand me up there. I know where she lives. I—

My phone buzzes, and I bark out a high-pitched "Shit!" A few scantily clad girls turn in alarm and stare at me. I blush, thankful for the green gunk I bought to go under my foundation, and fumble my phone out of my bag.

Hey u! Are u there? We're inside—in the corner, by the door! See u in a mo, yeah? Axxxxxxxxxx

I clutch my phone. She says she's there. But she might not be. She still might be playing a cruel trick. I text back:

I'm outside.

Oh! Cool! Can u see me? I'm waving!!

And lo and behold, when I look up I can indeed see the shadowy form of someone waving out of one of Sanford's windows.

She wasn't lying. She is here. And she texted me to make sure I was coming. I'm not sure whether I want to laugh or cry.

25: #HELL

Bars in the UK are odd beasts. Some are light, airy affairs with award-winning menus and organic ales on tap. Others are dingy holes with dartboards and sticky floors and a clientele seemingly made up of elderly sex offenders. Then there are the "family" ones, which sell generic beer and chicken nuggets and chips, with sad-looking "gardens" tacked to the back, filled with desperate smokers and a slightly terrified-looking family who actually took the sign at face value. There are also ones that look more like cottages, where everyone seems to own a Labrador called Jasper and they all drink expensive gin and tonics. And then there are the town pubs, catering mainly to students and people hoping to smash pint glasses into the aforementioned students' faces.

Sanford's is definitely the last one. No organic ales or canine Jaspers (although potentially quite a few sex offenders). The music is deafening as I enter, and despite knowing exactly where Amy is, I feel that familiar swell of panic rise within me. A few people turn and watch me come through the door, which doesn't help. Just stop it. Stop it and go back to whatever you were doing. You don't need to watch me. I'm nothing to you. Finally, as if hearing my silent entreats, they stare back at their phones.

Amy hares across the bar, a vision in chiffon and pink sparkles, looking like she's raided the dress-up section of a toy store. Suddenly I don't feel quite so self-conscious about the skull dress.

She flings her arms around my neck, squealing, "You're here! I thought you might not come!" I awkwardly hug her back, hoping I don't suffocate her with my arm flab.

"Everyone's here," she continues to squeal, and takes me by the hand to drag me over to the corner.

By *everyone*, she means three people from her halls. I recognize Paddington Patrick immediately. He grins widely at me as I approach the table. One of the others is Dizzy, who looks like she's been forced to suck eighteen lemons off at once. Next to her is another stick insect—this one has painfully fashionable rainbow hair and a pierced lip. She doesn't have to say anything. I already hate her. Amy introduces her as Indigo, because of course she's fucking called Indigo. She sips on a straw and gives me a narrow-eyed smile that on the surface could look friendly if you scrunched your eyes up a bit, but we both know better. Indigo is a Beautiful Person, I am Fugly, and never the twain shall meet—well, until someone like Amy comes along, anyway.

I say a quiet "Hi." Dizzy all but ignores me; Indigo mouths a tight "Hi" back. Patrick booms, "Big Bird!!" I know it's coming, but my cheeks flame nonetheless. I wonder if I could fit under the table.

"Paddy," Indigo says, with no small measure of contempt.

"Do you want a drink?" Amy says, breathless with excitement. "I like your dress. Very new-goth. You should have got some gauzy wings to go with it. Was the bus ride okay? I'm so glad you're here. Shall I get you a drink? Yeah. I'll get you one. They do two for one cocktails here. I'll get us the same, and then we can be drink-sisters! How cool is that?" And before I can even begin to sort through what question I should answer first, she's off, skipping up to the bar. It's a miracle they're serving her, to be honest. She looks about twelve.

Dizzy and Indigo share a look, and Patrick beams at me.

"Tinks said she'd invited you. Good job you could come. Might have someone with the poundage behind them to keep pace with me, huh? I like a bird who can drink."

He winks at me, and I don't have the heart to tell him I rarely drink, mainly because I don't have anyone to drink with. I let the Big Bird stuff slide, too, even though it smarts like hell. It's perfectly okay for fugly chicks to say they're fugly, but for someone else—no, not cool, bro. Still, Patrick's got this sort of full-on affability thing going on, and so I kind of forgive him. At last he's willing to engage with me, unlike The Poison Twins who are busy muttering at each other and rolling their eyes. Yes, I'm *so* sorry that I'm somehow polluting your oh-so-perfect airspace with my fatness. How dare I even come within twenty feet of you, you stuck-up, skeletal bitches?

I wrap my arms around myself but then self-consciously unwrap them again when I remember how that makes me look like I've got an innertube. Oh, Christ, this is horrible.

"Anyone seen *Bake Off*?" I ask, desperate for common ground. "I'm team Fahmida, but I think Alison might win . . ."

The Poison Twins each give me a disdainful look, obviously wondering why I'm even bothering to speak to them. The go back to their own whispered conversation. I chew on the inside of my lips. Where is Amy? I know the bar is busy, but come on. I'm not sure how much of this I can put up with. I knew this was a bad idea. I just knew it.

"Oh yeah," says Patrick, "that cooking thing with the weirdo in it? Had a banging little chickadee in it earlier—what was her name? Ruby? Robin?"

"Rachel," I all but whisper.

"Oh, fucking hell, yes, Rachel! Amazing tits. When she bent down to open those ovens—woof woof!" He waggles his eyebrows, and I feel kind of sick.

Suddenly, like a tiny, sparkling angel, Amy appears, bearing two violently colored drinks, a straw stabbed in each.

"There you go!" she says triumphantly. "Cheers!" She grins at everyone. Patrick roars heartily in return and takes a massive gulp of his pint, draining it. Dizzy and Indigo sneer and continue sniping together. I take a tentative sip; it's so sweet it almost tastes metallic, and the alcohol makes my cheeks burn immediately.

"It's good, isn't it?" Amy says. "They call it the Attitude Changer. Dread to think what that means, huh?"

"I'll tell you what it means," Patrick beams. "One for the chicks, to get them ready for us fellas, hey, am I right, girls? Yeah!"

He nods to himself while the rest of us stare awkwardly at the table.

"Has he come out with us, or is he waiting for someone?" I whisper to Amy.

She shrugs and takes another long slurp of her drink.

"Indy and I are going off," Dizzy says, standing up. "Petra is meeting us in Bombshell's with McNeil and Pengy. See you later, Tink."

They don't even nod in my direction.

"Babes! What? What's going on here? You can't leave!" Patrick whines.

"We're going, Paddy," Indigo drawls with an unmistakable air of finality. "See you later."

She doesn't need to add on the *don't follow us*—it's obvious from the way she looks at us.

"Oh, bollocks, the totty has upped and left," Patrick says. "Oh well!" To my shock, he slings his arms around me and Amy. "What do you say, ladies? Jägerbombs all round? I think so." He winks at us again and then lopes off.

"Do you think we could just . . . go?" I stammer.

"Go? Why? We can't leave Paddy here by himself."

I hear a guffaw from the direction of the bar.

"I don't think he's going to find it too hard to find new friends," I say. "I'm just finding him a little bit—you know."

"Aww, he's not that bad," Amy says, but I can tell by the guarded way she stirs her drink with her straw that he *is* that bad and probably more besides. I stare into my drink for a bit and check my phone. No messages. I don't know why I thought there would be. Then Amy nudges me.

"Okay, let's split. Paddy'll be okay. Let's down these and go find some fun."

◆◆◆

Go find some fun translates to wandering around town for bit, trying to find a bar where the bouncers will let us in. Despite us completely adhering to all dress codes (if anything, Amy's the one on shaky ground, wearing a hot-pink tutu), we're turned away from three other pubs. The fact that two of them seemed quite happy to let Amy in when they thought she was a sole agent says it all, really.

In a way, I wish the last one we went to had sent us on our way, too. Then I'd have had the perfect excuse to go home and put all of this behind me. But no, this dive's bouncer gives us a distasteful look but waves us in, and now we're huddled in the corner, drinking bottles of cider, our voices drowned out by the music. I think they're having a nineties rave night here. We try to talk, but it's futile. Maybe we should have stayed at Sanford's after all.

I steal a glance at my phone, mainly so I can see how late it is. *10:15.* Blimey, I can't remember the last time I was out this late. Usually I'm cruising the highways and byways of the internet now, surveying my domains, terrorizing the locals. Instead I'm cowering in a corner drinking something that might be apples dissolved in battery acid, trying not to make eye contact with anyone. Oh, how the mighty have fallen.

Finally Amy gestures that we should leave and all I can do is hold in a big sigh of relief. Now I just have to suffer a couple of hours in a student nightclub, and then I can go home.

26: #WORSE

I will admit that I've been harboring a secret hope this evening. I still don't have my student card, so I'm kind of praying that they won't let me in. Then I can act all disappointed, say sorry to Amy, and head home. Okay, so it means running the taxi gauntlet, but I'm going to have to do that anyway at some point tonight, so why not get it over with sooner rather than later?

The bouncers at the door of Disaster Zone (I maintain that it's a stupid name for a club) don't seem to be so picky as the Guardians of the Beautiful People at the pubs, in that they barely look at us. As long as you've got what looks like a ticket in your hand, they're allowing you in. Bastards.

Amy's giggling with excitement, or maybe just nerves, I don't know. The way she's acting, you'd think she'd never gone clubbing before. I mean, okay, so *I've* never actually been clubbing before, but she could show a little dignity.

The whole place stinks of cheap aftershave, stale beer, and BO, with a faint undertone of piss. It's pretty dark, so actually seeing who you're trying to talk to/dance with/run away from is pretty much a nope. Lights strobe at a dizzying degree, making me worry if photosensitive epilepsy runs in my family.

The dance floor is everything I dreaded it would be. The atmosphere is similar to that of a low-rent strip club (or so I imagine, given I've never been to a strip club either—one for the bucket list, I guess), with bulgy-eyed males (I hesitate to call them men, but it feels spurious to call them boys, given most of them have beards, and the rest badly maintained stubble) gawping at the dead-eyed dronettes who gyrate to a thumping beat, desperately trying to figure out who they might be able to cop off with, hoping to fill their various orifices to plug the emptiness that yawns within them.

I feel like David Attenborough again, observing the actions of a troupe of bonobo monkeys just before everything hits the freaky-time fan. It's horrible and I want to get away, but at the same time, I'm mesmerized by the scandalous clothes, by the gyrations, by everything, and a little part of me howls in jealousy that I will never do this, that I will never be one of those girls twerking in a pair of hotpants so short they may as well be a thong . . .

I tear my eyes away from the animalistic display and follow Amy to the bar, once again in pursuit of colorful alcoholic beverages. I don't catch what this one is called, but it tastes of coconut and industrial solvent and has a kick like a mule. Since apart from the odd snowball at Christmas I'm basically teetotal, I'm actually beginning to feel a little fuzzy—four drinks in and I think I've had more alcohol this evening than the rest of the year combined. My cheeks burn and I find that I am grinning, which is a bit embarrassing. Amy keeps grinning back and giving me little thumbs-up signs. I am struck by just how adorable she is, and yet again wonder exactly what kind of freak she is that she's seemingly settled for me as a friend. Still, I don't complain. As long as I don't look at the heaving mass that is the dance floor, I could probably kid myself into thinking that I am actually having a good time.

The tunes change, and the DJ mumbles something at the crowd. Amy's eyes widen as she proclaims, "I LOVE this track!" Next thing I know, I'm being dragged onto the hated dance floor, where she begins her own manic-pixie-girl version of the gyrating mating call dance. I am so out of my depth, I don't know what else to do but jiggle—it isn't really dancing, but it isn't really standing still. I must look like I'm being zapped with a cattle prod.

My dress feels too tight. Every now and then, the strobe lights find me and blind me momentarily, forcing me to blink away bright purple spots from my vision. The drink Amy got me is too strong—what I really want is a nice, cool glass of Coke, but I can't really ask for one of those here, can I? Maybe if I sling some vodka in it, that would be okay. Amy twirls in front of me and throws her arms around my neck. For a moment, I freeze, unsure of what to do, but the drink has loosened me, and I find myself wrapping my arms around her waist, and before I know it, we're hugging, and Amy is laughing, and I'm laughing, and for once, everything is good—

Until I notice the slinking pack of hyenas.

There's four, possibly five of them, all of the badly-grown-stubble variety. They're nudging each other and winking. One says something to his mate that is obviously the most hilarious thing ever.

I pull away from Amy, who twirls in front of me again. The good feeling's gone, replaced by an acute desire to flee. Amy's oblivious, though. Or maybe she's not. Maybe this is normal and I'm freaking out over nothing. I jiggle to one side. Maybe I might be able to sidle away? But that would leave Amy alone, and I'm not doing that to her.

One of the hyenas breaks from the pack and sidles over to

us, behind Amy, making a crude cupping gesture toward her backside. His friends find this the epitome of wit and roar with laughter. Amy frowns and mouths "Fuck off!" at them, but this seems to egg them on, and I am reminded of all those horrible romantic films where the male character remarks that he likes a girl with spirit.

In defiance, Amy keeps dancing and takes my hand, trying to encourage me to do the same. It's admirable but futile; the hyenas continue their circling until I can't keep all of them in my line of sight, and before I know what's happening, one is behind me in a cloud of cheap deodorant and aftershave, trying to snake his arms around me so he can get his hands on my tits.

I freeze. This is worse than the bus. Amy's usual childlike expression of glee turns ugly and she pushes past me, screaming at the lowlife to fuck off and leave us alone. For a moment, I think she might actually punch him.

This is obviously the most fun he and his friends have had all evening, and they're not about to give up their game just yet. Behind them, a couple of the Skinny Girls are smirking, their eyes wide, whispering behind their hands, no doubt saying, "fucking hell, she deserves it," and maybe I *do* deserve it, because I knew something like this would happen. It's inevitable. It's my punishment for even attempting to be normal.

The groping hyena now has his hands up, feigning innocence whilst Amy jabs her finger at his chest, snarling at him like an angry Chihuahua. All I can do is stare. The more he smirks, the more a tight, spiky ball in my chest grows; my heart thuds as adrenaline pounds through my system and my inner MidnightBanshee fights back.

This is not right. *THIS IS NOT RIGHT.* Come into my domain, little boy, and I will destroy you. I will hunt you down and I will tear you limb from limb. You'll never be able to show your face in public after I've finished with you.

Except none of that is going to happen because this is Real Life, not the internet. I yearn for Tori because I know she'd be able to find out who he is.

The hyena cackles one last time, shakes his head in mock disdain, and finally slinks back to his mates, who offer him high fives.

And you wonder why I don't go clubbing.

♦♦♦

After that, Amy loses her taste for dancing. She says it's because the track is crap, but I know that's not true. I glance toward the dance floor; the hyenas have picked a new target. I can see them circling her and wonder where the bouncers in this god-forsaken place are.

It's my turn to get the drinks, but I have no idea what to buy. I settle on Jack and Coke for the both of us. At last, something with a name I recognize.

"Dickheads," Amy seethes as she takes furious little sips from her drink. "Who the fuck do they think they are?"

I don't say anything, but I know exactly who they think they are, and exactly who they think we are, too.

"There's always one," I say. "Or, in this case, five."

"Well, I'm not going to let them ruin our night. Fuck them. Come on, drink up. We're having fun tonight. Let's get another one in."

27: #ANOTHERONE

After yet another horribly sweet and stupidly strong cocktail, Amy drags me back to the dance floor—the edge, thankfully—where she can shake her groove thang and I can sort of sway in a hopeless attempt at mimicking what humans call dancing. The music's actually not too bad. The overhyped corporate pop shite has now given way to something a little harder and a little darker, possibly mirroring the night as a whole, but hey, I can't complain too much.

The hyenas are now bothering yet another group of girls. The one who went for me is leering at the plumpest of a group of four. She is obviously a prize in a "pull a fatty" competition. It's heartbreaking; I have no doubt that the poor girl knows exactly what's happening, but she's helpless to stop it. Tell them to piss off, and you're a frigid bitch. Play along and you're a gullible idiot. Try to play them at their own game, and you're a presumptuous little whore who needs to be taught a lesson. No matter what avenue she takes, she's going to lose.

Another guy, not one of the hyenas, is now chatting to Amy, who is making gooey eyes at him and giggling. I kind of don't blame her, as he is pretty cute in a scruffy, doe-eyed sort of way. Technically, she's still dancing with me—but yeah, who am I kidding.

After a minute, Scruffy-but-cute wanders off toward the bar.

"He's going to buy me a drink! Oh, I can't believe it! Isn't he just adorable? Tight little buns in those tight little jeans!"

"Yeah, he seems nice," I say. "What's his name?"

"Uh, Petey, or Piers, or something like that. It begins with a P, anyway. Or it could be a B. It's hard to hear in here."

Ah, the joys of hooking up. Meet a guy, he gets you a drink, you have no idea what his name is, but you're probably going to cop off with him anyway, because that's how we do it. Everything's anonymous: anonymous review, anonymous Twitter handle, anonymous shag.

Scruffy saunters back and hands Amy her drink. Nothing for me, of course, but then I'm not the one he wants to expertly seduce. And anyway, I don't want anything else to drink. I'm already feeling a little too fuzzy round the edges, and quite honestly, I don't want to end up like the hyena victim, who is currently snogging one of them while he gives his mates a thumbs-up and they laugh hysterically . . . I wonder if that's her first kiss. It would have been mine, if Amy hadn't stepped in.

Scruffy and Amy try to chat, which involves lots of leaning closely into one another. I can't help but wonder if he's telling her to ditch her mate so they can go off and have some proper fun.

I stare at my phone. The reception in here is terrible. Even with the signal booster, it's struggling to find one bar. Just enough to check Facebook—the little icon spins round and round and round and round and nope, not even that. Bollocks. No one to text, no internet to amuse me, and . . . oh, great. Scruffy's got his tongue down Amy's throat now. I mean, what do you do? Stare, vaguely horrified, in the other direction? Cool indifference, as if sitting next to two people groping one another isn't awkward in the slightest? Get up and give them some privacy, running the risk of losing the only person you know in this dump, while looking like a complete billy-no-mates? None of these options are very attractive. Maybe this is why so many people take drugs when clubbing—to dull themselves to whatever squelchy things their friends are doing not two feet away from them.

Finally, Scruffy and Amy break apart. He gives her a look that I'm sure she finds most alluring, but I think it just makes him look like he's stoned. He takes a gulp from his drink, touches Amy on the cheek, and jumps up, which I think is quite a feat, given what he's just been up to.

Amy turns to me, her lipstick smudged, her eyes luminous. "I can't believe it! I think I've pulled!" she squeaks.

I'm not quite sure what to say to that. He willingly came over to her, bought her a drink, made small talk, and then shoved his hand up her top in public. Oh, and yep, there he is, making his way back, smiling as he does so. What other evidence does she need? A verbal contract? Something signed in blood? Jesus. Open your fucking eyes, girl. You've pulled. Go you—

I stop myself. My inner troll seethes, but the human part of me backs up and feels a bit awkward. Amy's lovely. Why shouldn't a guy be interested in her? No one else in the room deserves it more than her. And then it strikes me. I'm jealous. I don't *want* to be jealous. I want to be above such petty nonsense, but I can't deny it. For all her kookiness and her manic-fairy demeanor, Amy is still a Beautiful Person. Possibly the most Beautiful Person I've ever met.

I just don't think she realizes it.

An uncomfortable thought occurs to me. If I had found her online first, would I have seen this? Would I have seen her sweetness, her open heart, her positivity in the face of this soul-crushing world? Or would I have just seen the kooky clothes, the perma-cute grin, the snub nose, and condemned her to Troll Hell? How many others out there are oblivious, posting snippets of their life, only for me to come and tear them down—

I drain my glass in one big swallow. The club spins, as does my stomach.

I need to get out of here before I'm sick.

✦✦✦

So, here I am. Alone. Crouching against the wall outside the club, phone in hand. At least the reception is better out here.

I don't feel quite so queasy now. The cold air's been good for me. Turns out, Tori's been on Facebook. I missed her. She even left me a message.

Amy knows where I am. I didn't just bail on her—I told her I needed to go out for some air, which wasn't a lie. And to her credit, she said she'd come out with me. But then Scruffy started to whine, telling her not to go. I don't blame him, not really. To him, I'm just Amy's fat mate, the chubby millstone around her neck that is stopping them from having some real fun.

Amy wavered for a bit but ultimately chose the dick over the friend. Hell, I don't blame her either. If it was me, I'd probably do the same. Okay, maybe not, but you never know. It could happen. Stop snickering at the back.

The ground is damp, so I can't sit down, and my legs are screaming at me. The bouncers keep giving me weird looks; I don't think they know what to do with me, as I'm clearly not out here because I'm blind drunk, which means they can't just order me on my way, but at the same time, they can't let me crouch here like Gollum's fat cousin. To spare them, I straighten up, wishing I smoked so I'd have an excuse to be out here.

Maybe I should just go home. But what if something bad happens to Amy? What if Scruffy is a secret date rapist? What if he ditches her, drunk and alone near a canal, and she falls in? Okay, so we don't *have* a canal here, but that's not the point. The point is, if I did go home and something did happen to her, I'd never be able to forgive myself. Or her, for that matter.

But I can't stay out here all night. I glance up at the sky, as if the answer might be written in the stars, which is a futile endeavor given that this is the UK and the stars are hidden behind a smothering layer of cloud.

Fuck it. I'll text her. Then toss a coin. Maybe gut a rat and see what its entrails have to say. Lord knows, there must be enough of them around here.

> Hey, u ok? Where r u? With . . .

Balls. What's his name? Can't call him Scruffy. Did she even find out before she let him slobber all over her like an overexcited labradoodle?

> . . . blokie?

I cringe. Oh well, best I can do. I send it.
And wait.
And wait.
And w—
"Hey! Big Bird!"
Oh, God.
"Hi, Patrick," I say wearily.

146

"Lost you back at Sanford's. Found Jonty and Mikey, though, so that's tip-top."

Holy fucking moly. The boy's a walking stereotype.

"So why are you out here?" he continues. His two friends smirk at me, but Patrick doesn't. He actually seems . . . genuinely concerned? Yeah, I know. I'm struggling with it, too.

"I'm here with Amy. She's hooked up with some dude, so I'm catching some air."

"Oh, eww. Know how that feels. You should come with us!" He beams at his friends. "We're off back to Jonty's to partake in some spliffola and play some violent video games. You'd love it!"

"Ahh, no, I can't. I need to make sure Amy's okay."

"Come on, Big Bird! Tinkerbell will be fine with her Peter Pan, I'm sure. You look like you could do with some cheering up."

Jonty and Mikey are both giving Patrick the side-eye now, so I shake my head. Patrick might be the biggest, most oblivious oaf I've ever met, but his heart seems to be in the right place. Shame his mates don't sing from the same hymn sheet, so to speak. Although I do wonder if they'd be sharing looks of horror if I'd been Dizzy or Indigo . . .

"C'mon, Paddy," says Jonty or Mikey, not sure which one. "It's fucking freezing out here."

"Sure I can't tempt you?" Patrick says.

"Nah, I'm fine. Thanks for the offer, though."

"Ah well, suit yourself. See you later, Big Bird."

He meanders off. Both his mates share a relieved look and follow him.

And I am alone again.

Well, apart from the bouncers. But I'm not sure if they count as human.

28: #HOMETIME

I'm actually pretty angry now.

It's been half an hour since I texted Amy, and she hasn't replied. Probably because she's too busy getting off with Scruffy. Or he's dragged her off into somewhere secluded and is—

No, not going to think like that. Amy's fine; she's just ignoring me. That's why I'm angry, remember? God, I gave up a night of mucking about with Tori for this. People are always saying, "Get off the internet and out into the real world." Yeah, no thanks, not when this is what the real world has to offer.

Well, if I can't find Amy, I can at least see if Tori's around. I open Messenger.

Now, how to start this? Can't kick off proceedings with whining. Something short and sweet should do it. A *hey*. Yeah. You can't go wrong with a *hey*.

Hey. You there?

Nothing.

Oh, for fuck's sake . . . but, no, wait . . . a "seen" check mark! She is there!

Hey you! Was wondering where you might be. You ok?

I am now.

Argh.
Made the mistake of going clubbing
and am now outside
freezing my ass off
cos it's hell in there.

You went *clubbing*?
Why the fuck did you do that?
That's reserved for wankers and students.

The latter.
Uni friend wanted to go out.
She caught me in a moment of weakness.

Shiiiiiit. Poor you. Lesson learned, huh?
Is that the girl who is always posting shite on
your FB wall?

Yeah . . . she's sweet, but does do my head in sometimes. She's currently eating the face off some twat so I
said "later" and fucked off.

So you on your way home?

No, I'm hovering around outside, dithering, because I am incapable of making a decision on my own. But you don't need to know that.

Will be soon when my uber
shows up.

Ugh. Uber. Let me know where you are
so I can keep track of you,
so you don't end up being trafficked
to Lithuania or something.

Aww. She's seen actual pictures of me, and she still thinks I might be a victim of sex trafficking. That's quite sweet, if you think about it.

K. Hang on . . . location pin sent!

:) Awesome. Now go get your Uber, Batgirl!

:)

Talk about misrepresentation, because the last thing I feel is "smiley face." "Slightly terrified face" is more like it. I tuck my phone back into my bag and actually consider walking home, which, coming from a fat chick, is saying something. I could call an Uber but I'd probably have to wait a few more minutes for one to show up, and there are a lot of ordinary taxis already here, parked up like shining beetles. Might as well just grab one of them.

I have nothing against taxi drivers. I'm sure the vast majority of them are lovely. And I'm positive that, even if their intentions were less than pure, they're hardly going to go for me when there are hordes of scantily-clad drunk girls around. Still, approaching the line of cars is nerve-racking.

I try to remember the advice from those safety videos we watched in school. Look confident. Don't look like a victim. Head up, shoulders back. Only not that much, because it makes you look like someone with a botched boob job trying to join the Ministry of Silly Walks. Relax. *Relax.* Hundreds, if not thousands, of people are probably doing what you're doing now, and they're all fine. So be fine.

I sort of totter over, and instead of asking confidently if he's available, I do that "Uh, you? Yeah. Great. Thanks mate," thing. The cab driver is a middle-aged bald bloke, and I know without looking at his badge that he's called Steve or Bob or Dave. I get in the back (screw getting in the front; he might try to engage me in conversation, and the last thing I need tonight is A Proper Englishman's Perspective on Brexit), give him my address, and fish my phone out again, hoping he'll take the hint.

He doesn't.

"You have a nice night, love?"

Urrrgh. Love. Why? For all he knows, I'm a militant feminist kickboxer who could punch his Adam's apple right out of his throat.

"Uh, yeah."

"You on your own?"

I stare at my phone for a bit before giving in. "Yeah. My friend lives on the other side of town."

"Oh, right. Student?"

Oh, for God's sake, enough with the questions! I just want to ride the ten minutes home in uncomfortable silence, then mutter "Cheers, mate" as I tip you. Is that so hard?

"Yeah. She's in halls."

"Ahh, you're not though?"

I bite back a sigh. "No. I live at home."

"Sensible. Life's expensive these days. All those university fees. Weren't like that in my day. Only the brainboxes went, rest of us went out and made a proper livin', you know, payin' our way. But then everyone got told they were a special snowflake and could be anything they wanted." He says that in a sing-song voice. "And all of a sudden everyone wants to go and study fucking pointless things like media studies and women's studies and psychology, you know what I mean? What you studying?"

"Psychology."

"Oh."

He stares at the traffic lights for a bit.

Well, at least he's stopped talking. I don't think I could cope with the inevitable immigrant rant that I could sense was coming next—

"Of course, it wouldn't be too much of a problem if it wasn't for all those bloody immigrants . . ."

I sigh inwardly. Is it too late to put on a Polish accent?

29: #SOBLESSED

I smile and nod and grimace the rest of the way home. Steve or Bob or Dave has two kids and a baby grandson, as well as strong opinions on everything that's wrong with this once proud country, including people under the age of twenty-five (his daughter not withstanding), students, the Liberal Elite (which seems to be anyone who can count without using their fingers), and those benefit scroungers like the ones you see on TV. It's all quite horrifying, but I still give him a tip at the end of the journey, because I'm nothing if not terribly British and therefore fear any kind of confrontation, ever.

"Oh, cheers love," he says when I give it to him. "You enjoy the rest of your night, yeah?"

Okay, maybe he is taking the piss after all.

The house is silent when I go inside. Thankfully, Mum remembered not to put the chain on, or I'd be forced to sleep on the front step.

I don't turn any lights on. I don't need to. Since Dad ran off, nothing ever gets moved around. The whole house is trapped in a time warp. Before, Mum was always shifting things, complaining that she hated the house, forever peering into estate agent windows, picking out what, to me at least, looked like near-identical houses to the one we already live in. But after

Dad left, all of that stopped.

Everything stopped.

An eerie, flickering light plays along the corridor wall, telling me the TV's still on. I poke my head around the door. Mum's asleep on the sofa, covered in her blanket. I tiptoe over, fumble around for the remote, and turn the TV off. The room is plunged into darkness. Mum fidgets in her sleep. I hold my breath. She does not wake.

Relief washes through me, and then I feel bad. I shouldn't dread my own mother waking up. But I do, even if it is simply because life is easier when she's asleep.

I creep upstairs and log in.

So you got home safe and are not on your way to Lithuania? The night's a success!

I have to laugh at that, and instantly feel a bit better.

Yep, home safe. There was this one moment when they tried to stuff me in the boot, but I fought them off with my mad ninja skills and then ran over the rooftops until I got home ^_^

Lol! Did you chuck poison-tipped throwing stars at them while you disappeared off into the night?

You know it! Cos I have such good aim and everything :P

imagining bastard taxi drivers gurgling in the gutter with throwing stars embedded in their necks while Beth runs off in her catsuit, two katanas slung over her back

Something swells in my chest, and I can't help but grin.

You wanna play on Twitter?

Ahh, Twitter rampages. They're always fun. I imagine my targets are the hyenas from the club, and it feels so good. But out of nowhere my mind switches to Amy, the Oblivious Beautiful Person, and suddenly I'm not so sure. I don't want to disappoint Tori. But still, no matter how hard I try to smother it to death with Twixes, that horrible, nagging feeling—that I don't actually know these people, so who am I to judge?—keeps gnawing at me, and for the first time since I met Tori, I go to bed feeling less than euphoric.

I don't know what's wrong with me. Must be the booze.

◆◆◆

As it happens, Amy did cop off with Scruffy. His name was Dylan. I say *was* because he disappeared Saturday morning, and she hasn't heard hide nor hair of him since. She is, naturally, devastated, meaning I've had to lay off the *first-years are fresh meat* comments. To be honest, it's enough to make me glad I'm not attractive in any way, shape, or form. Why would anyone want to put themselves through it? It borders on the masochistic, if you ask me.

Turns out, I give good hugs. After some tears and "What's wrong with me?"s and "He's such a fucking bastard!"s, she bounces back quickly enough.

The days turn to weeks, and before I know it, a month's flown by. It's okay, though; by day, I go to lectures and spend most of my lunchtimes at Amy's. By night, I'm with Tori and her whole host of wonderful sockpuppets. I never thought I'd say this, but life ain't too bad. Dad even calls a few times and tries to sort something out for Christmas; we're invited to his place, which would be a first. Mum's not invited, though, so I don't think I'll go.

The only real fly in my ointment is a certain Denise Reitman. Yep, the lovely Dizzy, with her superior attitude and inability to treat Amy like a human being. The final straw is when one of her tops gets caught up in Amy's laundry and she accuses Amy of nicking it. Of course, Amy's done nothing of the sort—it was a genuine mistake—but Dizzy makes Amy cry, and so Dizzy must pay. With any luck, she'll also lead me straight to that sniffy bitch Indigo too, and I'll have both the Poison Twins in my sights. A little thrill chases its way down my spine. Revenge is like ice cream—very sweet and best served cold.

Dizzy's Instagram account is a goldmine of selfies, "healthy student food" snaps, and twee inspirational quotes. It looks like she documents her every move here, and there's such a smorgasbord of attack opportunities laid out, I'm not really sure where to start.

Eventually, I send Tori a link to the account, and she takes the initiative, going for a particularly ripe selfie. She's such a connoisseur.

So here we are, ready to teach the bitch the lesson she'll never forget. We can't say *too* much right now. Not if we want to trap her good and proper. Like building a house, you have to lay the foundations first. Let them settle. Then expand on it brick by brick. Create detractors. Fake defenders. Photoshop a few images. Make a few memes. You wanna go viral, honey? Yes, but not like this? Too late . . .

Shame we have to stop. So much more fun
if we could just keep at it.

Yeah, I know.
But if we don't, mods get suspicious . . .
And we get banhammered before we can reap
any real rewards, I know, I know. You're totally the
yin to my yang, hun.

I smile at that.

Haha. Lookit, ppl coming in now . . .
oh, and I do believe I might know one of them.

It's the lovely Indigo, indignantly telling us both to fuck
right off.

Oh? Another biatch to take down a peg?

You know it

We take a moment to peruse Indigo's account. If anything,
Indigo's an even bigger target than Dizzy. Mega-healthy vegan
meals photographed? Check. Pouting selfies of her in a string
bikini as she perches on the edge of an infinity pool somewhere
exotic? Check. Artfully posed snaps of her doing something
bendy that hints to any muscled hunks out there that she's not
only skinny but flexible too? Check and check and check again.
She quite literally embodies everything I despise, and everything I want to be.

Fucking hell.
This one needs something spiky

shoved up her perfectly pert ass, and soon.

Tell me about it.

The 2 of them look at me like I'm a bit of dirt
they've scraped off their shoes.

Poison Twins. They need destroying.

Oh, they will be, my sweet, they will be.

Let's just strategize for a bit. We need to plan this.

Oh? Any ideas?

A couple. I know you're not into hacking much,
but I could really fuck them over with something
really nasty.

Some dog shots, or something.

This is where I get a bit queasy. Although we've had hacking fun before, doing it here kind of feels like crossing the line. Whether I like it or not, I know these girls. The aim is to wind them up to the point where they destroy *themselves*, not force myself into their lives and trash everything I find there. Plus, even I draw the line at extreme porn. That shit's nasty.

I dunno. . . Why don't we see how things turn out
before you crack out the big guns? Give them a chance
to respond, and play them that way?

Oh, Beth! You're so sweet.

You've got to stop worrying about what other people think.

Umm, no, not so much worrying about what other people think, more worrying about Special Branch smashing down my front door and confiscating my laptop.

Nah, just don't see that it's necessary.

Maybe later, huh?

Right now, let's just destroy her externally.

Ok. :/ You need to chill!

Fucking hell, I thought you liked the adrenaline rush.

Maybe I was wrong.

Ugh.

In the end, Tori amuses herself by posting pictures of slaughtered animals all over Indigo's page. I'm not all that comfortable with it, but I go along with her because the last thing I want is for her to think I'm a wuss, or even worse, boring. Plus, I'm the one who told her to destroy the Poison Twins. I can't unleash hell and then complain that a bunch of demons have burned the carpets.

Still—half-skinned calves? Yeah, it's going to take me a while to get that image out of my head. Mac and cheese for tea tonight, I think.

30: #HOT

In between the devastation on Instagram, Tori and I also have a quite sweet, quite normal exchange on Facebook. Because Facebook is the domain of middle-aged mothers talking about gin, we actually feel pretty safe here. I don't look up Dizzy or Indigo, and since they'd have no reason to look for me, Tori and I exchange a few silly cat memes and compliment each other's photos.

Until Amy joins in.

Who's this Amy?
Second time she's crashed our party.
Is this the chick you stole your name from?
What gives?

I wince. This isn't awkward at all.

Nothing.
She's just a friend from uni.
I used her name cos she was the last person
to text me.
Nothing else!

A weird prickling crawls over my skin. The last thing I want is for Tori to get the wrong idea and target Amy—which in itself is weird, because in the past I wouldn't have given two hoots what Tori might do to Amy, but now I do, and I have a sneaking suspicion it's because (whisper it) I actually like her. She's sweet, kind, and completely harmless—unlike Tori, who's caustic, a bit scary, and absolutely, wonderfully exciting; kind of like the difference between a kitten and a Siberian tiger, I suppose.

I switch over to Instagram. A shiver of delight trickles down my spine and roots itself deep in my belly, sending a warm flush of intense pleasure to my nethers. Tori's abandoned the gruesome animal shots (thank goodness) and is now dancing circles around Dizzy, exposing her for the fraud she is.

I don't even have to join in, Tori's such an expert. Doesn't mean I *don't* join in, because of course I do; I can't help it, it's like dancing naked in the rain with batteries strapped to your nipples—dangerous, electrifying, and deeply, deeply satisfying in only the way doing something so wrong can be.

Dizzy's now trying to block our accounts, but each time she does, the random IP generator conjures up another, until she might as well be trying to swat wasps with wet tissue paper.

And then, like that, she's gone. I let out a crow of delight. Tori joins in on Metachat.

Ha ha! Lolololol!! She deactivated!
I know! Can't stand the heat, get outta the kitchen!
Oh, you were perfect! You know you've done it right when they lose the ability to construct a coherent sentence!
And then you went all grammar nazi on her!
I thought I'd die laughing at that!
Cos she's doing a fucking English degree and everything!!

I couldn't resist it.
Sometimes you don't have to shock,
you just have to be really fucking annoying . . .

                    I know! And you did it perfectly!
                       You totally showed her up,
           god that was amazing, better than sex!

Better than sex?
I dunno about that.
It was good, but orgasmically good?
You get off on this stuff? ;)

Okay, that's a sudden change in gear. My heart speeds up, and my palms go a bit sweaty, forcing me to wipe them down my thighs. Did I really mean that? I don't know. I don't really have any reference points—hang on, what's this? A picture?

I click on the file, and it unfolds before me—Tori, in her underwear, giving me a peace sign. She's winking and poking her tongue out.

You like?

Oh, I like. I like very much indeed. I feel all floaty, like this isn't quite happening.

                    Omg. I dunno what to say.
             Other than you're killing me here.
                      WOW! xxxxx

Hehehe.
Thought you might like that.
Do I get one too, or are you gonna make
me beg, babe?

The floaty feeling flees. She wants a picture like that of me? I can't do that! Jesus fucking Christ!

Or maybe I could. Maybe I should just throw caution into the wind and give her something. Not a full underwear shot—talk about running before you learn to crawl—but . . . a cleavage shot? Would that do? It would mean taking my T-shirt off, but if I worked on the lighting and took my hair down and smooshed my arms like this . . . okay, maybe not like that, because how the hell am I going to hold my phone to take the picture? Okay, if I lay on my front and angle myself a bit like this and then hold my phone there, and . . . oh, crap, that looks dreadful! Try again. Uh, and again. And, oh fuck me, that one's being deleted straight away. Aaaaand . . . is that one all right? Okay, so to me it looks awful, but it isn't as awful as the rest of them, and it's kind of the best I can do given the material I am working with—

Babe, what are you doing? Did I scare you off? :/

No! Course not! Just trying to get a good pic . . .

Ooooooo! Now I'm all excited! Like Christmas, only hornier!

Ooooooookay, I'm not going to be able to get out of this, am I? Go on, Beth—take a risk for a change. Just send it. Upload it and send it. It's just a bit of fun. She might send you more pictures if you send this one. Come on, girl—you can do this, you curvy diva!

Uploading . . . oh God, am I really going to do this? My heart is going like the clappers, caught between terror and excitement. Then, before I can change my mind, it's gone, into the Metachat ether, and into Tori's inbox.

I hold my breath.

Now that's what I'm talking about!
Woo hoo, hun—you look gorgeous.
If I could bury my face in that cleavage just once,
I'd die a happy girl . . .
Can't believe how much I love you. I'm so lucky.
You're everything, the whole package—funny,
smart, sexy . . . ♥

I love you.
That's it. There. Instantly, I reply:

I love you too.

I've never felt anything like this before. Oh, I had silly schoolgirl crushes when I was younger, but this is something completely different. Love. Proper love.

If you'd asked me a week ago if I thought such a thing possible, I'd have told you not to be so stupid, but now? I'm a believer, baby. I may not have met Tori in the flesh, but I don't have to. This is the beauty of the internet. Here, it's all about the mind, the soul, our very inner beings, not appearances or what we wear or what bands we like, but something far deeper and far more profound. People say you can't make friends on the internet, that relationships forged are a thin emulation of the real thing, but they're wrong.

This is as real as anything I've ever felt.

31: #HATEMYBRO

I go downstairs at ten to grab myself a snack. I've been so wrapped up in Tori and the new level our relationship has reached, I hadn't realized how quiet the house is. I stick my head round the living room door, and yep, there's Mum, playing zombie. All that's missing is the rat-a-tat-tat of fake gunfire from the room above.

I creep back upstairs, my euphoria slowly leeching away. Is Bratley even in? He should be. Maybe he's in there, doing horrible teenage boy things to awful porn? I don't want to see that again.

But what if he's not? What if he's not even here? If he isn't, then where is he? But, then again, why should I care?

You care because he's your little brother, a voice pops up in my head.

Is that true? Maybe, once upon a time, when he was a blond-haired moppet who wanted to share his Pokémon facts with me. But now? No. I don't care, I just don't need him piling any more stress onto Mum.

I hesitate by his door. I could just walk on by, go back to my own room, scarf down biscuits, and cocoon myself in Tori's digital embrace. I could. No one would blame me. I'm not his legal guardian. But his legal guardian isn't exactly in any fit state to legally guard him, is she?

I gnaw on a biscuit for a bit and then tentatively knock on the door.

"Brad?"

No answer.

I turn the handle. There's no lock, but the door catches on something. An unpleasant smell wafts out of the tiny crack. I push the door a little more, but it just bounces off whatever is on the other side.

"Brad?"

My fear of his teenage wrath is replaced by something deeper and more nebulous.

"Are you in there?"

No reply.

I shove the door and cringe as something crashes down. Now the door opens easily. The foul stench of unwashed clothes, BO, cheap deodorant, and an indefinable musk (which isn't unidentifiable, unfortunately) rolls out.

"Jesus Christ," I mutter as I cover my nose with my hand.

I find the source of the door's resistance pretty quickly. Brat tied some string to a pile of heavy books, which he then looped around the door handle. There's enough give to slip a hand in to untie it, but because I didn't know about it, the books have crashed off the shelf and onto the floor. Well, screw him; I'm not picking them up. I don't care if he knows that I've been into his room.

I glance around. Dirty clothes litter the floor and piles of gaming magazines and tissues are scattered around the bed. Eww. I'm not going near those. Posters of scantily clad women line the walls, broken up only by the odd game poster. His current game is paused, his characters frozen in time. No sign of any schoolwork. Lots of evidence of him pissing his life away. Nothing whatsoever that might give me a clue as to where he might be.

I wonder how long he's been doing this. The thought strikes me, hard. In the evening, I'm usually so wrapped up in my online world that I have never really given his whereabouts any thought at all. Has he stayed out like this before? When did he leave?

Is he ever coming back?

I don't like that thought. He might be a colossal cockwomble, but he is still my little brother.

Back in my room, I grab my phone and bring up his profile. A flashing on my laptop screen catches my attention—Tori, asking me if I'm okay. My heart swells at that. She does care. She really does.

> Soz. Went to get a snack, noticed
> my brother isn't in.

Problem?

> Could be. He's 14 and annoying af.

> I . . .

I pause, my fingers hovering over the keys. I don't talk about my family much, especially online. I prefer to keep them out of that world, slotted into different little compartments in my brain. Telling Tori about Brad would basically be like dragging him into the room.

And yet I'm feeling the need to share, the need to confide, and I realize it's because I want her in my offline life as much as my online one—

I take in a shaky breath.

. . . I don't know where he is, and that's an issue. My mum's not well and so doesn't have a great grip on him. He's going off the rails, tbh.

God, hun. Sounds shit.

Yeah, it is. I think he's been bunking off school, and now he's fucking off at night. I dunno where he goes or what he's doing. I was gonna text him, but I don't reckon he'll reply.

That is worrying. He could be doing anything.

Give me his number. Might be able to track him?

Oh. I hadn't thought of that. Brat doesn't feature in my online world—we're not on each other's social media, and I have no idea where his main stomping grounds are or even what his usernames are. But I do know there will be ways to track him via the GPS on his phone. I don't have the expertise, but I have a feeling Tori does, so I give her his number. She tells me to wait, so I spend a tense few minutes sorting through my empty candy wrappers, jumping each time my screen flickers. I'm getting notifications for Project Destroy the Poison Twins every two seconds; normally I would've been on them like a whippet on a rabbit, but now I'm ignoring them.

Finally, Metachat flicks up, showing me a screengrab of a Google map. It's the park just down the road from us. At its center is a little red dot.

Near you?

Yeah. It's just down the road.

The little *shit*. Here I am, worrying myself sick, and he's a five-minute walk away? I can see him now, in my mind's eye, sitting on the swings with his dickless little friends, swigging cheap cider, possibly sharing a badly rolled joint, thinking they're the Big I Am because they're out at night, when in reality they're just showing themselves up as the stupid little kids they are, and all the grown-ups they're so desperate to emulate are sitting in their nice warm homes, drinking their proper drinks and smoking their expertly rolled joints, possibly while watching a nice film or maybe eating a nice dinner or lazily making love. The one thing they're *not* doing is huddling around the kiddies' play equipment, pretending they're rebels while freezing their tiny bollocks off.

You ok?

> Yeah. Just pissed off.

You gonna go get him?

> Are you kidding? Let the little fucker freeze.
>
> I don't care.

Lol. Atta girl.
At least now I can tell you where he is if he does this again.
Saves you from worrying.

    She is so considerate. I am so lucky. Sure, giving out my brother's number without his permission might seem a bit foolish, even wrong, but he shouldn't sneak off at night. And she's totally come through for me, managing to make me feel better in a split second. Why couldn't she have come into my life earlier? It's a shame she lives so far away—well, at least I think she does. Remind me to ask her some time.

Come on. Forget your shitty bro. Let's go and
have more fun.

We do. Lots of it. Indigo's online now. For all her mindfulness and veganism, she's got a tongue like a lash and swears like a docker. It's enormous fun—as the old saying goes, I like a girl with spirit.

Soon I'm laughing so hard, I think I might actually wet myself. Most of that is down to Tori's caustic commentary on Metachat. Indigo and her little fan club try to wrestle back control, but it's absolutely futile. Me and Tori and our legion of sock-puppet accounts are merciless, and in the end, after blocking and reporting half of our accounts, the lovely Indigo goes the way of the equally lovely Dizzy and shuts down her account.

Two in one night? It's a new record, people.

32: #HEREFORYOU

Downstairs, the front door slams. I jerk my head up, my heart hammering. I'd been so wrapped up in my online world that I'd forgotten about the dreary real one. I glance over at my clock: past midnight. Has Bratley seriously been sitting in the park this whole time, freezing his nuts off—for what? Some booze? A drag on a spliff?

And people say those of us who have full online lives are sad.

<blockquote>Wait a sec. Brat's home.</blockquote>

Oh, shit. Your mum okay?

<blockquote>Dunno. Can't hear her.</blockquote>

<blockquote>She's probably asleep.</blockquote>

<blockquote>She's on some pretty serious meds.</blockquote>

Are you gonna say anything to him?

That's a very good question. I feel like I should. I am his big sister. I'm supposed to look out for him. But do I need the hassle?

<blockquote>Dunno. What do u think?</blockquote>

I'd go for the throat.

Well, of course she would. That's because she's brave and daring, everything I'm not. Not in real life, anyway. But what would Tori think if she knew that? That I'm not the cool, fearless person she thinks I am, but rather I'm a big fat coward who gets her kicks making other people feel bad about themselves? I don't want that. I really don't want that.

Right. Brb.

I get up off my bed and peer out into the hall. Bratley's groping at his door, obviously trying to deactivate his little trap. His movements are sluggish; he's at least a bit drunk. I glance back toward my laptop. Tori's Facebook page is displayed, alongside the little Metachat window. I was looking through her meager collection of photos of herself, as if that might bring her closer to me somehow. She'd do this. Be brave. Brave like Tori.

I open my bedroom door. "Brad?"

"Beth," he yelps. "What the fuck?"

"Uh, excuse me? I think I should be asking you that. What the hell are you doing, sneaking off and then not coming back until after midnight? You've got school tomorrow!"

"Oh, like you give a shit!" He's slurring and stinks, rather predictably, of cheap cider. "It's none of your business, bitch."

The casual way he tries to dismiss me rankles, and I'm glad I intercepted him. No more being afraid. Time to deal with the beast.

"Look, Mum's ill, and you acting like this isn't helping. You think you're the only one with problems? Think again."

"Oh, just fuck ooofff . . ." He tries to push his door open, but the books that fell over earlier must be blocking it, meaning he can't just slip inside and slam the door on me. Instead, he's got to spend some time trying to figure out how to get into his room in his addled state.

"No. I'm not going to fuck off, because you're fourteen, and sitting in the park getting drunk is—"

"How do you know I was in the park?" he slurs.

Oh, crap.

"Because I'm not a complete idiot, unlike you."

He screws his face up and shakes his head, as if that might dislodge me from his vision.

"You . . . you . . . you think you're so important," he says when I don't miraculously disappear. "That . . . that you're so much better than anyone else." His face is screwed up in an ugly pout, his eyes blazing with drunken indignation. "You're not, though. Better than me. You're just a stupid, fat bitch who can't face reality. Poor sad, mad, fat Bethany, can't cope with real life, so she drowns herself in chocolate, talking to her imaginary friends—"

"Shut up!" I hiss, my hands clenched into fists. "I'm not the one worrying Mum sick—"

He snorts. "Yeah, right. You keep telling yourself that. Between Dad and you, Mum hasn't stood a chance. Neither have I."

He says the last bit quietly, framing it as an afterthought. The ember of fury flares in me again. How dare he blame me for what Dad did? That's about as low as you can go. He's the one who needs to face up to facts. He's the one who needs to sort his life out.

We stare at each other for a few seconds more. A sneer curls his lip, but his eyes are oddly bright. He then shoves his door open and disappears inside his room, and I turn away, sharpish, back to my own sanctuary, wishing I hadn't bothered trying to tackle him in the first place.

♦♦♦

So, how did it go?

Tori's message is waiting for me when I settle myself back down, but I'm not sure if I'm ready to tell her yet. I'm angry, and there's now a lump in my throat that just won't melt, and I don't know why.

He's a shit.

Oh. Not good, then?

You could say that.

I can piss off if you want.
But you can tell me. I'm here for you.

And, at last, the lump loosens—only rather than disappearing, the tears it contained flood out of me, and I find myself typing madly, telling her everything Brat said, and how life's shit since Dad left, and that I don't think I can cope with Mum's illness and Brat's awfulness all at once.

Tori doesn't interrupt me. She says nothing about my spelling mistakes or my repetitions. She lets me get it all out over the course of four messages, and I am grateful. When she eventually replies, she says just one thing.

I am here for you. You know that, right?

And I cry again, this time with happiness.

33: #YOLO

She knows how to cheer me up, that Tori. It's now two thirty in the morning, but I don't care. Tomorrow will take care of itself. I need to revel in the right now. YOLO and all that. She sends me her favorite *Banshee and Midnight Jim* strips—there's a lot of crossover with mine, but that doesn't surprise me. We talk about how great it would be to really be Banshees, deciding who lives and who dies, sending our own Midnight Jims after our enemies so he can envelope them in his darkness and leave nothing behind but a husk, their life force drained away into the ether.

Imagine if we could do that to Dizzy. Or Indigo.
Or one of those tossers who harassed you in the club.

That would rule so hard.
We could proclaim them void,
and Midnight Jim could feed. So cool.

Either that, or we could make him drown them in the sea.

Haha! I know, right!
Get in the sea, you fuckers.
Bother me no more.

Or off a high building.
Or get him to slit their wrists,
so it looks like they killed themselves.

A sharp pain lances above my right eye. Maybe it's time to go to bed.

Haha. Hard to fake that, tho.
Oh, I dunno. I'm sure it's not that hard.
Overdose first, then slashy-slashy. Easy-peasy.

A queasy feeling turns my stomach.

lol. Look, it's late, and I have lectures in the morning. Need to go to sleep.
Oh? All right. Shame.
But I've got work in the a.m. too,
so it's probably a good idea. Like all your ideas. ;)

Now I'm smiling again.

Night night, Tori. Speak tomorrow?
Try and stop me. Night night.

I pause. Will she log off first, or will I? Is she sitting there in her bedroom, wondering the same thing? I rest my fingers on the keys, itching to type something, anything, but what—

Something to help you sleep. Love you, babe.

Another photo, this time of her blowing me a kiss. I close my eyes in joy. This time, the courage to take another photo comes easily, so I send one of me doing the same back.

love u too, hun.
And we log off, together.

34: #LIVINGTHEDREAM

I'm not sure where I read it, but I know I liked the idea.

Living online.

Not just logging in and talking over the net. Actually, physically plugging yourself into a virtual world, forgetting about your physical body, living purely in your mind in a digital world. Imagine, no more worrying about what you really look like, because you can craft your own appearance. No worrying about eating—your body would be plugged into some kind of cryo chamber, keeping you in suspended animation. Want to smite your enemies? Feel free. It isn't real, after all. You're not committing murder, you're just playing a game.

If I was clever, I'd be working on this. Then Tori and I could be together, forever.

35: #DREAD

I wake up pretty late. My morning lecture is a write-off, so I flop back in bed, trying to ignore my full bladder.

My phone buzzes. A text from Amy.

Where r u? xx

Soz, overslept. Be in soon.

Ok. Text me when ur in xxxx.

I yawn, and my bladder wins out. I pad out to the bathroom. As usual, the house is quiet. I hesitate by Brat's door, wondering if he's in or if he's actually gone to school today. I give myself a little shake. Why should I care?

Back in my room again, I check my laptop. No sign of Tori. I wonder if she's slept in too. In a way, that would be like us sleeping in together, which is an image I like, so I linger on it for a bit. I imagine her dark hair trailing over the pillow beside me, the warmth of her body next to mine, the soft, steady rhythm of her breathing. For a moment, I'm lost in the fantasy, and it is greater than any dream of fictional characters, because this is something that could happen, may already behappening.

To celebrate this, I find a cute little meme, featuring a kitten showing someone unconditional love in many and varied ways, and share it on Tori's page. I'm such an old romantic.

I skip morning coffee and grab a granola bar to keep me going. Mum's still in the living room, but she's awake. She smiles at me when I go in and give her a kiss goodbye. I don't mention Bradley. Why ruin an otherwise perfect morning?

Outside, it's drizzling, but I simply don't care. I even manage to ignore the other bus wankers at the stop who are waiting with me. As soon as I can, I'm back on my phone—Tori has "loved" the meme I left her and has sent me one with a silly frog that's completely twee and stupid, but I "love" it anyway, blushing to myself.

I hear the chug of an engine in the distance and look up. It's the 21, so I stuff my phone in my pocket and flash my bus pass at the driver with a smile. He grunts in return. Well, you can't please everyone.

On the bus, I text Amy to tell her I'm on my way and then stare wistfully out the window. No more messages from Tori; she's obviously either on her way to work or is trying to weasel the day off—

"Hi, Beth."

I look up.

It's Jenna Thwaites from school.

"Oh. Hello." I try not to stare as I regress back to being thirteen all over again. What the fuck is she doing, talking to me? This has to be the first time she's willingly acknowledged my existence. "What are you doing here?"

She shrugs. I notice that she doesn't have those cloth daisies in her hair anymore. "Going into town. I moved away, tried the whole uni thing, but it's not for me. I'm thinking of coming back. Too expensive to live on my own." Without waiting to be asked, she sits down next to me.

"That's a shame," I say, feeling extremely awkward as

old memories fight their way through ancient scabs to bleed once again.

"Nah, not really. It's cheaper this way—means I can at least try to save some cash. I'd like to go traveling at some point, but I was forking out nearly everything on rent. It's ridiculous. You off to uni?"

"Yeah. I overslept, so I missed my first lecture. Can't miss my second."

She smiles at that, and despite myself, I'm reminded of all the reasons I once hated and adored her.

"It's good you're doing well," she says. A pause. "I always knew you'd do all right."

A little stab of panic erupts in my chest. "You did? Oh." The bus rumbles on. "I'm sorry. This is my stop."

"Oh. All right. Might see you around?"

Seriously? After everything you put me through, you *might see me around*?

"Yeah. Maybe." I press the bell, which chimes my desire to get out of this nightmare.

"Love to your mum, yeah?"

Funny. I'd forgotten her mum was once friends with mine. "I'll tell her. And love to, uh, your mum too."

She nods. The bus stops. I get off and let out a long, cleansing sigh of relief.

♠ ♠ ♠

Amy's waiting for me in what I'm beginning to think of as her usual spot. Her other friends, Nicki and Carla, aren't standing with her. They're there, just not with her. Over the last few weeks they've kind of drifted away from her, and I kind of feel sorry for her. Is hanging out with me really so damaging to one's reputation?

Not that Amy seems to care. As soon as she catches sight of me, she waves, her face breaking into a broad grin. I find myself following suit—although I keep my arm pinned to my side and just wave with my hand; last thing anyone needs is the sight of my bingo wings billowing in the wind, even if they are covered by my coat. Maybe this is what friendship actually is. Geographical convenience, the ability to tolerate one another, and waving. Even I have to admit, there are a lot worse things in the world.

"Hey," I say as I stroll up. "Did I miss anything?"

"Nah. All basic stuff. A brainiac like you could catch up in minutes. Brice says he's putting the slides on the intranet this afternoon, so it's all easy-peasy. Dunno why I even went, to be honest. I mean, if he's just going to go through a Powerpoint and then shove them online, what's the actual point of going to his lectures? Seems like we could all save some time there. Then again, I suppose he won't get paid if he doesn't teach. Anyway, have you seen about that open workshop thingie? What the fuck is that all about?"

"Uh, what open workshop?"

"It's this thing where they split us all up into small groups and we all have to psychoanalyze each other using questionnaires, or something. They emailed out the details yesterday, but the names are on the bulletin board. Did you not get it?"

A slick feeling of dread oozes around my stomach. "No . . . I didn't check my email yesterday, though."

"We could go look on the board? It would be so cool if we were at the same workshop!"

"Yeah, uh, maybe later. If we go look now, we'll be late for Grindle's lecture."

She play-slaps her forehead. "Duh. Of course. Lecture first. Always getting ahead of myself!"

She slips her arm through the crook of mine. I try to ignore the way my stomach flips. Open workshop. That doesn't sound like fun. That doesn't sound like fun at all. That sounds like role-play and team games and all the things people! Who! Talk! In! Exclamation! Marks! find fun, but the rest of the population despises. I shiver and hug my folders tightly to my chest.

Just when you think things are starting to go your way, eh?

♦♦♦

I'm kind of getting used to not sitting at the back now. I'm not saying I like it, but it's sort of like eating broccoli or using mismatching cutlery.

The lecture's pretty interesting—historical methods of diagnosis—and leaves me with a distinct sense of gratitude that I wasn't born a hundred years ago. The only thing that really bothers me is the looks that Nicki and Carla keep throwing me and Amy; furtive, nasty little looks that leave me in no doubt that we are their topic of conversation in the DMs they're so obviously sharing. No whispering, just tippy-tapping away on their phones while Grindle drones on about electroshock treatment. Makes me wish he had a shock button on his desk. Not paying attention? Bzzz! Making up nasty little lies? Bzzzz! Gossiping? BZZZZ!! Heh heh, I think I could do with one of those. I'd have my brother on the straight and narrow within one afternoon.

As the lecture ends and we all start to pile out, there's a call from the front of the lecture hall.

"Miss Hardcastle!"

Amy frowns and gives me a facial shrug.

"What does he want?" I whisper.

"I dunno. I've done all my work. Better go see."

"Can't you pretend you didn't hear him?"

"Miss Hardcastle? Can you come over here?"

"Not really. I think he's spotted me."

She turns and weaves her way easily through the crowd, like an otter gliding through water, leaving me to stare after her as people jostle me on all sides. I want to follow her, but at the same time, I most definitely don't, and so I allow the sea of students to carry me out of the room and back outside, where they break up into small groups. I hover at the edges, waiting for Amy to come back with the terrible news that she's inevitably receiving. I glance up at the sky; it's gray, like always. I gnaw on the edge of my thumb, biting off squidgy chunks of skin that I know will sting like hell later, but right now, I don't care, I just need to let my mouth do something, anything, to ease the tension.

Jesus Christ, how long is he going to keep her in there for? Maybe he's chucking her out. Or telling her to pull her socks up. Or, or, maybe they're having some kind of sordid affair, something she is forced to keep from everyone, or, or, or—

"Hey. Thanks for waiting for me," Amy says. I jump. "Are you all right?"

"Uh, yeah. Of course." I swallow, hoping it will steady my voice. "What did Grindle want?"

"Oh, nothing. Just to clarify one of my sources. Said it was a clever find. It was one of yours, so no surprise there, eh?" She pauses. "Are you sure you're all right?"

When people say *all the color drained from her face*, I'm never really sure what they mean by that. Oh, of course, I know what they *mean*, but it's something you see written, not in real life.

I still don't know what it looks like, but I now damn well know what it *feels* like.

"He asked about a source?"

"Yeah. Said it was a clever link. I think he was probably trying to work out if I was plagiarizing someone, but I said it was something you'd found and had helped me with." She gives me an impish smile, like she's done me a massive favor. "It felt wrong, stealing your thunder. I wonder why he picked it up in my essay and not yours, though?"

All that color that had drained from me suddenly rushed back in one big burning hit. "I dunno. Maybe he hasn't marked mine yet."

"Yeah, must be it. Shall we go and see what work group you've been put into for the workshop?"

No. I don't want to traipse all the way over to the Richmond building to see what fucking group I'm in for this pissballing workshop. I don't want to *go* to this workshop. I wish this workshop didn't exist! For fuck's sake, I thought uni would be lovely lectures and libraries and studying and basically being left to my own devices, not being made to spend time with a bunch of wankers who'll inevitably hate my guts! Gah! Just drop it! Please!

I don't say any of that, of course. Instead, I put on my best apologetic face and make up something, because lying is something Beth does best: "Oh, sorry, I can't. I've got to get home. I'm babysitting, and I need to be there early."

"Oh, bummer. Would have been good to see if we're together. I might wander over there anyway. I can text you your group."

She gives me a hopeful *Has Amy Done Good?* look that makes something in my heart twist painfully. I chew on my lips so I don't yell out, "For God's sake, no!"

"If you want. Don't go out of your way, though."

"Cool!" She beams at me again and hugs me goodbye, and I kind of hate her for it. And then I kind of hate myself too, because there is literally nothing to hate about Amy.

36: #PANIC

When I get on the bus, I wish I was as tiny as a mouse and that no one could see me. I sit as near to the back as I can manage. (The *very* back seat is taken by two scary-looking men chugging Monster energy drinks.) I'm huddling against the glass as if I might meld into it and become invisible. Sparks of panic are crackling all over my body; my breathing is all over the place. It seems like ages since I felt this way. I suppose Tori has to take the credit for that. She sure can keep my mind off the horrible stuff.

I wonder where Amy is now. Is she already in Richmond building? Or has she decided not to bother? I hope it's the latter. I *pray* it's the latter. Oh, I should have told her not to bother, it's probably online, I'd find out that way. Then I could ignore it. This was *so* much easier before I found a friend. I should have known other people cause complications. Just look at my family.

I've run out of fingers to chew on, so I resort to the inside of my cheek. It isn't long before the skin starts sloughing off, and I taste the bright tang of blood. I suck on this, hoping it will give me something to focus on, but it doesn't help. The worries won't be silenced, even with a blood sacrifice.

I want to eat. I want to gorge and gorge and gorge until I can't think of anything else but how wonderfully, painfully full I am, drowning myself in a world of taste and texture. Crunchy, smooth, wobbly, stringy, hard, chewy, lumpy, crisp, chunky . . . I go through the words of food, and my heart rate begins to slow. I might order in a burger for lunch. And fries. And onion rings. And those little jalapeno popper things—

My phone buzzes, and I almost fall off my seat. Behind me, one of the Monster-drinking men snorts in unmistakable amusement.

Hay! Just looked on the board—ur name isn't on the list? Maybe u shud ring ur tutor? Axx

My mouth runs dry. All thoughts of my lunchtime burger feast flee. I turn my phone off.

I'll deal with that later.

◆◆◆

Mrs. Olgive has just left for her class, and I still haven't turned my phone on. Haven't checked Facebook, either.

If I don't read it, I don't have to deal with it. If I don't acknowledge it, I don't have to accept it.

The kids want a bedtime story, so I read *Sometimes I Like to Curl Up in a Ball* to them. It's a cute story about a wombat who likes to curl up with his mum at the end of the day, because that's where he feels safest. I used to like that too. When I was small, I'd curl up into a ball with my mum and my dad. Can't do that now. Don't think I'll ever be able to do it again.

I toy with my switched-off phone. Its surface looks like a black void in the low lights of the kids' bedroom. They snuggle down under their covers, and I run my hand over both their silky heads. Oh, to be that small, that innocent again. When your biggest worry was what your mum had packed in your lunch box, or whether your friends would want to play with you at breaktime. Those worries felt so huge then; right now, I'd do anything to go back to those days, to when the world was simple and made perfect sense.

I snap the light off as I leave and linger by the door.

"Sleep tight," I murmur.

"Ni-night," they chorus back to me, sleep already infecting their voices.

I creep downstairs, my insides growing heavier with each step. My laptop is on the sofa. I know I can bypass all my Beth accounts and go straight into troll mode, but for some reason I'm not that into it tonight. I kind of want to talk to someone— Tori, mainly—but at the same time, I kind of want to be alone. But I also don't want to be alone with only my own thoughts for company, because they scare me and I don't want to deal with them, and I need to switch my phone on just in case Mum needs me, but I can't because Amy's going to be on there, asking where I am, what I'm doing, have I spoken to my tutor yet, workshop, workshop, workshop . . . I close my eyes, my heart thrumming in my head, making it ache so badly that I feel sick.

In my bag, I have three Mars bars. I mainline the lot, and for five blissful minutes, I let my mouth calm my mind. Chew. Swallow. Savor. Get lost in this. No one can harm me here.

I switch on the TV. Mrs. Olgive has Netflix. Netflix is another good way to waste time and forget yourself. I put my phone in my bag.

Out of sight, out of mind.

It's the only way, really.

♦♦♦

I awake with a little snort. Must have drifted off. My right hand feels all weird and fizzy. Shit. Are the kids okay? What woke me up? Is Mrs. Olgive home already? Only feels like five minutes since I sat down.

It's longer than five minutes, but only just. Out of sheer habit, I reach for my phone and switch it on, and the world crashes into me.

My home screen is flooded with messages, mainly from Amy. It takes all I have not to fling the fucking thing at the wall.

Okay. Okay. Okay. All I have to do is say, *Thanks for looking—I'll ask and find out.* That's it! Just that, and this nightmare will be over.

Except it won't be over, because then she'll want to know whose group I'm in and what did my tutor say and who is your tutor and all sorts of little questions that I simply don't want to deal with, so I drag my laptop over and log straight in to Metachat, where I know Tori will be waiting for me. I send her my chat key and sit there, waiting, waiting, waiting, oh, come on, where are you? It's never taken you this long before, come on, Tori, I need you, I need you to tell me everything's going to be okay, to reassure me that I'm fine . . .

No reply.

For the first time since I met her, Tori isn't there.

37: #STUPIDCHECKMARK

I keep one eye on Metachat while I half-heartedly watch something sci-fi-y that features the heroics of some impossibly beautiful people. Yeah, I'm pretty sure they don't have eyeliner and hair straighteners in the far dystopian future, and even if they do, it's hardly going to be a priority when you're reduced to eating rats.

I drum my fingers on the arm of the sofa. Mrs. Olgive left me a Penguin bar, and I'm allowed as much tea as I want, but what I really want is my burger feast (which I didn't get earlier because I don't have enough cash, hence why I'm here, babysitting), or more chocolate. Anything to take my mind off my crushing anxiety.

My phone is buried back in my pocket. I hope the simple act of switching it on hasn't sent anyone that check mark that says I've read their message. I *hate* that stupid check mark, always watching me, always telling tales. Okay, so I use it to keep tabs on the people I've messaged, but I never said I was perfect, or indeed, not a hypocrite.

Oh God, oh God, oh God, what am I going to do? I'm catastrophizing and I know it, but I can't help it. My life currently feels like a loose association of strings, all wriggling off down their own little terrifying avenues, and I haven't a clue as to which one to grab and drag back first.

Still no Tori.

The big blue F is watching me from my laptop screen.

I have enough proxies to quickly log in and take a look. No one needs to know. I'm invisible. Like a ninja. Like a cowardly, anxious ninja. I check all my security protocols again, and then click on the F. My heart feels like it's going to burst out of my forehead and bounce around the room.

Facebook flicks open, and I mutter under my breath, "I'm invisible. No one knows I'm here," but I'm not totally sure of that because I've never actually tried this before.

A few new links sent from both Tori and Amy. Tori's are the earlier ones, sent this morning. Amy's are more recent. One message immediately stands out.

R U okay?

Now I don't just feel anxious—I feel bad too.

There are a couple of other notifications. One is a friend request from—get this—Patrick. I don't confirm his request, but I don't delete it either. The other notification is from Messenger. From Amy.

I gnaw on my thumb.

I wish I'd taken my security measures out for a trial run so that I could be sure they'd cheat the dreaded check mark. Because if Amy sees I've read her messages without responding, she's going to know I'm avoiding her, and for some reason, that really bugs me.

Ding

Metachat. I almost hit the ceiling.

Babe? What's up?

It's Tori, blessed, blessed Tori, come to save the day!

> OMG. So fucking anxious right now.
> Need to check something,
> but don't want other person to know.
> Have software but haven't run it yet.

Yeah? If you want I could just hack the back door,
retrieve messages for you
without anyone ever knowing I was there?

> Really? Seriously? That's high level stuff!

Hey, how do you think I get half my dirt? I'm a pro!

I smile. She sure is. She's a rebel.

I wish I was a rebel too.

Without thinking, I give her the nod. She warns me it'll take a mo—settle down, have a cup of coffee. She'll get back to me when I log back in.

Half an hour later, Mrs. Olgive is home. I gather up my things and run down the road. It's drizzling again, just enough for me to be uncomfortably damp by the time I let myself in. Mum's asleep in front of the TV, a half-finished plate of macaroni and cheese in danger of sliding off her lap. I rescue it and pick at the leftovers absentmindedly whilst I root around for the TV remote, which I find stuffed down the arm of the chair Mum's propped up in, and lower the volume to a more socially acceptable level.

In my room, I snap open my laptop and log in even before I plug the damn thing in. Straight away I clock Tori's Metachat ID. She's good. Very good. It's only been twenty minutes or so since Mrs. Olgive got home and she's already got something for me. I feel weirdly proud of this.

So? What's the verdict?

That Amy chick says you've been left off some list,
but no one was in the office so she couldn't find out why.
Then there's loads of "are you okay" type messages.
Seems a bit needy to me.

I feel like crying.

That's it?

Yeah, that's it. Why were you so worried, babe?

I lie back for a moment and let it all wash over me. Sure, it won't go away, but I can sort something out in the meantime. What's important is that my life is still intact.

For now.

38: #EMERGENCY

I spend the rest of the evening mucking around with Tori, building new extensions on our empire of hate and generally enjoying ourselves. Eventually I pluck up the balls to message Amy; I make up some bullshit about my internet going tits up and not having enough mobile data left on my phone, which she swallows hook, line, and sinker. Even so, in the morning I feel a twinge about that, to the point where I seriously wonder if I should even leave the house. But then I catch a glimpse of Mum, slumped on the sofa, a half-drunk cup of tea in one hand as she stares blankly at the TV. Sure, it's hell going outside, but sometimes, staying in is even worse.

It's raining again. I quite like the rain. People tend to mind their own business when it rains. Only major problem is the coat issue, and by the time I'm at the bus stop, I'm sweating like a pig.

I hardly have time to cool down before the bus comes chugging around the corner. I've arranged to meet Amy at our usual spot, which is enough to send uncomfortable tingles of anxiety through me. I know we have a lecture, but what if she says we should go to the office first? Not only is that a good five-to-ten minute walk away—not much of an issue if you're a normal person, but a huge, sweaty mess when you're fugly—but the whole . . .

I close my eyes. No. Just don't mention it. Avoid it, and it will go away. That's the Beth Soames way.

I get off at my stop and take a moment to pull my hood up over my head. The rain has eased up a bit, but I like the anonymity the hood gives me. Now I'm just another fat chick in the crowd. Say what you like, you don't know me, and so it doesn't matter.

I'm just about to cross the road when my phone buzzes. Damn thing has me on a leash, so before I can think about it, I'm looking. A text from Amy.

Won't be able to meet. Come to mine. Pls. It's an emergency. Need ur help. Axxxx

What? Why on earth would she need my help? Oh God, she hasn't hurt herself, has she? But why text me? Call a fucking ambulance! I end up sending *K* and then add *hope ur ok* and turn back.

◆◆◆

By the time I arrive at Amy's, I'm breathing hard and feeling more than a bit self-conscious. Thankfully, there's hardly anyone around, so I spend a couple of minutes trying to compose myself.

I press the buzzer to Amy's floor. It takes a good minute before anyone answers (why is it taking them so long—come on, you knew I was coming!), and although I can't work out exactly who says "Hello?" I can tell they're panicky.

"Hey, yeah, it's Beth—Amy's friend?"

They don't say anything else as the door releases.

Okay. This is weird. I hesitate by the lift, which, thankfully, is working. Do I want to get involved with whatever's happening up there? Fine, so Amy asked me, but it really doesn't have anything to do with me, and I quite honestly have enough on my plate as it is. Does that make me sound callous? It does, doesn't it? Oh, balls. My chest twinges, a nasty, twisting sensation that makes me feel sick. Okay, okay, I'm doing it.

The door to Amy's floor is wide open when I reach the top, and I can hear a lot of people talking in a wheedling way. An undercurrent of tension crackles around me, making the hairs on my arms tingle.

"Hey, anyone there?" I call out, rather than just enter. Gives them some warning. God knows what's going on.

"Yes!" I hear Amy squeak, and her head pokes out round Dizzy's bedroom door. "Oh, God, I'm so glad you're here!"

What is she doing in Dizzy's room? And why is she crying?

"Dizzy! Please, honey, let us in." It's Patrick, and he sounds both commanding and incredibly scared. I really, really don't want to go in there, but backing out now doesn't seem like a viable option, so shuffle in, giving everyone who glances my way an apologetic look. And everyone is in there—Amy, Patrick, Indigo, Richard, plus another annoyingly thin girl who I can only guess is friends with Dizzy—all of them looking worried.

"Oh, Beth!" Amy stage-whispers. "Dizzy has locked herself in her bathroom! Says it's all too much, that she can't cope— we've been trying to get her out of there for the last hour, but she's totally refusing to come out."

"What do you mean, she can't cope?" I ask, genuinely bewildered. I mean, for fuck's sake, what can't she cope with? Being perfect?

"Someone has been harassing her online," Indigo deigns to say. "Look."

I can see her trying to smother her instinctual revulsion at having to communicate with me as she hands me her phone.

And there it is.

Everything Tori and I have ever thrown at her, plus some more we simply encouraged.

On that little screen, in stark black and white.

Fake ass basic bitch.

Think ur something? Ur not. Ur no one.

Fuck u. So fucking vile.

Look at that fat ass. Fuck sake. Shouldn't be allowed.

And there's more. Stuff I wasn't involved in. Stuff I don't recognize. But what I do recognize are the various handles and the style.

It looks like Tori carried on having fun way after I bailed.

I swallow.

"That's horrible," I manage to croak.

"Yeah. I know." Indigo sniffs, and it dawns on me that it might not actually be revulsion that made her hand shake when she gave me her phone. Well, not revulsion at me, anyway.

"What do you think she's done?" I find myself asking. "Do you think she might have overdosed or something?"

"We don't know," Amy says.

"She used to self-harm," Indigo adds. "She plucked up the courage and told me a couple of weeks ago. She was bullied at school, and this has just totally torn all those old wounds open. She's an absolute mess. I mean, I kept telling her that they're just stupid little trolls, trying to wind her up, and that they don't really mean it, but she wouldn't listen to me."

My head's spinning. I'd quite like to be sick, but I force myself to gulp it back. Oh, they're trolls all right. One of them might not mean it, but the other one certainly did. Because the other one thought bashing someone better than them might make themselves feel better. And it did. Right up until this specific moment, it did.

"Dizzy, please!" Paddy implores through the door. "Just open up!"

"Fuck off." Dizzy's voice is thick with pain.

"Have you called anyone?" I ask.

"What? Like, who?" says the girl I don't know. She has a light, breezy voice that perfectly complements her light, breezy body.

"Like, an ambulance? If she's hurt herself, or worse, we really need to get someone out."

"No, no one has—I mean, they're really busy and we didn't want to waste their time . . ."

You didn't want to waste their time? *Seriously*. You're actually going to sit there, with your massive baby-blue eyes and your perfect, baby-pink hair and tell me this isn't an emergency? You dense bitch, you have no idea what's going on in there! If she's taken something, this could be it. She's been in there, what, an hour? AN HOUR!

I shake my head and close my eyes, stopping my mental rant.

"Okay. You need to call someone. Now. Someone else needs to find Hall security. They should be able to get the door open."

Richard, his eyes huge behind his thick glasses, nods at me. "I can do that."

"Good." He tears off down the stairs. Indigo's now talking to someone on the phone. Paddy's still talking to Dizzy through the door, which is also good. Baby Colors launches herself at me, falling into my arms so I have no other choice but to catch her and hold her.

"Thank you!" she sobs as I pat her awkwardly on her back, trying to make comforting sounds. All I can think is *I'm the last person you should be thanking,* but in a way, it's weirdly gratifying. No one has a clue that I'm partially responsible for what's happening. If nothing else, this proves that all my privacy paranoia has been totally worth it and all the measures I've taken to stay anonymous have worked. I know that sounds all shades of wrong, but look at it this way: None of this would be fixed by my cover getting blown. It could only get worse.

We sit in silence, apart from Paddy, who keeps up his wheedling, until we all hear sirens in the distance. The lift buzzes to life. A security guard strides in. She's a solid lass, older, a stern face like a bulldog chewing a wasp, and let's be honest, that's exactly what we all need. She barks orders at Paddy that might be questions; he stares at her, a deer caught in headlights, and points to the door. The security guard shakes her head and mutters something under her breath. How many times has she been in this particular situation? Judging by the way she whips out an electric screwdriver and takes out the lock, I'd say pretty often.

Next she says, very loudly and *very* firmly: "I'm coming in—stay back from the door!", gives it a few seconds, and then shoves it open. Before I can stop her, Baby Colors is up like a whippet and charges into the bathroom.

The sirens are now deafening, and blue lights strobe the room. I can hear the security guard saying, "All right, all right, you're okay, can you get out of here, I know she's your friend, but back off." Baby Colors stumbles back out of the bathroom, groping at the wall as if it might offer her some comfort. Before she can grope toward me again, two paramedics come charging in, with Richard reluctantly in tow.

The paramedics immediately set to work, asking us questions. I inch out of the room until I'm back in the corridor. Richard's there too. He's hugging himself and looks like he's about twelve rather than eighteen. It strikes me that for all the legal stuff we can do at eighteen, all the things that declare our fresh adulthood—voting, drinking, getting married, driving—most of us really haven't seen much of life, not really. Kind of unfair, when you think about it. Child, child, child, no, not old enough, nope, nope, n—yes! Eighteen. Adult now. Off you go. Adult away. What do you mean, you don't know how? What's wrong with you? Why not? Are you defective?

Amy wanders out into the hallway. "The paramedics say she'll probably be okay," she says. She's pale and visibly shaking. "There's no evidence she's taken anything, but they're going to run tests just in case." Her eyes well up. "There's blood every-where, though. She's really torn her arms up. Probably going to need lots of stitches. Oh, Beth, Indigo showed me some of the stuff she's been dealing with . . . it's so vile. People like that! How can they live with themselves? How can they sleep at night?"

I could answer those questions. In great detail. I could say that doing this actually makes their lives easier and that they sleep very well, thank you very much.

But I don't. Because that would be a lie.

Instead, I hug her, as much for my benefit as for hers.

39: #GUILT

There's that scene in thriller movies, you know the one, where everyone gets into one room and they all realize that one of their number is the killer/betrayer/alien/whatever, and they all go nuts with paranoia because they can't work out who it is.

I kind of feel like I'm in one of those scenes, except I'm the betrayer, the alien, or whatever.

And I know it.

We've been moved from halls to let the cleaners sort out Dizzy's bathroom. The university's offered counseling, but right now, we're sitting in the student union, each nursing a stiff drink, even though it's still technically the morning.

Dizzy's friend Baby Colors isn't with us. She and Indigo left with Dizzy. My last glimpse of them in the back of the ambulance showed them wrapped around each other, their shared grief almost a parody of some sort of illicit affair.

Amy's phone buzzes, and we all jump. She fumbles at it, cursing when it doesn't recognize her fingerprint the first time.

"It's from Indigo," she whispers. "Okay, she says Dizzy is okay, they're treating her now, but there are no signs of overdose." She closes her eyes, one hand on her heart. "Thank God for that. Okay, then it says that they're probably going to keep

Dizzy in, as her head is a mess. They've called her mum and dad, so hopefully she'll be fine."

Everyone stares at their drinks for a second before saying anything.

"I don't get it," Paddy says, his usually unctuous voice now thin and rough. "Why do people do it?"

Oh, I don't know. Why do you call me Big Bird? Knobhead.

"Because they've got nothing better to do with their lives," Amy whispers.

Even I have to nod in agreement with that.

"Why didn't she just ignore them, though?" I say. "It's just words."

The moment it leaves my mouth, I know I've said the wrong thing. From the way the others are looking at me, with a mixture of surprise and disgust, they have come to the same conclusion.

"*What?*" says Richard, his face screwed up in disbelief.

"No—I didn't mean it like that. Of course I didn't. I know better than anyone how much damage words can do. But— Dizzy? She doesn't come across as the type that would let something get to her so much. I mean, she's pretty and successful and popular . . ." I trail off under the weight of their collective stares.

"Dizzy has some pretty serious anxiety issues," Amy says. For the first time, her voice has lost its bounce, replaced with an icy brittleness I really don't like. "She was bullied really badly at school. She ended up being homeschooled because of it. She told me that uni was a way of starting afresh. You know, that whole 'be whoever you want to be' thing. Looks like she couldn't escape it, though. Fucking bullies still found her."

"Seriously, though," Patrick says, "they should be strung up by their balls, or whatever chicks have instead of balls. Their tits, I suppose. Totally out of order."

His lack of self-awareness is almost hilarious. I really want to shout that it's the likes of him, the ignorant ones who carelessly name-call and thoughtlessly make hurtful comments, who are the main problem.

But I don't. Because although I know I'm right, that would make me the biggest hypocrite in the room. Sure, Patrick's mindless nickname for me is horrible and derogatory and reductive—but it doesn't come from a place of malice, unlike my trolling. I troll because I want the beautiful people to hurt the way I'm hurting.

Only, I've never had to face any actual consequences of this before. I've read the online meltdowns, gloated over the closed accounts, laughed as they tried to block my accounts like someone trying to stamp out an anthill. But I've never actually *seen* it before, up close and uncomfortably personal.

How many of those girls I've tormented have ended up like Dizzy? How many of them hurt themselves? Once I've destroyed someone's account, I rarely revisit it (unless they come back cockier than ever, of course). How many of those girls I've tormented have ended up like Dizzy? How many of them hurt themselves? How many of those accounts were deleted, not to escape me and my ilk, but because their owners aren't around anymore to maintain them?

My stomach boils. I feel sick again. The old phrase is true, I suppose: It's all just a bit of fun until someone gets hurt.

"We should get her a card or something," Amy says. "Make one. Make it personal. Let her know we're thinking of her, and that she is special."

Special? Really? The sickness is now replaced with the bitter tang of anger. I glance at the solemn faces around me, and I feel a switch flip within me. Fucking Dizzy. Sure, she was bullied—but for what? Being too pretty? Too bright? Too god-damn perfect? Fucking snowflake. Try being fugly. Try having insults thrown at you every single day to the point where you're scared to walk down the road. No one wants to send me a fucking card telling me I'm special. Oh no, that's only reserved for the Beautiful People. Because they're the only real humans. Not us. Not the Fuglies. We can quite literally go to hell for all anyone cares.

♠ ♠ ♠

After we finish our drinks, Amy wants to go out and do some window shopping to take our minds off Dizzy. I'm not really feeling up to it, but don't have much of an excuse. I can't very well say I'd prefer to go to lectures, can I?

So I spend the next couple of hours being dragged in and out of shops containing clothes that will never fit me, trying to ignore the narrow-eyed glares of the stick-insect shop assistants who know damn well I shouldn't be in there. I halfheart-edly nod at each thing Amy shows me, occasionally daring to touch the shiny heels of shoes I would never be able to walk in without breaking them, or indeed, myself.

I genuinely don't think Amy sees how uncomfortable I am in these places. I don't want to upset her by making a big deal of it, but it does kind of hurt that she is so oblivious, especially after this morning's events.

"What about this?" she asks, holding up yet another pair of skinny-fit jeans, with holes artfully torn into them.

"Uh, yeah. They're nice."

"They are, aren't they? Shame my student loan won't cover that price tag." She sighs heavily and hangs them back up. "Oh well. Maybe when I'm a big-shot psychologist to A-list stars, eh?" She flashes me an uncertain smile, as if her little quip might be too much given the circumstances.

"Yeah. Maybe we could be in practice together. I'll do the Jolie-Pitt kids, you get the ex-Disney stars on drug benders."

"Oh, I want the Jolie-Pitt kids. More money there!"

"Yeah? Why do you think I called dibs on them first?"

She giggles, and I feel a little bit of the weight crushing my heart lift, just a teensy bit.

"Why don't you pick something?" she says, stroking a nearby top. "All this stuff is really nice, and it would so suit you."

I try not to stare at her in utter disbelief, and fail miserably. There's nothing over a large in here, and even those are thin on the ground, if you'll excuse the pun. For a split second, I'm not sure if she's trying to be nice or if she's taking the piss, but then it strikes me. She's being neither. She genuinely doesn't see that there is a massive problem with her suggestion—*massive* being the operative word. I shrug and half-heartedly flick though one of the rails of T-shirts, hoping the large might stretch enough to keep her happy. Of course, there aren't any in large, but there are plenty in extra-small, just in case you'd forgotten that was the size society thinks you should be, so I can't even pretend to play along and am in the end forced to admit that nothing would fit.

"Really?" Amy's face screws up in disbelief. "There's loads of sizes here. You're not that big!"

You're not that big. I know she means well, but she may as well have slapped me. It's like when people say you have nice hair, or pretty eyes, as if that makes everything okay. Newsflash: it doesn't.

I shrug and automatically try to find solace in my phone. No messages about Dizzy's state for me—I'm not important enough to have anyone's number except Amy's—but it means I don't have to look at Amy, who is now awkwardly checking out a tiny strappy top that might just about cover my left tit if I'm lucky. She holds it up and goes to say something. I catch her eye before she can say it, because I know what is coming, and no it *won't* do, and no I *won't* fit into it despite what you think, and no I'm *not* selling myself short, I'm just being realistic, so please, just put it down, shut up, and let me get the hell out of here before I end up screaming.

She hangs up the top.

"Wanna grab a coffee?"

That sounds more like it.

I can put sugar in a coffee.

40: #EVIL

Every now and again, throughout the rest of the day, Amy's phone pings and whistles, telling her various updates. My phone, in contrast, is fairly quiet. It did buzz once, but that was Amy tagging me into a status about Dizzy, so I'm not sure if that counts. The upshot is, I'm feeling pretty distant from something I was actually directly involved in, and it's making me want to quit and go home.

Eventually we bump into a couple of people Amy knows and, well, you know Amy—she's everyone's friend. After hovering for a few minutes I make the excuse of having to catch the bus, and I split.

It's only just past two, and as lectures don't usually finish until four, I feel kind of up on the deal. It's the closest you can get to time travel without knowing anything about quantum physics. I've managed to gain an hour and a half. Go me! Or that's how I would be thinking if I didn't just feel numb.

Indigo's last text said Dizzy's parents were on their way and that she and Max were coming back. I assume Max is Baby Colors, but who knows in this weird, hyper-connected world? On Facebook, people are talking about it on Amy's page, and it leaves me feeling incredibly uneasy. Surely it's up to Dizzy to tell people she had a meltdown that ended up with her being hospitalized? I know I wouldn't like any of my issues being aired out in public like this, whilst I was in the hospital waiting for my parents to turn up, trying to think up a decent explanation for slicing my arms up like so many tomatoes and breaking their hearts yet again.

And yeah, sure, people are being supportive now, but what about when the vultures come circling? For fuck's sake, she did this due to trolling. Talking about it openly just gives them a whole new playground to trash.

Except maybe not. Because while Dizzy thinks it was a group of people targeting her, it wasn't. It was just two. Me and Tori. And I'm not about to start trashing this playground. I'm not about to let Tori do it, either.

Yes, yes, I know. I'm the one who told Tori that Dizzy existed, but I just wanted to dole out some payback. She was the one who took it to almost criminal levels.

Dizzy's ripped-up arms are going to haunt me for some time. Too many memories I'd rather ignore being nudged awake.

I'm not nice.

And neither is Tori.

I almost clap my hand over my mouth, as if I've yelled it out at the top of my lungs rather than just thought it.

More thoughts come, thick and fast, piling up and up until they form a tsunami that teeters over me, threatening to crash down and drown me.

Never hacked anyone's account until you met Tori.

Never destroyed a man's marriage until you met Tori.

Never drove anyone to self-harm until you met Tori.

Never, never, never, Tori, Tori, Tori . . .

I cower in my seat.

I've allowed myself to be turned into a monster.

I just hope it isn't too late to turn back.

♣♣♣

When I get home, I don't even check on Mum. I log in to my laptop, careful to avoid Metachat. Knowing Tori, she's probably already worked out a way to tell if I'm logged in, despite it being supposedly completely anonymous.

First stop, new proxy. New VPN. New everything. I want to be as untraceable as I can for this. It takes a while to do it properly, but it's worth it.

Then, Instagram. My favorite stomping grounds. If I'm honest, I can't remember all the accounts I've shat all over, but I can remember enough of them to see a pattern—a wide trail of destruction and abandoned accounts. I stare at the screen. I can't lay all of this on Tori, as some of these were before her time, but it is telling that most of the closed accounts are from the days of us tag-teaming. And to think, I once thought getting people to close accounts was a win. Getting one over the Beautiful People. Now, all I feel is shame as visions of Dizzy lying broken on the paramedic's stretcher dance through my head.

How many more people have ended up like that? Not just at my hands, or at Tori's hands, but at the hands of all the trolls? How many people have we laid judgement on? Destroyed their lives, and for what? A brief high, where we get to vent our hate and our frustrations and punish those who don't live our lives.

Until we find out that they do live our lives. The struggles may be different, but we all have them, one way or another. I mean, what was I thinking? That Dizzy wasn't real?

Just goes to show how easy it is to forget when people are

an abstract concept, a few lines of code, a brace of photshopped pictures. To forget that they have feelings and emotions as real as yours, as legitimate as yours.

I stare out my window. A thin film of black mold is creeping up the seals, making the plaster bubble around it. Condensation has always been an issue in this house—it's old, not that well-ventilated—but Dad used to keep it under control with yells of "Open your windows and let the place air!" while Mum came round with bottles of mold-killer that made the house stink of bleach. She hasn't done anything like that this year, and now the price is being paid. I didn't even notice how bad it was getting until now. I wonder if it's too late to stop it. Probably.

Got to cut this stuff off at the root.

Back to the computer. Back to scrolling through page after page of hate. Less than half of it is mine, but that doesn't mean I don't feel responsible for it.

There's another ping from my phone. A text from Amy.

Just making sure ur ok Axxxx

I bury my head in my hands and cry.

41: #BFF

Teatime comes and goes. I make Mum a fish finger sandwich, and I have one too because I'm not up to any actual cooking. No sign of the Brat, but then again it's only five. Maybe I could nip out and get some ice cream? But that means going out, and I don't really want to do that. Apathy battles with my sugar addiction. This time, apathy wins. Hell, if it gets too bad, I can always eat the hot chocolate powder straight out of the tub.

Mum doesn't say much when I hand her the plate, and you know what? I'm fine with that. I sit next to her and eat in the fetid hole that was once our living room. Once upon a time, Mum would've gone mad if you'd worn your shoes in here; the mantelpiece was dusted to within an inch of its life, and God help you if you didn't use a coaster when you put your cup down. Now, the floor is littered with old tissues and the inserts from magazines, and I don't know the last time she undrew the curtains. Maybe I'll do that tomorrow. Open a window, let the place air a little.

Mum has yet to take a bite of her sandwich. Must remember to make sure she eats before she takes her meds. I swear that's the only thing she can do now, apart from sleep. Anything to forget. Sounds kinda nice, when you put it that way.

Once I finish my sandwich, I leave Mum in *CSI*'s capable hands. I know, I probably should've stayed with her, but it's hard. It's hard to look at the one person in your life you're supposed to be able to rely on forever and realize she's just as broken and as human as you are.

I sit on my bed, my laptop open. Metachat's blinking a code at me. I know Tori's there, but for the first time ever, I don't really want to talk to her. I don't want to lose her, but I don't think I can stand watching her gloat over one of our conquests, which now feel more like nasty, personal little terror attacks designed to cause as much heartbreak and horror as possible.

My phone dings. Another text from Amy.

Hi. U ok? I know this might sound a bit weird cos todays been so horrible, but I was thinking, maybe u would like to come over tomoz nite? I really think I need to do something to put my mind off this. Axx.

I read the message over a few times. The knot that always lives in my belly tightens.

I glance up. Tori's code is still flashing at me.

I look down at Amy's invitation.

> Hey A. Yeah I'm fine. U ok too?
> You're closer to Diz than me, and I found it
> horrible enough.
> I just can't get my head round it all.
> U wanna do something tomoz?
> What u thinking of? Bxx

Right now, I need fluffy. Sorry, Tori, I do love you, but sometimes it's better to cuddle a puppy than run with wolves.

Feels weird here. Everyone's all sad.
Even Paddy is quiet. Don't like it.
Was thinking you could stay over tomoz, have a sleepover?

We could do silly things—die hair, eat pizza, watch shit films . . .
Does that sound like fun? Axx

"Die" hair. It's an obvious autocorrect fail, but for some reason, it feels horribly apt.

Do I want to go hang out at Amy's tomorrow night? For, like, the whole night? I've only ever had one sleepover. I was twelve and it was hell. That was when I realized that frenemies were actually a thing. Year 7, just up from primary school, when friendships suddenly went from "we're vaguely the same age, shape, and species, cool, let's play" to "I both adore and despise you, and everything we do must now become a torturous game of one-upmanship, depending on who we are with or where we are."

How was I to know the sleepover was going to be a pecking-order sort out? That actually eating the pizza was a sign of weakness? That answering the Truth or Dare questions honestly would mean that everyone would know about my confusing crush on Ms. Pinter the following Monday?

I pinch the bridge of my nose, trying to remind myself that all that shit happened over six years ago and that Amy's not like that, and I'm a fucking grown-up now, even though I'm not really sure what that means, because I don't think I really feel any different from when I was twelve. Still as awkward, still as chubby (no pretending it's puppy fat anymore, though, so I guess things do change after all), still as confused.

I read the message again, looking for something that indicates this is all a setup, but of course there's nothing, and it dawns on me that this is something I probably don't want to screw up. I take in a deep breath in the hopes of steadying my wildly beating heart, and before my doubt-demons force me to change my mind, I rattle off, *Yeah, that sounds cool, really need it, thanx xxxx*, and then throw my phone on the bed as if it might bite me for my impudence.

Awesome! Am so pumped! Sort out deets tomoz, ok? Axxx ❤ *xx* flies back at me and punches me squarely in the feels.

This is so weird. I'm not used to this. I'm not even sure where to begin. I swallow as my eyes heat up.

Is this what I've been missing?

No wonder people will do anything to hold on to it.

42: #AVOIDANCE

Hey, hun. You there? Is everything ok?

It's Tori. I've been ignoring her Metachat keys, so she's resorting to Messenger, which is something she *never* does.

Yesterday, I would have crawled over broken glass to talk to Tori. When I'm with her, I feel I could conquer anything: move mountains, breathe fire, soar above mere mortals on wings of pure spite. Well, I did until today. Today, I still desperately want to talk to her, but each time I go to click the message, I can't help but think of Dizzy lying on the stretcher, her arms cut and bloody, her eyes dull with self-loathing.

I don't know how to begin to talk to Tori about this. How do I tell her that I love her but I don't know if I love what she does anymore?

In the end, I play Aeon Valhalla for a bit. It's been a while since I've picked it up, so it takes me a moment to get back into the story, which is suitably bonkers. I trawl around the countryside with Sable and Demonica at my side (seriously, where do they get these names?), seeking out random encounters to bolster my stats before I charge into the Ice Caves and kick the Ice Dragon's ass. It's a tough battle that leaves me muttering colorful expletives, but it's worth it. Ice Dragon armor and a crystal bracelet to upgrade Sable's iron one. Nice.

Except it isn't. Even though I've turned my phone off, it sits next to me, staring up at me, daring me to switch it on and check my messages. I'm keenly aware that I'm hiding, trying to make myself as small as possible, just like I do in the real world in the hopes that everyone will pass me by and leave me alone. Only for the first time I'm not hiding from strangers; I'm hiding from the people I care about most.

I save my game, fully aware that it is just pixels, its only purpose being to eat time. The victory is hollow, a fantasy achievement that solves nothing.

I pinch the bridge of my nose. Jesus. Maybe I should just get some sleep. I'm beginning to sound like some pretentious philosophy student. Lighten up, girl. We all know life's futile—you don't need to keep banging on about it.

I thought I'd really struggle to drop off, but nope—out like a light within a few minutes. I wake up pretty early, though; it's still dark outside, and the soft swish of rain against my window tells me it's another glorious British day out there.

Out of habit, I switch my phone on again and kind of regret it. A twinge of anxious shame twists my guts when I see that Tori's messaged me another three times, asking if I'm okay. I chew on my thumbnail, unsure of what to do. I want to answer, but that horrible, yawning pit in my stomach also wants to chuck my phone away and pretend none of this is happening.

I grit my teeth and open the messages: Nothing unpleasant, just a small collection of *You ok?*, *Where are you?*, and *Hope you're okay*s that make me feel even worse. Since I know Facebook would have tattled on me by now, I dash off a quick *I'm fine hun—wasn't online last night as I was feeling like utter shite*, which isn't really a lie, and hope that'll do the job.

I go downstairs and make a cup of tea. The living room is dark, which means Mum actually managed to make it to bed last night. That's good. She rarely does that nowadays. Maybe she's entering one of her "up" phases, where she starts to resemble the mother I once had. I pop another tea bag into a fresh mug and pour her a cup, too. She may not be awake, but I figure it's the thought that counts.

Back upstairs, I hover outside Mum's room, two mugs in hand. The door isn't shut, which is also a positive. It still smells pretty rank in there, though. Maybe I'll be able to convince her to open the window later, and maybe help her do more than bare-minimum laundry. Change the bedclothes. Let some light in.

Judging by her breathing, she's still snoozing. I creep over to the bed, sheepishly aware of how stupid this is; I have a cup of tea for her, so how is not trying to wake her going to be help-ful? Still, it's habit. I set the mug on the bedside cabinet. There are at least five empty pill packets on it, and for a moment, my heart jumps as I worry she's taken them all at once and the breathing I heard was just a figment of my imagination—

She snorts, and I spill my tea over my hand. Habit makes me suck back the "Fuck!" that tries to escape me, because you don't swear in front of your mother, Bethany.

"What time is it?" Mum mumbles, waving her hand in the region of where her alarm clock was ten years ago.

"It's a quarter to seven," I say. "I know it's early, but I made tea."

"Quarter to seven?" she yawns, and goes to roll over.

"Yeah. Remember, you have an appointment at nine."

"I do?" Her body slumps under the duvet. "Oh, yeah. I remem-ber now."

I'm amazed I do, if I'm honest. I hadn't even been thinking

about it, which only goes to show how much you can squirrel away when you have to.

"Shall I call a cab for 8:30?"

Mum doesn't reply, and suddenly I'm struck by the absurdity of the situation. I'm the teenager—shouldn't she be the one struggling to get me up?

"I'll call a cab," I say. "And I'm out tonight."

"You are?" That makes her sit up.

"Yeah. Amy's invited me over for a girls' night in. Is that okay?"

I can see it: the battle going on in her head as she struggles to settle on an appropriate response. This is all she's ever wanted for me—to go out, to have friends, finally to be normal . . . but at the same time, I know she needs me here to do all the things she should be doing but can't.

"It's just one night. I'll be back tomorrow."

Mum gives me a tight nod. "Of course. That's fine. Thanks for letting me know. Have fun."

I nod back, amazed that the slight fizz in my stomach isn't nerves or anxiety or dread, but something else, something I never thought I'd feel—the simple excitement of going out with a friend, a real friend, not an online one but a honest-to-goodness flesh and blood one, one I can touch and laugh with and whisper stupid things at.

Back in my room, a message is waiting for me.

Boo. Hope you're feeling better now. Love you. xxx

The fizz dies down.

Is this . . . cheating? Going to Amy's, that is. It kind of feels like cheating. Should I tell Tori I'm going? No harm if I do.

Hey, Tori, I'm out tonight. Yeah, going to my friend Amy's. Yeah, the one I'm at uni with. Yeah, she's a flake, but she's sweet. Okay, speak later. Love you.

A totally normal conversation. Thousands of people have similar ones every day. So why do I feel like I'm betraying her?

> Morning, hunny. Yeah, I feel ok now.
> Migraines suck.

Not that I suffer from migraines, but hell, they're always a good excuse.

Urrr, migraines. Tell me about it. You free now?

The fizz is replaced by something spiky and made of lead, making it hard for me to swallow.

> Nah, sorry babe. Got uni in a mo.
> Busy day.

Well, that sucks. I'm at work atm but no one is here so I'm having a play. Was hoping you'd join me . . . ^_^

Normally I'd jump at the chance, but not this morning. This morning, I'm glad I've got an excuse not to go online and play her vicious games. Still, have to keep up the pretense. You never know, by tomorrow, I may be over this newfound attack of conscience.

> Aww, jealous now. No excuses today tho. Test day.

Nerd alert! :P Speak later, yeah?

> Yeah.

Love you. ❤ xxx

Yeah, love you too xxx

I still get a flutter at that, a shameful little thrill. Maybe I should just blow Amy off. Sit in with Tori. Continue to live my life in the shadows. Yeah. I'll do that. So much safer than pretending I only want one slice of pizza.

Still, better shove some deodorant and a spare pair of knickers in my bag. You know, just in case.

43: #FLASHBACK

The rain hasn't eased up, so by the time I'm at the bus stop, I'm soaked inside and out. Sometimes I wonder why I bother with a raincoat—I end up sweating so much, I think the rain might actually be preferable. Thank God I brought my deodorant. At least I won't end up stinking like a dead whale later. See, it was a good idea after all. Beth Soames, ready for anything.

Except today. I am definitely not ready for today.

The bus turns up on time, which is good. Quite a few empty seats, good, which one to choose, a window one for preference, God, where did my headphones go, escaping down my top—

That's when I spot him, looking at his watch with that slightly dramatic motion people who still wear watches use. I don't know why I chose to look at the exact moment he moved. It's a gift, I suppose, a sort of hyper-awareness that means nothing gets past me. It comes from a lifetime of barely-disguised disgusted glances, or the tuts that come when you can't quite get out of someone's way, despite trying your very hardest. Anyway, my spidey-senses must have picked up on something, because there's no way this was simply a coincidence.

The man with the watch is the pervert. The one who groped me. Given everything that has happened to me recently, I'd almost managed to forget him. Almost, but not quite.

My heart thumps once and begins to race. The edges of reality go fuzzy. I stumble past him and duck into the nearest seat, staring, bug-eyed, straight ahead, my headphones forgotten. All I can hear is the roar of blood in my ears.

He gazes out the window, oblivious.

I chew on my lips. I should say something. Be brave. Be strong and stand up for all the other girls who go through this shit every day. Maybe someone will record it on their phone and it'll go viral, brave girl stands up to her harasser, gives all other girls hope, shows them they can fight back . . .

The bus slows, and he stands up.

Two seconds later, and he's wandering down the aisle without a care in the world.

And then he's gone, off the bus, melting into the crowds of people trying to get to work, his paper held over his head to keep the worst of the rain off.

I think I see the flash of a wedding ring before he disappears.

◆◆◆

Two stops later and it's my turn to disembark. I try to stop my hand from shaking when I press the button for the bell.

I pull my hood up and cram my hands into my pockets, hunching my shoulders in a futile attempt at making myself smaller. It doesn't work; I still bump into two people. Because they're terribly British, they apologize, but I can see the seething annoyance in their eyes. Sometimes I wish we were more like the Americans and were freer with our emotions, but today I'm glad of our stiff upper lip. I think if one of them had shouted at me, I might actually have cried.

Outside Richmond building, crowds of students are milling,

all with their hoods up, all faceless. A growing sense of panic builds within me again: Where's Amy? I'm not up to this today. Maybe I should just go home. Maybe I should just—

"Hey, Beth!" My heart thuds. "I waved, but you didn't see me. You okay?"

I'm not quite sure how I didn't see her, as she's wearing a bright pink mackintosh and matching Doc Martens. I smile faintly.

"Heya. It's hard to see out from under this hood. You okay?"

"Yeah, I am—and I know, right? When will this shitty weather end, eh?" She's grinning, but it's strained, like she's forcing herself to be normal, to talk about normal things.

"How's Dizzy?" I say, cracking first. An unmistakable look of relief crosses Amy's face.

"She's okay. Last thing I heard, they were discharging her and she was going home. Back to her parents, not here," she adds, as if that even needed to be clarified.

I nod, unsure of what else to say.

"You were great, you know," Amy says. "You really helped. I dread to think what might have happened if you weren't around. You're such a rock."

I swallow, my cheeks flaming. I try to mutter something along the lines of "No, I'm not," but it comes out as a grunt. Amy's giving me one of those *aww, bless you* smiles because she thinks I'm being bashful and self-deprecating, when in reality, the urge to yell "She only did it because of me!" is getting quite hard to resist.

Amy links arms with me. I tense, but I don't think she notices.

"Come on, you lovely person. Door's open. Let's get out of the rain and plan tonight."

44: #ITSAPLAN

All the way through our lecture, Amy's scribbling stuff down on her notepad, little questions about what we can do, little shopping lists for things we could buy, little hopes, little dreams, little plans for The Best Night Ever. She's so damn adorable. I don't have the heart to tell her that it all sounds a bit like my idea of hell. But after talking about Dizzy, I'm feeling bad again, and it strikes me that a distraction might do me good. Plus, a night out is the perfect excuse to put off talking to Tori a little longer. She can't complain—I'm a student. That's what we do. We go out on a Friday night.

Which in turn makes me feel weird, because being a stereotypical student who goes out on a Friday night is veering dangerously close to Everything I Hate. But then, why bother even going to uni in the first place if I didn't want a chance of belonging?

I screw my eyes up and massage my temples with my fingertips, as if that might help me order the chaos in my head.

It doesn't work.

Amy slides her pad in front of me, nudging me as she does.

U ok?

Oh, God, she even *writes* in text speak. She really is a lost cause.

I glance over at her and nod. She's giving me a concerned look, so I scribble: *just a headache.*

She pulls her pad back.

Break in a min. We'll leave early. No one will notice. Start the prep early.

It's all I can do to stop myself from beating my head against the bench in front of me.

◆◆◆

After the lecture, it's still raining, but that does nothing to dampen Amy's enthusiasm.

"First we'll go to Superdrug and look at hair dye. I'm thinking of going Harley Quinn—what about you?"

"Uh . . ." But before I can answer, she's off again.

"Doesn't matter, there's plenty of colors to choose from. Then we can go to Tesco and grab some snacks and loads of booze!"

So it's Superdrug first, followed by a supermarket. I should be grateful. She could have suggested we buy new pajamas—

Pajamas!

Oh crap, I forgot those. I brought spare knickers and deodorant, but I was so sure I wasn't actually going to do this that I didn't think about pajamas. Will I even *need* pajamas? Or will we be up all night? I bet Amy has those posh silky ones, rather than the slightly graying cotton nighties I still have to suffer wearing—

"You okay?" Amy trills as she hands me a box of baby-blue hair dye. "Hmm, I think I'm going to get some peroxide, too—my hair's too dark for this color." She reaches out in front of me and grabs another box and drops it into our basket. "You found a color you like?"

I scan the shelf. "Uh, this one?" I pick up a box of burgundy dye, the one color everyone gets away with.

"What? That? Really? I think my mum uses this color." She wrinkles her nose and picks up a violent shade of violet. "How about this one? Still purple, but a bit *more* purple, if you get what I mean? I never understood why people chose basic colors. If you're going to dye your hair, then fucking well dye it, right?"

She reaches past me and grabs a pink box and chucks it in the basket to join the blue and the peroxide. I take the violet box from her. I will admit, I'd love to give it a go, but do worry I'll end up looking like a Teletubby.

"I don't know . . ."

"Oh, go on. Live a bit. How about this?" Fire-truck red. "Or this?" I can't see what it's actually called, but I'm going for Hulk Green, which is NOT a comparison I wish to draw to myself.

I take the red off her. "I think this one. Loud, but not too weird."

Amy screws up her lovely little nose. "Where's the fun in not being weird? Okay, you can have the red, but I'm going to lighten your hair first so it really pops."

Forget the Hulk, I'm going to end up looking like a chubby Pennywise the Clown if Amy gets her way. I put the red back and pick up the purple again, which makes Amy grin and exclaim, "That's my girl!" It really is a pretty color. Live a little. Purple it is.

She pays for everything. Don't get me wrong—I offer to pay for my own, but Amy waves me away and sticks it all on a credit card.

I'm beginning to suspect that, for all her protestations to the contrary, Amy's quite rich.

After that, it's off to Tesco, where Amy fills a basket with as many freezable cocktail slushie things as she can carry, a bottle of cheap vodka, family-sized Galaxy bars, microwavable popcorn (sweet, of course), and more flavors of Pringles than even I know what to do with. Again, everything goes on the credit card.

"You sure you don't want me to chip in?" I ask, feeling rather guilty, and again Amy screws up her face in disbelief and mutters, "No, of course not," at me.

We gather our spoils and trek back to halls. Even though the bags aren't all that heavy, I kind of want to call a cab, but it really isn't that far, so admitting I want a cab would in fact be an admission that I don't really like walking. When we get back to Amy's, I'm trying to hide the fact that I'm breathing a lot heavier than she is—not that she seems to notice as she continues to chatter and we get in the (blessed, oh so blessed) lift that takes us up to her floor.

There's a weird moment when I flash back to yesterday, and judging by the way Amy hesitates by the door, I can tell she's experiencing it too. I wonder how long it will be before we can get the image of a bleeding Dizzy being hauled away on a stretcher through this very doorway out of our heads. A month? A year? Blood has a funny way of lingering in the psyche long after it's been mopped up.

There's a crash from the direction of the shared kitchen, followed by some rather ripe language. We traipse in to find Paddy up to his armpits in suds, valiantly tackling what looks like a month's worth of dishes. A smashed mug lies forlornly at his feet.

"You wouldn't believe what these absolute cockmunchers have done. They've only gone and left all the washing up to me.

So unfair." He raises his hand out of the sink and waves at me. "Hey, Big Bird! How's my favorite girl doing?"

His favorite girl? Yes, I'm confused too.

"It's all yours, Pads," Amy says, emptying her bag of cocktail slushies into the freezer. "We told you, we're not your slaves. You make a mess, you clean it up."

My chest twinges with pride, just a little bit.

Paddy rolls his eyes dramatically. "Always nagging me, that one. What you got there, Tink?"

"Cocktails. And they're not yours. They're for me and Beth, so don't drink them."

"Wouldn't dream of it!"

"Paddy, I mean it. They're for us, tonight." Amy straightens up and looks almost proud. "Me and Beth are having a girls' night in. We're going to get absolutely wankered and eat loads of pizza. Right, Beth?"

"Yep." I nod, trying to look as sincere as possible. "Booze and pizza warriors, that's us. If you value your life, you'll stay out of our way." I risk a little smile.

"Really?" Paddy grins broadly at me. "Will there be silky nighties and pillow fights, too?"

Amy narrows her eyes at him. "Fuck off, pervert. Come on, Beth—hair dying time!" She shakes her other bag at me.

I lift the remaining bag of snacks I'm carrying. "What about these?"

"Bring them with us, otherwise Porker over there will trough the lot."

"Oh, I resent that remark!" Paddy grins, and I'm struck by just how easy this whole back and forth is, as if all the awkwardness of a few weeks ago has just melted away. It's sorta, kinda nice.

"Anyway, I don't need your stash. Going out for drinkies later with the rugger team." He gives me a shrewd look. "Actually, you ever thought of playing, Big Bird? You'd be really good. I know the ladies' team is after—"

"Paddy!" Amy says. "Don't be so fucking mean."

Paddy looks hurt. "I'm not being mean. The ladies' team really is looking for new players and I think Beth would do really well. I could just see her, striding across the pitch, flattening the opposition like some kind of warrior woman of old. Yeah. Boudicca Beth."

"I don't know, Paddy," I say. "Not really into violent sports." Apart from ones in a virtual world, of course.

"Oh, rugby's not violent," Paddy says. "It's intense, but no one wishes anyone any ill-will. Have a think about it. I'll talk to Katie. Just give me the nod, yeah?"

I don't know what to say to that, so I shrug.

Amy sticks her tongue out at him and drags me off to her room. "I can't believe him sometimes," she says as she dumps her bags on her bed and begins to organize our Trial by Hair Dye. "So sorry. He totally has no idea whatsoever."

"It's okay. He wasn't being mean." And it strikes me that Paddy's suggestion doesn't actually hurt. He thinks I should play rugby. I don't necessarily agree, because despite my generally low opinion of myself, I do actually value my ears and my nose, not to mention my knees. But there's no getting away from the fact that Paddy looked at me and saw something other than a tub of lard for once. He saw a potential sport-playing person. A warrior woman, no less.

Before I know it, I'm standing with my head bowed over Amy's sink, a slightly musty-smelling towel draped around my shoulders. The water's a bit hot, but I don't dare say anything.

Amy's already got her peroxide on, and the fumes it gives off make my nose tickle as she smothers my hair in her leftovers. I'm quite glad she's decided to take on the role as hair-dyer-in-chief. Those little gloves they put in the boxes are always too small, and the last time I tried to do my own hair, I ended up resorting to sandwich bags to cover my hands.

The door outside bangs, and Amy skips over to peek outside.

"Oh hey!" she squeaks, and Indigo pops her head round the door. She's smiling.

"Hey Beth, you all right?" she asks, as if she's actually interested. I nod, relying on a slightly sheepish *yeah, okay, right* smile. "Amy said you were coming over tonight. We're all going down to the union later. You interested?"

I try not to let my eyes widen in panic at that. What is going on? Who is this girl? Why is she talking to me like this? I literally don't understand.

Luckily, Amy comes to my rescue. "Maybe. We really were just planning on chilling out."

"Oh, okay, well, that sounds like fun too. If you change your minds, you'll know where we'll be."

It's Indigo's turn to try on the sheepish smile. "By the way, Beth, I don't think I ever properly thanked you for your help with Dizzy. None of us knew what to do. I dread to think what might have happened if you hadn't been there. We really owe you one."

"But I didn't do anything," I say, as a nasty red flush creeps over my chest and up the sides of my neck. I can only hope Indigo mistakes it for embarrassment and not the deep, burning shame that's still eating me from the inside out.

"Credit where credit's due, Beth. You girls have fun, yeah?"

"See you later, alligator!" Amy sing-songs as Indigo's head withdraws. She jerks her thumb toward the now-closed door. "She's so lovely. Isn't she lovely?"

And it dawns on me that she probably is.

45: #PARTY #YAY #MAYBE

Those supermarket cocktails aren't very strong, which is why Amy bought the bottle of vodka. We're now on our third one—margaritas topped off with voddie—and I'm well on my way to being a little bit squiffy.

"I so love your hair!" Amy says for about the squinchillionth time, and strokes it. I actually kind of like that. It makes my spine feel all fizzy and melty. Maybe this is why cats arch their backs when they're stroked. "You look like someone's poured pure liquid amethyst over your head." She slurs a little over "amethyst," which comes out more like "ameshyst." This makes me giggle and take another long suck on my straw. I wince. God, that's strong.

"And you look just like Harley Quinn," I say. "She always was the best and mosht beautiful." And she does. One side turquoise, the other pink. She looks even more like a fey creature than usual, with her enormous liquid brown eyes and her sculpted cheekbones and those pink, slightly parting lips . . .

Jesus Christ. I think I need to slow up on these cocktails.

As it turns out, Amy's idea of a Proper Girls'-Night-In Entertainment isn't some crappy rom-com but is in fact a bunch of nasty, low-budget horror DVDs she cadged in a three-for-a-tenner deal. Color me surprised. She also ordered half the pizza menu after declaring that she was "shtarving" and clutched her nonexistent stomach as if that would emphasize the point.

She's poured out another cocktail-slushie for us. We're dangerously low on vodka now, something I think is probably for the best. I hope she doesn't suggest going out to get more— she's half my size but is definitely handling the huge amounts of alcohol better. I literally have no idea how she does it. Metabolism? Must be. Either that or she really is a moon-child from beyond the stars who was raised on mead and little else.

The buzzer to the flats goes off just as we're anticipating yet another contrived-yet-secretly-terrifying jump scare, and I have to stop myself from screaming, which makes Amy laugh hysterically. She asks me to pause the film and then runs out of her room shrieking "Pizza! Pizza! Pizza!" while I sit awkwardly on her bed, blinking in an attempt at trying to stop the room from spinning.

A few moments later, Amy comes back bearing gifts . . . and what gifts they are. Three large pizzas, garlic bread with cheese, potato wedges, mozzarella sticks, BBQ chicken wings, sour cream dips, and a large bottle of Coke. I have to stop myself from drooling as she lays out the feast on her floor. She plonks herself in front of it and pats at the space next to her, inviting me to sit with her. I grab what remains of both our cocktail slushies and pick my way through the food mountain to join her.

"Need a plate?" she says, with a mischievous grin.

"Are you kidding me?" I quip back.

And she laughs, long and hard, before picking up a quite frankly enormous slice of pepperoni and cramming half of it in her mouth. I think it's safe to say that it's one of the sexiest things I've ever seen in my life, and I stare to the point where she has to nod meaningfully at the food while saying something that might be "tuck in" if her mouth wasn't already full to bursting with pizza.

I reach out for a slice, grinning, and then hesitate as the *don't eat in front of others* instinct kicks in. I've said it so many times to myself now that I've conditioned myself; can't be greedy, don't eat that, mustn't let them think I actually *like* this, where's the salad, the salad, the savior, my last bastion of defense, something green, something healthy—

"You all right?" Amy wipes her mouth with the back of one hand, her half-eaten slice drooping from the other.

I glance at her. She's put her hair up in pigtails. There's a smear of tomato sauce on her chin. She doesn't care. She's never had to care. Look at her. She's perfect.

The old, hated jealousy unfurls like an infected flower within me. Why can't I be like that? Why can't I eat whatever I like and not have to worry? Why can't I sit there, with tomato sauce on my chin, and still look like a fucking goddess? It's not fair. It's not fair, because it's ruining something good, making me hate someone I actually really like, someone who genuinely seems to be able to accept me for who I am, or at least I think she does, I hope she does, I—

Fuck it. I grab the next slice and defiantly chew off its point. Screw that voice. Screw *all* of it. This is my moment of rebellion—true rebellion, not a virtual, made-up one—and it tastes *sweet*.

"Oh! Forgot! Film!" Amy staggers to her feet, cramming what's left of her pizza slice into her mouth. She grabs the TV controller, sending the potato wedges flying. "Whoops!" she giggles, and flicks the movie back on, catapulting us both back into a world of almost pornographic violence. "You gotta watch horror when you eat pizza," Amy explains. "Cos pizza and violence, pizza and violence, they go together like a horse and carriage . . ."

She sings the last bit, badly.

"That doesn't rhyme," I giggle back.

"Oh, fuck it, it doesn't need to rhyme! Eat, my amethystial beauty—eat!" She picks up a bit of garlic bread and feeds it to me. I try not to choke, both on cheese and on joy, because *this* is what it should be all about. Not petty sniping and insults and making people feel bad, but laughter and sharing and not giving a crap what anyone else thinks.

And there it is. The revelation. I reckon there's a choir somewhere, hitting the high notes as something fundamental clicks into place within me.

When Amy reaches for her phone to take a selfie with me, for the first time ever, I don't protest. I don't even flinch.

I want this moment to be remembered forever.

46: #DRUNKTALK

"This bit's really funny. Wait for it . . . wait . . . Ha! Chainsaw to the face. Classic!" Amy takes another huge gulp of her last cocktail slushie while I try not to imagine her as a closet serial killer. This is literally the most fun I've had in forever.

There's pizza devastation laid out in front of us, hideous gore on the TV, and no more vodka left. The world feels fuzzy and soft, and my head spins. I haven't checked my phone in hours; I've only used it to take photos so I have a lasting memento of tonight's events—proof, if you will, that it happened, insurance in case I start to doubt (or indeed, it never happens again). Amy rests her multicolored head on my shoulder, and I lean into it, resting my cheek against it, and my world fills with the strange scent of synthetic coconut and harsh chemicals. I could put my arm around her . . . but I don't. Why spoil this by pushing too hard? It's already far beyond anything I'd expected.

Amy yawns, and I follow suit. The movie is stupidly violent, so over the top that it could never be considered scary, just ridiculous.

"Do you want that last piece of garlic bread?"

I shake my head, surprised that it's true. Usually, when presented with this kind of bounty, I eat until I puke, but not tonight. "You have it," I say.

"Hmm, garlic bread . . . ," Amy says, doing a perfect Homer Simpson impression as she dangles the last bit in front of her mouth before cramming it all in. She giggles through a full mouth, saying something that sounds like, "m sush a foo slug," which I *think* roughly translates to "I'm such a food slut." Speaking as a fully paid-up food slut, I know she isn't one, but I don't disagree with her. I get it. Temptation and sin are fun when you're the one in charge.

To my surprise, she throws her arms around my neck, and all but nuzzles into me. My heart leaps and I have to force myself not to jump away from her; sudden physical contact, especially of the affectionate kind, is not something I am particularly used to.

"I am so glad we met," Amy slurs. "You're my best friend here, you know that?"

"Best" sounds like "besht," and "you know that" comes out as one word; all of this is nonsense drunk-talk. But I don't care. I smile at her to disguise the fact that my eyes have suddenly— and alarmingly—begun to well.

"Yeah," I whisper. "Me too."

A woman on the TV shrieks, signaling her impending doom. Talk about psychic dissonance.

"You still don't say much, though. Not much of a talker, huh? Oh, Beth Beth Bethie Beth . . ."

"Yes, Amy Amy Amymie Amy?"

She sniggers. "Amymie? Wow, you stretched that one, huh?" She sits up and punches me playfully on the shoulder. "You know your problem? You let other people run your life. You let other people tell you how you think about yourself." She looks a bit confused. "I think that makes sense. Anyway, you know what I mean."

Yep, Amy, I do. And I don't like it. The squishy, fuzzy feelings from before have fizzled away, leaving behind the greasy taint of junk food, the metallic tang of cheap alcohol, and the incessant, shrill screaming of a woman who really should have known better than to go into the basement.

"No, Amy. It's not like that. I just don't do drama." The magnitude of the lie almost chokes me.

"Pshaw. Look at me!" She waves an imperious finger in front of my face. "You, Bethanany Soames, are a lovely person. You got that?"

"Great. Next you're going to be telling me I've got nice eyes, or that my hair is lovely." It's out before I can't stop myself, and it's steeped in years of bile.

Amy doesn't seem to notice, though. She grins at me and twiddles a lock of my hair between her fingers. "Your hair *is* lovely. All amethysty and shimmery." She hiccups. "S'cuse me."

"Why are you saying these things?" I ask, suddenly tired. "We were having such a nice night."

"We still are having a nice night!" Amy looks a little offended. "I just wanted you to know that you're my best friend and I love you, that's all."

I know this is drunk talk. The very definition of drunk talk. Said in that imperious way only the truly intoxicated can get away with. Doesn't stop my heart from migrating up into my throat and contracting into a tight little ball that makes it hard to breathe, though. No one outside of my own family has ever said they loved me. Yeah, okay, so Tori said it over Metachat, but I now realize there's a hell of a gulf between someone typing it on a screen and someone saying it to your face. Even if the one saying it to your face is completely off her tits on cheap booze.

"I love you too," I manage to croak, just getting it in before my stunned pause turns decidedly awkward. Amy grins like a loon and wraps her arms around me again, nestling her head against my shoulder. It's painfully intimate, and I have no idea how to react. Is this what friends do, or is this more than that? Is this just-friends-love or the first shoots of love-love? Just what is going on?

"My parents didn't want me to come here," Amy says, rubbing her head against my cheek. I try to ignore the way her hair tickles. "I know I'm a disappointment to them. My parents. Never did anything right. Rob was all straight As and piano playing and 'Oh, Daddy, I'm going to study law, just like you.'" She makes a raspberry noise. "Fuck them. So fed up with being in his shadow. Everything is 'well, when Rob was your age' and 'well, Rob did this.' You know they actually threatened to cut me off if I came here? Yeah, they did. Thank fuck this place gave me my only offer. Couldn't badger me to go to fucking Oxford if fucking Oxford won't have me. Doesn't stop them from trying to make me apply for a transfer, though." She sits up and throws her head back. "They want me to go to a 'proper' university and study a 'proper' subject." She air-quotes *proper*, exaggerated moves that speak of deep disdain and even deeper pain. "I mean, why can't they just accept me for who I am? So I'm not that bright. Is that such a crime?" She gives me an expectant look.

"Of course not. And you are bright. Of course you are," I say dutifully.

"Not compared to Rob, I'm not." She rubs her face with one hand. "Sometimes I hate my brother, but then I feel bad, 'cos it's not his fault." She sighs heavily, lets me go, and flings herself backward across the cushions and pillows we have strewn across the floor. "Oh, fuck this. Fuck this! You know what we should do?"

"Um, no?"

"We should go traveling. Yeah. Around the world! We could go to Kathmandu and Hawaii and, and, and Magaluf—"

"Magaluf?" I grin. "In Spain? 'One of these things is not like the others' much?"

"Hey, it's a party resort. I wanna go there. Better than fucking Portugal."

Considering the farthest I've ever been on holiday is Wales, I'll have to take her word for that.

"Just imagine it. Every week a different town, a different beach. No one would know us, so we could be exactly who we want to be, rather than being stuck doing the same stupid things over and over again."

I have to admit, it's tempting.

"Sounds nice, but I'd never be able to afford it. Unless the minimum wage for babysitting goes up to a couple of grand an hour, I'm kind of stuck where I am."

"Oh, Beth, you're so sensible. But you don't have to be sensible all the time. We can dream. Lighten up!"

Oh, was that one of those moments when I was just supposed to go along with it all? I wish someone could have told me, because Amy's now fiddling with her phone, and I have a horrible feeling that I've managed to break whatever moment we were having.

"Smile!" she calls out, and before I have a chance to at least attempt to rearrange myself into something that might be considered a flattering pose if you stretch the definition out as far as you can, the flash goes off, blinding me. I blink, trying to clear the little floating blobs in front of my eyes, wondering if I could get away with confiscating Amy's phone.

"Ha ha! Look at you! You look evil. All red eyes and everything!" She waves her phone at me, and I am mortified at the sight of my own mountains of flesh, bared for all to see.

"Please don't post that, Amy," I say, trying not to sound too pathetic.

"Why not? It's funny," she says, fiddling with her phone.

"Please, just don't. Don't. I—I don't think I can cope with that being on the internet. I don't like people taking photos of me at the best of times, and you might have noticed I don't post many of myself, so please . . ." I leave my plea hanging.

Amy cocks her head to one side, like a little bird. "Okay. I won't. I promise." She shuffles closer to me, her brows drawn. "Are you all right?"

"Yeah, I'm fine. I just don't like photos. I'm not exactly photogenic."

Amy shrugs. "So? None of us are, not really. I take photos to remember things. Don't you want to be able to look back years from now and see how things were?"

It's my time to shrug, as if that's enough to explain that no, I don't want to look back and see just how fat and pathetic I really am. If anything, I want to forget it—no photographic evidence means it didn't really happen, and once I figure out how to con a doctor into giving me a gastric bypass, I can pretend most of *Beth: The Fat Years* never happened.

But I can't tell her that, because I can just tell she'd never get it. Not because she's a bad person, but because she's the exact opposite: she's a good person, the best type of person, the type who desperately wants to see the best in people despite their flaws, which will inevitably lead to them getting hurt, or even worse, being completely disappointed by the people they want to believe are also good people, but we're not, we're not good people, we're bad people, and now I just want to leave, just go home, because I love Amy, I do, she's the best friend I've always dreamed of and I don't deserve her, because deep down I'm a terrible person, an awful person, a person who will probably just end up disappointing or, even worse, hurting her—

Outside, the door to the communal hallway bangs open, breaking my train of thought. Amy looks up from her phone, jumps up to her feet, or at least tries to; it takes her a couple of attempts, but eventually she hauls her bedroom door open.

"Tinkerbell!" Indigo's slurry voice rings out. "Why didn't you come out?"

"Oh, sorry, Indy—we stayed in. We had pizza. It was yum."

"Piiiizzaaaa?" Indigo says the word in a drawling whine. "I love pizza. I'm not supposed to have pizza, but I love pizza. Is there any left?"

"Yeah!" Amy is nodding enthusiastically now. "Beth, get the pizza."

I lurch across the floor, a willing little acolyte, and fetch up the remaining slices into one box, which I offer up to Indigo, who, despite being blasted out of her mind, still looks gorgeous. Behind her, a walking beard in skinny jeans and a stick-insect with bright red hair lounge.

"Pizza!" Indigo says again and groans as she takes a slice of pepperoni.

"It's gone cold," I say, and I hate the apology in my voice, like it's my fault.

Indigo ignores me and keeps eating, making orgasmic grunts as she chews.

"Uh, Indy?" The Hipster Beard peels himself off the wall.

"Do you want some?" I ask, unsure of what else to say.

If in doubt, offer food. It's a good principle to live by, in my experience.

Hipster Beard eyes the pizza the way a ravenous lion eyes an injured impala. I can see he's tempted, but he shakes his head. "Can't. Vegan." He gives Indigo a piously disgusted look; in return, she rolls her eyes and pulls a face.

"Oh, fuck off, Trent. What are you going to do, call the vegan police?"

The redhead next to Trent gives me a smile that is half mischievous, half apologetic, and reaches in for a slice.

"What the fuck?" Trent says, throwing his hands up into the air.

Indigo grins at that and winks at me. "So, you two had a good time?"

I let Amy field that one. She jabbers on while Indigo pinches the last slice, and I think I actually see a thin tendril of drool trickle from the corner of Hipster Trent's puckered mouth. It's kind of amusing to watch; I don't think I've ever witnessed that level of desire crossed with that level of revulsion before. Beside him, the redhead nibbles on her slice like a mouse, her eyes darting between Indigo and Hipster Trent, as if weighing who she wants to please more.

It's all absolutely fascinating. It never even entered my head that the Beautiful People might have a hierarchy like this, and that it can all come tumbling down via too much drink and the temptation of illicit pizza.

Amy's now flicking through photos on her phone, and an icy dread punches me squarely in the chest—she'd better have deleted that photo.

"Oh, that's so funny!" Indigo brays. "You two look like you've had so much fun." She pouts. "Still, you should have come out with us." She turns to her friends. "You know Tink, but this is Beth—she helped us with Dizzy!"

"Oh, awesome," Hipster Trent says, nodding in what could have been mistaken as approval, if I wasn't completely suspicious of where this was all actually going. "Fucking hell, though, huh? Poor Dizzy. Sad day when you can't just go about your life without someone charging in and shitting all over it. Someone should arrest those fuckers. Seriously, five to ten, no parole. Attempted manslaughter. Boom."

I try to swallow, but my mouth's gone dry. The dread in my chest is like the beating of a nasty drum. All I can do is nod. If these people cotton on to the truth, then I'm toast, of the *hold her down while I tear her a new one* variety. Hipster Trent is quite a big guy, despite his veganism, and I have no desire to tussle with him, or anyone else, in real life.

Amy's chattering again, and Indigo is replying, as animated as I've ever seen her. She's actually quite intimidating; she holds herself with confidence and laughs loudly, waving her arms around as if it might reinforce her point. Hipster Trent interjects every now and again, and I can't help but wonder if he fancies her. Well, why shouldn't he? She's gorgeous. I can now see how she managed to fend off Tori and me for so long—

Tori!

Oh *shit*. I completely forgot to tell her I was going out tonight! Everything happened so fast . . . I didn't think it was possible, but my stomach sinks even lower, and the desire to throw up all over everyone steals over me. My face feels hot, my clothes tight, and no matter how much I try to fight it, the desire to run from this situation is gaining on me. I mean, what the hell am I thinking? I don't belong here. This is a ridiculously Instagrammable moment: four Beautiful People (just ignore the fugly one in the corner) having a very photogenic conversation in their hip uni halls well after midnight. I wonder if I could just back away. No one's paying attention. Okay, I know, I'm not exactly small enough to just slip away undetected, but I could slope off with the pizza box under the pretense of throwing it away—

"I like your hair."

I snap back to the real world.

"Pardon?"

"I like your hair," the redhead says, a nervous smile playing around the edges of her lips. "I had it that color once, and I loved it. It really suits you."

I self-consciously touch my hair. "It does?"

"Yeah. Brings out your eyes. I'm Becky, by the way." She gives me another one of those half-mischievous, half-apologetic grins, and leans over to me. "I wish you had come out," she whispers. "It would have been nice to have other people to talk to."

I stare at her. After a second I shrug, the universal sign for *I have no idea what to say to you, but I have to be polite, so* . . .

Becky nods at this, and I can see it in her eyes. She gets it.

I don't understand how, or why, but she gets it.

47: #99PROBLEMS

Amy's fast asleep, sprawled across her bed. To my surprise, she snores. It never once crossed my mind that someone so dainty and cutesy might do something as base as snoring, even in an inebriated state. She still looks like an angel, despite the snoring. This is an odd little privilege. If you think about it, it's the ultimate expression of trust. For all she knows, I could be a serial killer. We haven't known each other that long in the grand scheme of things. She's told me more about her than I have about me, because she's on the right side of normal when it comes to being a proper, authentic human being.

And the more I know about her, the more I hang out with her, the more I'm coming to the conclusion that my own problems might not just stem from my fugliness. Maybe that's just the way I've rationalized it. Maybe there *isn't* this big conspiracy against me and the other Fuglies, and we *do* hold our destinies in our own hands.

Maybe it's me. Maybe I'm the one with the problem.

And maybe that's *always* been the case.

I shake my head. I don't want to think like this. Damn alcohol. Should be banned. But I can't just blame the cocktails and the vodka, can I?

I've done bad things. I was once proud of them, which, in a

way, makes it even worse. They weren't mistakes. I deliberately went out of my way to crush Dizzy, just because she's pretty. I told myself it's just online, it doesn't count, it isn't really *me* . . .

. . . but it is.

I roll over onto my back and stare at the ceiling. Amy's stuck little glow-in-the-dark stars on it, because of course she has.

I sit up and fumble in the dark for my phone. It's 4:16 a.m.— not quite morning, but definitely not night. A weird time of day, really, one that no one but cats and people working night shifts knows very well.

I have some messages. Lots of them. All from Tori.

My breath hitches as a nasty, crawly feeling infects my chest and belly.

Due to the way Messenger works, I get the last one first.

Where the fuck are you?
Who the fuck is this?
Isn't she that little slut Amy?
Wtf are you up to?
Are you fucking her or something?

A photo of a drunk me pouting at the camera with Amy is attached.

The dread intensifies. I scroll back.

The messages start off okay. *Where are you, are you there, what are you doing*, etc. etc. Then they step up a bit: *are you ignoring me, what have I done, wtf is going on*. That then escalates to a full-on *why are you ignoring me, I know you're there, that bitch is posting photos of you on her page, why the fuck would she be doing that, where the fuck are you* . . .

I should have told her I was going out. Just a quick message and that would have been that. Why do I do this to myself? Just one simple thing would have saved me all this shit. I cower in front of the screen, my thumbs clumsily mashing the keys on my phone until autocorrect manages to decipher the core of my message:

> Sorry. Was invited out by my uni friends.
> I meant to msg you, but signal was shit

Interesting lie, but hey, whatever calms her down, right?

> Sorry again. Wasn't ignoring you.
> We literally just ate pizza
> and watched shitty horror movies.
> Nothing else, I promise.
> I'll be home soon,
> then I can explain in more detail xxxxxx

It does cross my mind that Tori's lost it a bit—she doesn't own me and I am allowed out once in a while, but I'm so worried that I've upset her, I squash that down. I did say I'd be online tonight. Oh, why didn't I just message her? Stupid, stupid, stupid!

I clutch at my phone, willing her to be there, aware that it doesn't look great that I'm replying at four in the morning. Her last message was just after 1:00 a.m. and they started at 8:30 p.m. Oh, God, I feel even more terrible now. She sat in, waiting for me for nearly five hours . . . It's about the closest I've ever come to legitimately standing someone up, and it's a horrible feeling.

Nothing. Not even the bloody check mark tattles on her. She's probably doing what all sensible people are doing right now and sleeping, which is what I should be doing but can't because I'm too wired, too scared, feeling too goddamn sick to even contemplate lying down, even though I know it's ridiculous and that I should at least try to get some shut-eye, oh *God*, what have I done?

❦❦❦

I finally hear back from Tori at 8:48 a.m.

Oh. You were out? Why didn't you just tell me?
I was worried.

And that's it.

I feel even *worse* now, if that's possible. I ping back a load more apologies, explaining how I didn't really want to go out, but I couldn't say no when everyone else was going, all the while completely aware that the photos Amy has so stupidly shared show just the two of us—I mean, come on, you don't have to document every fucking moment of your life on social media! No one's interested, and all it does is make you look like either a desperate, needy twat or a complete narcissist. What makes it even worse if the people you drag along with you have no say in being part of your online freakshow, which, by the way, is totally selfish . . .

. . . though not exactly the most heinous crime imaginable either.

I glance over to Amy, who is still asleep. She has one hand curled under her cheek, and if I squint, I think I can see the child she once was. She looks so peaceful. I wish I had her life. Okay, not the whole brother/parent thing (although at least they're basically normal, rather than being a nonfunctioning depressive and a fucking delinquent), but that ability to switch off; to do stupid, selfish things like post pictures all over the internet when you know damn well the other person doesn't like having themselves plastered in public spaces, and still be able to sleep like a baby . . .

I press the palms of my hands into my eyes. My stomach growls.

Crap. We gave away the last of the leftover pizza last night.

I know. I'm sorry. If it's any consolation,
I know I would have had far more fun with you.
I feel bad. Can you forgive me?

A few moments later and *ping!*

Of course I can, babe. You're my special girl. I didn't mean to go off on you, but I saw the photos and thought you'd ditched me—which, let's face it, you kind of did—but hey, you had fun, so I should be happy if you're happy.

I can't help but frown at that. On one hand, it sounds like she's forgiven me and is apologizing for going over the top, but on the other . . . passive-aggressive much? Is this normal? I don't know—it's not as if I have much to compare it to. Maybe she's trying to be cool with it all but is struggling a bit because I hurt her feelings? That would make sense, I suppose. Oh, why didn't I just *tell her*?!

Again, I'm so sorry, Tori babe.
It was totally one of those off-the-cuff things.
Next time, you'll be the first person I tell, k?

Another pause, then:

K. Are you free? I got us a whole new
playground . . . ;)

My stomach twists again.

No. Will be soon, tho. Look forward to seeing what you
have for me! ? xxx

Although that is a lie. I'm in no mood to fuck someone's day
up for shits and giggles. Last time I did that, someone almost
died.

. . . You're not at home?
Where are you then?

Oh GOD! Just drop it, Tori!

I crashed at Amy's. Closer to town than my house.
Oh. I see.

I sigh heavily, as if that might relieve the pressure building
up in my head and chest.

Babe, it's not like that.
It's not like anything.
I just needed somewhere to crash.
You know I love you. B&T forever, remember?
Yeah. I remember. Are you leaving now?
Soon. Just need to find my stuff.

And say goodbye to Amy, maybe help her tidy up, you know, the basic ways you demonstrate that you're not a total jerk. But I don't think I'm going to have time for that; I get the impression Tori wants me home five minutes ago.

K. Message me as soon as you get in.

No kisses, no "babe." Not a good sign.

Will do. Could be an hour or so, tho—
need to get the bus
and you know what they're like. xxxx

I know she's read it as the check mark has given her away, but she doesn't reply. And given she knows how to bypass the check mark, she obviously wants me to *know* she's choosing not to reply.

I stuff my phone into my pocket.

"Amy," I hiss. "Amy!"

No reply. Not even a grunt. She's still totally dead to the world. I lean over and give her a little shake. She swats my hand away with a small groan.

"Amy, I've got to go."

"Uhh!" She pulls a pillow over her face. I clench my jaw. I don't have time for this.

"Amy, I mean it. I need to go. I'd stay and help you clear up, but I—I've just got to get home. Sorry."

"No. Stay here and feed me coffee . . ." Amy whines plaintively.

"I can't. I have to go."

"Why?" She pulls the pillow off her face. Her mascara has

smudged, but she still looks way too good for someone with a raging hangover. "I thought we could have coffee and then get bacon sandwiches from the greasy spoon down the road. And anyway, why are you so awake? Why aren't you hungover? You're inhuman!"

That pulls me up. My excuse—that my mum needs me—dies on my lips. She means it as a joke (or at least I hope she does), but she's right. That I was even thinking of using Mum as an excuse to get away from her so I could talk to Tori . . . that's a bit of a red line, isn't it?

"Okay, look, I'll fix us some coffee and help you clear up, but then I have to meet someone."

Amy hauls herself upright. "Ooo, you do? Who?"

"Just . . . someone," I say, refusing to look at her.

She peers at me, and a slow grin spreads across her face. "Someone important?"

I shrug, giving her one of those noncommittal grimaces that some people mistake for smiles. "You could say that."

Amy claps her hands in glee. "Oh, how adorable! When did you meet them?"

"A little while ago," I say, way too quickly. "Online."

"Oooo, an online romance." Her grin broadens.

I feel a blush creep up the sides of my neck. "Yeah, well, I said I'd be online in an hour and, you know, I need to get home, so . . ."

"Aw, why didn't you say so? I can clear up. I don't want to get in the way of some serious Romeo and Julieting. Although . . ." Her grin dissolves, replaced by a small, concerned frown. "Be careful, yeah? I know online dating isn't a new thing and everything, but even so—there's loads of dicks out there who like to take advantage of people."

She doesn't say it, but the *like you* after the *people* drops neatly into place.

"It's okay. I know all about the creeps online. I'm not about to give anyone my life savings. We just met on a forum and like the same stuff, that's all."

"Oh, okay. I wasn't trying to lecture you or anything. Like I said, loads of people meet online now. I just don't want you getting hurt. After Dizzy and everything, I don't think I could cope with another friend being messed about."

I snort. "I'm not going to pull a Dizzy." Amy's face falls. Okay, so that was a bit harsh. "What I mean is, I'm careful. I'll be okay."

"Yeah, sure." Amy smiles, but it holds none of her usual sparkle.

48: #HOMETRUTHS

I stay long enough to help Amy clear away the worst of the mess. I even take the greasy pizza boxes with me to the communal dumpster on my way out. I can tell Amy would like me to stay, but she's being gallant about it, trying to be encouraging, asking where my "special someone" lives and whether I'm going to meet them.

When I tell her I'm not sure exactly where Tori lives, she seems a bit shocked but doesn't say anything, and suddenly it does strike me as a little bit odd. Maybe I should have asked by now.

When I leave, Amy gives me a big hug and tells me, yet again, to take care. This time I don't hesitate in hugging her back; it feels nice, and quite frankly, I wish I could stay here, warm and secure in the arms of another human. But I can't, so when I leave, I give Amy a proper smile—not a smirk or one of those carefully-constructed half-smiles designed to minimize chinnage, but a proper, unguarded grin. I want Amy to be someone I can grin at, chins and all.

She grins back at me, all wrinkle-nosed and crinkly-eyed, and I feel a rush of affection for her, because she's my friend. There, I've said it. The F word. The really important one.

I actually feel pretty good when I get on the bus. It's on

time, and it's one of those cold-but-clear days that make late autumn my favorite time of year. I get home just after 10:30, which is excellent; on a usual Saturday I'd try to sleep in till now, so in reality, I haven't really lost any time with Tori at all.

There isn't any sign of anyone when I get in, so I fix myself a cuppa, and lo and behold, there's food in the fridge, so I make myself some cheese on toast, too.

I text Amy as the cheese is melting under the grill, just to let her know I've gotten home safe. She pings back a *Thnx for lettin me no! xx* ❤ *xx*, and I find myself smiling at the terrible spelling rather than being irritated by it.

Upstairs, I change out of last night's clothing and into my lovely, comfy pajamas, fling open the curtains to let the weak winter sun in, and log on to my computer. A Metachat login is waiting for me.

It doesn't take Tori long to show up.

You're home now?
> Yeah. Just got in.
> had to help do a bit of tidying up,
> but got back asap. are you still mad at me?

Tori doesn't reply immediately, and my mood drops a notch.

I wasn't mad. Just concerned. You had me worried.

> Yeah, I know. You've already told me, like, a thousand times already. Jesus.
> I know. I'm sorry.

A wild idea strikes me.

Wanna skype?

Again, a horrible pause stretches out, further and further, chaining seconds into minutes. A fluttery feeling starts up in my chest. Have I pushed this too far?

Sorry—I don't do skype.
You might as well hand the feds your life on a silver platter.

It's my turn to pause.

Oh, ok. Just an idea.

I can't deny it—I'm disappointed. I'd hoped we'd get beyond worrying about security issues and the nebulous "them" that patrol the internet. Plus, whether I like it or not, Amy's words keep playing back in my head, and a small but irritatingly insistent voice keeps saying, *Is this normal? Really? This doesn't feel normal. Is it normal?*

It's okay. I don't skype anyone.
Not worth the hassle.
That's how people get caught.
Anyway, we have fun here, right?
While you were out with that dozy bitch yesterday,
I found some new victims.
You'll love them. Come on, let's play!

And it strikes me: I don't want to *play*. Is this all we've got? Being horrible to other people on the internet? That's it? No skyping, no arranging to meet, no trying to organize a future together—just bile and spite and a constant stream of insults. Like calling Amy a dozy bitch. I don't want Amy called a dozy bitch. She's neither dozy nor a bitch. She's my friend, one who will eat pizza with me and watch movies with me and go out drinking with me . . .

I massage my temples with my fingertips to try and ease the headache that's building there.

> Nah. Not in the mood. Would rather just chat.

What?? Come on, Beth,
you bailed on me last night,
don't bail on me now, babe!

I lean back from the screen. What is her problem? Why is she so keen for us to go trolling? There's more to us than that. There has to be. I try a different tack.

> There's a new Banshee strip. You seen it?

Yeah, course. Not as good as the earlier ones.
Getting too commercial. Left a review. ;)

A link appears. I copy and paste it into a new tab (no hyperlinks on Metachat, for obvious reasons), and there's Tori's "review":

What is this? I used to love this strip, but it's fallen into a well of shit recently. Seriously, do yourself a favor and step in front of a very fast train. I can't believe you'd even think this was good enough. We deserve better, you hack. This is fucking crap. Sort it out, or give it the fuck up.

. . . Wow. Okay, so maybe the strip isn't quite as fresh as it was a couple of years ago, but it's one thing to say you don't like it and quite another to advise the creators to kill themselves.

How do I respond to this? She's obviously fishing for approval, but I *don't* approve. At all.

> Bit harsh. I thought Midnight Jim devouring the chili-obsessed guy was quite funny. Sure, it's a bit lame, but Banshee's face when Jim thinks he's going to melt . . .

Are you fucking serious? It was SHITE.
I can't believe you'd even say that.
Wow. What did you have for breakfast, basicmoronOs?

Uh, okay, what the fuck is her problem? I'm used to people being aggressive to me when I'm stirring up shit, but this—this is new, and I don't like it. It's like she wants to pick a fight with me.

> Uh, are you ok, hun?

Very tentatively.

Yeah. Of course. Just feeling twitchy.
I've got some bitches that need a good spanking
and you're giving me major blue balls.

Seriously? This is all *my* fault? She's pissed off because I don't want to troll. Or is it more that she's pissed off because I won't do what she wants me to do?

That is not a comforting thought.

I take in a deep breath. Time to take the bull by the horns.

Tori, look, I'm sorry. I know you want to go and play, but I need to take a break. Not from you—I want to be with you, of course I do—but I want to take a step back from the trolling. Had some trouble recently that really affected me and I need to get my head together. So can't we just have a nice chat? I love chatting to you. You get me and that's what I need right now. You. Not the Troll You, but the Real You—the one who likes to send me photos and cat memes and new AE fanfics, the adorable you that you hide from everyone else.

xxxx

Another agonizing pause.

You had trouble?

That's it? Three words? There's no way it would have taken her that long to type three measly words. No acknowledgment that I've basically just poured my heart out to her. No comment whatsoever on how I'm feeling, on my mental state. Just the bit that might affect what she wants to do, the bit that might put a damper on her trolling plans. The rest of it obviously doesn't count.

Yeah.

It's hard to type, my hands are shaking so much—but not out of nervousness. Out of something I never thought I'd feel toward Tori—pure, simple anger.

You know that girl Dizzy?
The one we took down the other night?

Yeah, I remember. The one you wanted taking down a peg cos she was giving you a hard time, if I remember right . . .

I may be many things, but I'm not an idiot. I can see someone setting up blame deflection from a mile off.

Yep, that one. Well, it turns out she's not as bad as I thought. I'm not too proud to lay it out as it is— I was wrong. I'm sorry, cos I dragged you into it and I take full responsibility. But it's made me think about things a bit, and how there's always more to these things than we think.

Wait . . . what. The. Fuck? Are you telling me you feel bad about what we did? You saw her profile! So what if she's okay in real life—she's one of Them! Are you going soft or something?

Soft. Just because I have a shred of humanity left.

No. Just had a dose of reality. Tori . . . she hurt herself. Badly. As a direct result of what we did. I was there when the ambulance turned up. It was fucking brutal. Never seen anything like it, and tbh, I don't want to see it again. Ever. That's why I was out last night—we all wanted to try and forget it for a bit. As it turns out, Indigo is actually ok too. I mean, yeah, she's still an insufferable Instagram whore, but she's not a bad person. And neither was Dizzy. Turns out she wasn't deliberately being nasty, she was just shy and so came across as a bit abrupt, cos she was bullied a lot before uni. The others said she came here hoping to make a

new start, to get away from it all, and we just brought
it all back. She probably thought her old bullies had
found her and there really is no escape . . . and I guess
that's something I can relate to. Anyway, it made me
think. Sure, having a pop at the beautiful people seems
ok cos they seem bulletproof—but what if they're not?
After seeing Dizzy on that stretcher . . . I don't want to
do that to anyone else.

Once I start typing, it all floods out. I can't help it. The
guilt is literally eating me alive. Once, Dizzy was just like the
others—a caricature, a cartoon character. Like all the others, she wasn't real—until, of course, she was, in unmistakable
ways. There's nothing realer than blood, after all.

Still no reply from Tori, but I know she's typing. There's no
way she'd just leave it at that. If we were on Messenger, I'm sure I'd
be seeing that little *dot dot dot, incoming message* flag. I gnaw on my
thumbnail. I know I'm right, but that doesn't stop me from letting
out a little involuntary squeak when the wall of text arrives. As I
read, my eyes widen, and a yawning pit opens in my belly.

Are you fucking serious? Actually, genuinely serious?
That whore was a total bitch to you, and she couldn't
handle it when you dished it back at her. That's it. That's
all that's going on here. Fucking hell! Don't you get it?
THIS IS WHAT THEY DO! Treat people like shit and then
can't handle any kind of criticism back! Oh, it's perfectly
ok for them to bitch and exclude and act like they own the
place, giving you filthy looks and making sure everyone
else knows you're some kind of untouchable pleb, but the
minute one of us fights back? Oh no, can't cope, they're

so mean, must cut myself because that's what all the cool kids are doing right now, to show that I'm a real human being rather than a vacuous twat with nothing to offer the world but pictures of my perfect hot-dog legs, oh waa waa, pity me pity me, I'm so fucking authentic. Fuck them! Fuck them all! I bet you a million quid that dozy bitch will be back online within a week, posting her sob story, capitalizing on all of this, telling the sheeple who follow her that she's ok now and oh, don't punish those who hurt her cos she's so fucking magnanimous, and there will be loads of pictures of her looking a bit sad with some bandages round her arms and the sheeple will fawn over her, telling her she's so brave, so forgiving, so fucking wonderful just because she's pretty. What if it was us, huh? What if we'd decided to cut ourselves up because some knob shouted something at us in the street? Would we have hordes of people telling us how brave we are, and how wonderful and strong we are being? Fuck off! We wouldn't get any of it cos we. don't. matter. We don't give people a boner when we put on a bikini, we can't pull off the fucking scorpion pose, and we don't look angelic whilst nibbling on vegan power balls that we simply whipped up that morning cos we're oh-so-fucking-perfect. So don't you feel bad about it. Don't you even DARE. That bitch deserved everything she got.

I read the rant over and over, trying to twist it around so it computes. Once upon a time, that would have been no problem at all. A month ago, I could have written that. Hell, maybe even a week ago.

And there is still a little, vicious part of me that agrees with every word she says. The Beautiful People do have it easier. But that doesn't excuse what we did. What I did. It's not their fault society is built that way, and it certainly doesn't make them any less human. Okay, so they don't *have* to document every single aspect of their lives online. They don't *have* to go out of their way to make sure they have an adoring audience. They could just be hot and anonymous. But, hell, who am I kidding? I get it! I know how strong the lure of the internet is. Am I really any different? They post pictures to make themselves feel that someone cares and that they are someone who matters. I troll those girls because, in some twisted way, that means I can steal a little bit of that power from them.

When I troll, I am their equal. It makes me feel powerful and clever and dangerous—all the things I'm not in the real world. Where they have their physical perfection, I have my perfect anonymity. I'm as hopelessly caught up in the web as they are. Without the internet, their lives mean nothing. Without them, my life *is* nothing.

Or, at least, that's what I once thought. But now Amy's introduced me to another way. A way that doesn't involve sitting on your own in the dark spitting venom at people.

I close my eyes and let out a long, shaky breath. I've been so stupid. I was so caught up with Tori and her seductively dangerous ways that I didn't even see Amy there, doing what friends are supposed to do, being what friends are supposed to be.

And now, that's all at risk. If she discovers what I did to Dizzy, she'll be gone and all I'll be left with is a shell of a family and spite spewing from a computer screen.

I gasp. Now that I realize how huge this is, tears aren't enough. I actually feel physically sick. Because even if I manage to keep all of this to myself, I still have to live with it. I still have to live with Dizzy and that bloke's marriage and Freedom-chick's online disappearance and the unknown fates of count-less others like her, other people who admitted defeat and qui-etly slipped away . . . maybe in more ways than one. Despite never picking up a weapon, I've got blood all over me. And it is never going to wash off.

Beth? You there?

I glance at the time. Shit. I've been sitting here, paralyzed, for nearly ten minutes.

Yeah.

I have no idea what to say next. I mean, how do you tell someone you love that you not only think they're wrong, but that you now think they've been wrong all along, and that you were too, and you kind of wish you'd never started this whole sordid business in the first place, without seriously hurting them?

I need chocolate and I need it now, in vast quantities. I rummage through a treasure trove of empty wrappers, hoping my bedside cabinet holds at least one I've missed, but I come up empty. Even chocolate has deserted me. I am truly alone.

More minutes tick by. What do I say? What do I do? Agree with her and go along with whatever she wants to do? That would be the easiest option. Just pretend all of this was noth-ing more than a silly misunderstanding, sorry babe, don't know what came over me, sure let's do it, that bitch deserves every-thing she gets, btw that pic of you in that T-shirt is gorgeous, can I have a more private one later, if you know what I mean, wink wink . . .

Yeah, I could do that. I could take the easy way, the coward's way.

But if I do, I may as well kiss my friendship with Amy goodbye, because there's no way I'll be able to look her in the eye ever again. What we did to Dizzy didn't just hurt Dizzy—it hurt everyone around her, even me. And while self-sabotage is definitely another of my talents, even I realize that sticking my head in the sand and carrying on wouldn't just be that, it would be full-on engage-self-destruct mode. Warning: radioactive person ahead.

> Tori, I'm sorry, but I can't agree.
> Not this time. I know we've been hurt
> by others in the past and punishing them
> was our way of dealing with it . . . but this time it's dif-
> ferent. You weren't there. You didn't see the blood, or
> how scared everyone was, how miserable and vulner-
> able Dizzy was. It made me realize that our targets are
> real ppl. Real women, with hopes and fears and inse-
> curities that we don't know about. Sure, what they're
> doing is stupid and vain, but be honest. If you looked
> like them, wouldn't *you* be doing it?

I take in a deep, shuddering breath. Time to lay my cards on the table.

> Cos I know I would.

There's a boom deep in my chest, like someone's detonated a bomb in it. I start shaking as I continue trying to type, my head swimming at the enormity of my confession.

I punish those girls cos they are everyhtin Im not. I hate them cos I love them. I want to be them I want wat they have. I wanna do yoga on a beach and have millions of ppl fawnin all over me. We all do, deep down. Even, I think, you.

I have no idea if Tori is replying, but as far as I can tell she hasn't logged out, so maybe she's now doing a me: she's questioning herself, and in reading my words, she might find a grain of truth in there. I really hope so, because I do love her, I do, and if we can just get over this, we can carry on as usual—well, not as usual, but as . . . as . . .

Beside me, my phone buzzes. I glance down. A Facebook notification from Amy. Yeah, I know. Even I can see that might be a sign.

My laptop screen flickers, heralding the arrival of Tori's reply. Well, the moment of truth has arrived.

How dare you make those assumptions? You don't know me. You want shitty fawners? Then fuck you. I thought you were different, but no, you're just like the other superficial whores out there. I can't believe I once thought you might be someone special, someone different, and that we might have something special, that we were together against the world, but it looks like I was wrong. You're right—you are no different from them if that is what you truly aspire to. You led me on, letting me think that you were on my wavelength, when all along you were just taking me for a fucking ride, and now you think you've taken the higher road with your touchy-feely bullshit. I seriously cannot believe you would do this to me, like it's my fault,

like you're blaming me, like I made you do it, cos I didn't—
YOU DID IT! And whatever happens, you will NEVER be
like those girls. You're never going to have their life, you're
never going to have their popularity, you're never going to
compare to them cos you don't have it, you don't have the
bikini body or the diet or anything they have, bitch, GOD I
cannot believe you, cannot believe this, FUCK YOU! FUCK
THEM AND FUCK YOU!!!

I have to read it three times before I can even begin to
make sense of it all. She's jumping all over the place, throwing
blame at everyone except herself. The backs of my eyes sting
and my throat turns bitter. Is this what she really thinks?
Is this how she truly views the world? That anyone who aspires
to be, well, *anything* beyond being a stone-cold bitch to everyone is somehow a fraud?

The fact that her rant is so disjointed makes it clear that
I've managed to really hurt her. That she doesn't just do this
for fun; she really believes she's *righteous*—which is mental. I
mean, even I knew what I was doing was wrong, when all is said
and done.

Before I can even think of replying, Tori's message dis-
appears and Metachat shuts itself down. I stare at the screen,
blinking furiously. Looks like Tori just left the building. Did
Metachat always do that when she logged off? I can't remember.
I was always too full of thoughts of her to even think about how
Metachat shuts down. Maybe I should have paid more attention.

I run both my hands through my hair. Oh shit. Oh shitty
shitting shitty shit. What do I do now? Am I losing her? I literally have no idea. I don't know how these things work. Sure,
I've been bullied before and had shouting competitions with

just about every member of my immediate family, but this is different. I hated my bullies. My family is, well, my family—you're *supposed* to argue with them. But this? Is this just a tiff, or is this one of those *I never want to see you again* deals? I don't know, and it's making me want to puke. And maybe jump off a building. Or build a time machine so I can go back and erase the last hour. Or maybe the last week. The last month?

Oh, God, why did I say those things? I am such an idiot! Stupid stupid *stupid*! Why didn't I just keep my mouth shut, or say I was busy, or that Mum had called me, or, let's face it, found an anonymous Beautiful Person to torment just to keep her happy—okay, so I'd have to live with the guilt, but at least Tori would now be happy and would be sending me messages of love rather than . . . whatever that was. It's all my fault. All of it. What the fuck is wrong with me?

My phone buzzes again and I jump about eight feet off the bed. Another notification from Amy. Shakily, I open up Facebook. She's tagged me into a few things—a couple of memes, nothing serious, just Amy-stuff. And there's a friend request.

From Indigo.

I stuff a hand into my mouth to stop the sob escaping.

A few months ago, I was alone and miserable. Now, miraculously, I have friends—and they're judging me on what they think is my personality, my qualities as a fellow human being, and not a number sewn into the back of my shirt. This is utopian stuff! Or it would be, if it wasn't all built on lies, the biggest of all being that I'm a good person, because I'm not, I'm a bad person, a very bad person, and I don't know what to do about it. At all.

Well, Indigo is going to have to wait for a moment. And Amy—sorry, you too. I need to find Tori. I need to say whatever it is I need to say to make things right between us. I don't care what it is or what I have to do—I just want things to go back to where they were, rewind to some arbitrary point where everything seemed okay and I can actually live with myself.

I click through my posts. Funny, I can't find her.

Okay, contact list. Scroll scroll scroll . . .

She's not there.

I check again.

Still not there.

Okay, forget the phone, stupid shitty phone, can never find anything on that. Check on the laptop. Aaaaaannnnd nothing.

In the few minutes since she pulled out of Metachat, Tori has unfriended me.

I think I've just been dumped.

49: #FML

Three days.

Three days of staring at the screen, of hitting refresh every thirty seconds, of logging into Metachat just on the off chance a miracle key might be waiting for me.

Three wasted, miserable days.

I haven't gone out. How could I? I might miss her. Well, okay, maybe I did go and get some chocolate, but that's it. It was, what, fifteen minutes, twenty at the most. One shop, a fiver's worth, yeah they're all for me, you judgmental knobhead.

I've trawled Facebook, trying to find her, but there's nothing. Not even a *you must be friends with this person to view their profile*. We had no mutual friends, no mutual connections. I don't even have the know-how to reverse-engineer the posts she once commented on to somehow find something resembling an IP address. It's like she never existed. All I have are the pictures I secretly downloaded. I stare at them, trying to resist the urge to stroke the screen, as if that might bring her back into my life.

I've had a couple of messages from Amy asking if I'm okay. I end up telling her I'm sick, which isn't a lie because I am sick, heartsick, so sick I'm beginning to wonder if it's time to call it on this miserable life. I can't ever see it getting any better; get older, get fatter, get more and more desperate . . .

I pinch the bridge of my nose, my eyes screwed up tight. This isn't right. Gotta do something. Gotta sort this out. Can't just sit here and rot. It's all a bit ridiculous, if you think about it; all I did was say I'd had a change of heart over being a total bitch to strangers. It wasn't as if I'd decided to dedicate my life to Jesus or Kanye or a commune. Sure, we'd had fun before that fun nearly managed to kill someone, but that wasn't the be-all and end-all of our relationship—was it? We had more than that. We had to. I think of Tori and my heart flutters. I feel physically sick when she's not around. That's love, isn't it? Maybe I should be flattered that she's had such an extreme reaction. Maybe this proves that she loved me more than she ever admitted, even if that also proves that it's all a bit twisted? Maybe, just maybe, she's sitting in her room, staring at her screen, wondering how she's going to fix all of this and invite me back into her life.

I let out a shuddery breath, because that last thought is the most painful of all. That Tori is still out there, waiting for me, wanting me, just plucking up the courage to get back in contact. It's painful because it fills me with hope—horrible, insidious hope, a little scrabbly thing that runs around your body, lighting fires along your nerve endings, forever whispering *what if* and *maybe* even though that kind of shit only happens in movies.

I rummage around in my bedside cabinet until my fingertips brush against something solid through the whispery wrappers of my misery. I pull the candy bar out—a Snickers, not my favorite but it was a quid for four and hell, who am I kidding, they're *all* my favorites when I'm this desperate—and tear into it, mechanically chewing and swallowing, not really enjoying it but eating it anyway because it's the closest thing to actual, genuine comfort I can get around here.

And all too soon, it is gone: just another empty wrapper joining its brethren in the cabinet. Together they twinkle like jewels in the light of my bedside lamp, shiny slivers of fleeting happiness, heavy reminders of soul-ripping shame. I'm running my tongue over my teeth to savor the last of the salt-and-sweetness you get when you mix chocolate with peanuts when my phone rings. It makes me jump, because it doesn't ring that often. I mean, who would call this stinking loser?

Turns out, Amy would. I should have guessed that, I suppose.

I could ignore it. I don't know if I'm up to her relentless perkiness. But, at the same time, can I really risk alienating anyone else?

"Hey," I say, trying to keep the weariness from my voice.

"Hello," Amy replies, sounding oddly officious. "Not coming to lectures again?"

"No, not today. I'm not feeling great. Sorry."

"Oh. I see."

Again, she sounds clipped, like I've somehow upset her. Oh, this is brilliant! I don't even need to be around people to piss them off now. Just my mere existence will do that.

"Yeah, I think I've picked up a bug. Feel terrible."

"So I take it you're not going to be coming to that workshop tomorrow. That's nice and convenient. Did you ever find out what group you were in?"

My stomach drops a note. I'd forgotten about the workshop. I swap my phone to my other ear so I can wipe my sweaty palm against my thigh. If I didn't know better, I'd say Amy sounded angry. But that can't be right. Amy's never angry. *Angry* doesn't even feature in her emotional dictionary.

"Uh, no, I forgot to do that—not that it matters, what with this virus. Are you okay?"

"Yep," she snaps.

"Oh. All right. It's just that you don't sound yourself today. Has something happened?" Ohshitfuckbollocks, has she found out about Dizzy? Does she know it was me?

"I don't know. Why don't you tell me, Miss 'We've never heard of Bethany Soames'?"

My heart rockets up into my throat and sits there, quivering, until I think it might suffocate me.

"Pardon?" I manage to squeak.

"I went to lectures today. I thought I'd do something good, so I apologized for your absence. Said you were ill but you'd be back soon. Imagine how I felt when Grindle looked at me like I'd grown another head. Turns out, he has no idea who you are. I thought it was a bit weird given you're pretty good at his subject, but hey, we all know what lecturers can be like, especially when it comes to first-year undergrads, so I let it slide. Having nothing else to do because my best friend's ill at home, I decided to go into the office and find out what group you were in for the workshop, just in case you were back tomorrow. So I looked at the list—and lo and behold, your name wasn't on it. So I spoke to the secretary, and guess what? She'd never heard of you, either. She looked you up on her computer and everything, but nope, no sign of Bethany Soames. Or Beth Soames. Or Elizabeth Soames, or any Soames at all. What the fuck is going on?"

She gets progressively louder until she's all but screaming at me. I try to swallow, but I can't.

This is worse than Dizzy. This might even be worse than Tori.

My whole life. My whole identity.

A lie.

I'm frozen, my phone wedged up against my ear. She's

breathing heavily, betrayed, waiting for me to answer.

I don't know if I can.

"I . . . I . . . I . . . ," I stutter. I can't help it. It's not even a ploy to buy me time—literally cannot say anything. If I was a computer, it'd be the blue screen of death.

"Yeah? And?" Amy's voice is like ice.

"I . . . I . . ."

"Oh, forget it. If you can't even think up an excuse, then why bother?"

The line cuts dead.

Amy's gone.

50: #PERSONALHELL

I stare at my phone. First Tori, now Amy. What's the third thing going to be? I start the fucking apocalypse?

I've got to fix this. And quickly. My window of opportunity is ticking away, and fast. So, what? A text. I'm better with those. So much easier to express yourself virtually than actual talking.

Well, it usually is.

Amy . . . I dunno how to say this so I'm just gonna come out with it. I wanted to be at uni. Like, properly. I applied last year but didn't get in. But Mum was so pleased I'd gone for it, I couldn't bear to tell her I'd failed . . . so I told her I got in. She was over the moon. Things were difficult after Dad left and she got ill and it was the only thing that seemed to lift her. When the rejection came in I had no idea what to do, so I decided to . . . ignore it. She threw me a little party. Just me and her and brad, but it was nice. Kind of like how things used to be in the old days. She was so out of it, she didn't ask about how it was going to work, you know, the money and every-thing. I wasn't going to go ahead with the charade, not really, but then I turned up at the beginning of the year and all these people were going inside and no one was checking anything so I just tagged along and before I knew it I was in the lecture. It was that easy. If I'm honest, I wasn't even going to keep it up—just go to a few lectures, let it fizzle out . . . Mum would never have noticed. But then I met u in the library and I got in too deep. I didn't mean to do any harm—it was something to do to keep me occupied, and was a perfect opportunity to reinvent myself. You know, play the student, maybe make some friends.

I pause as my thumbs twitch.

I didn't mean for any of this to go this far, but I'd spent too long kidding myself that I kind of bought into the lie . . . I'm sorry. I definitely didn't do this to hurt you or anyone else. I suppose I could have told you the truth, but in a way, I wanted to believe the lie myself. Please don't hate me. I am so sorry. xxxx

It's a hell of a long text, probably the longest I've ever written, and it hardly scratches the surface of what I really want to say, mainly because even now, I don't really know what I want to say. I pretended to be a student because I'm a loser and just wanted something to fill my time? Something to give me a semblance of normality? Something that made me feel like a functioning human being rather than a complete waste of skin and air?

I shake my head, burying my face into my hands, phone and all. Ugh, is there anything worse than a self-pitying fat girl? Time to face up to the truth. I did something stupid, and I fucked it up—badly. How the hell did I ever think this would end in any other way? I have literally no one to blame but myself. All I can hope is that Amy will reply and give me a chance to make amends, which, let's face it, is probably more than I deserve. And even *that* manages to sound whiny.

My phone buzzes against my cheek. It's not a text but

another call. I don't want to answer it, but I kind of *have* to answer it, because this is Amy replying, and I did just pray for that, so . . .

"Hi," I croak.

"What the fuck are you on about? You were going to stop pretending to be a student, but you didn't because you met me in the library that day? Are you blaming *me* for your colossal fuckup?"

She doesn't shout at me. No, she's beyond shouting and into angry hissing territory. I cringe back, my eyes screwed up tight, shame infecting every single part of my body.

"No—no, of course not. I—I—" I'm starting to hyper-ventilate, the shame giving way to panic, because I don't know how to make this all better. "I knew it was wrong. Know it was wrong. But I wanted to be normal so badly. To have a second chance. And you gave that to me! I even tried to keep you at arm's length at first, but—but—you're so nice and so sweet, and you wanted to be my friend, and I've never had that before, and—and—" I can't carry on. If I do, it's just going to come out as one big Chewbacca-esque sob.

"You lied to me, Beth, and that is not okay. That is never okay!" There's a horrible, crackly quality to Amy's voice now; I think I preferred the angry hissing.

"I know! I know. I—if I could go back and change it, I would, but I can't. Amy? Please don't cut me off. I'm still me. The uni thing was the only lie, everything else is true. Amy, please . . ."

My breath is hitching now, and so is hers.

"P-pretending to be a student is wrong," Amy says. "You're not just lying, you're s-stealing, too! People pay loads to go to uni. How long were you going to let me think you were legit?

Until graduation? How were you expecting to sit exams? Seriously, Beth, I just can't understand how you thought this was going to work!"

"I know, okay! I know. It's ridiculous. I'm ridiculous. I just wanted to join in, be like everyone else. I didn't want to be a loser anymore. Is that so hard to grasp? I just wanted a clean slate and a chance to be normal, to do things normal people do—"

"Normal people don't pretend to be things they're not!"

"You don't have to tell me that. I am totally aware of how mental all this sounds, but when you're in the thick of it, looking for a way out, you do whatever you can. You don't care how stupid it is, or how it might affect other people, or even what the consequences might be for you. You just—do it. And then boom, it's done, and you're stuck. Catch twenty-two. I couldn't tell you because I didn't want to hurt you, so instead I just kept pretending."

That's it. If I say anything else, I'll just be rehashing old ground. If she doesn't get it now, I don't think she ever will.

"Amy, I can't say sorry enough. You're my best friend, my first, proper, real best friend, and I don't think I can stand losing you too—"

I clap my hand over my mouth to stop the sob from escaping, because I know if it does, it'll never stop. I can hear Amy breathing on the other end of the line: short, ragged little gasps that speak of grief and betrayal.

"I trusted you, Beth. That's the bottom line. I trusted you, and you lied to me."

Not the only thing she's lied about, buttercup! my internal nemesis squawks gleefully. *You wait until you find out about all the other nasty shit she's done—you'll *puke* . . .*

I close my eyes. "I know," I whisper. Well, what else am I going to say?

"Truth is, I don't think I even know you. Not really. If you can lie about this, how can I be sure about anything else?"

I can't answer that. But I'm going to have to try.

"You do know me. Everything else is me. Okay, so I'm not a student, but I'm still Beth . . ." I think. I'm on shaky ground here, because even I'm not sure who I am most of the time. "Please. I'm not asking for you to pretend this never happened, but you're my friend, and I love you, and I don't want to lose you."

I love you. I've said that more times in the last few weeks than I ever thought I would in my whole life. There is a power to that phrase, one I didn't realize it had. It isn't just an expression of feelings; it comes in so many forms, with all kinds of baggage and a whole host of responsibilities—the first of which is "don't stomp all over the person you claim to love."

I kind of feel like I've fallen at the first hurdle.

My fingers curl around my phone, gripping it so tightly I think I might crush it.

Finally, Amy answers. "I don't know, Beth. I—I need time. This is a lot to process. I'm sorry. I'll call you later."

The phone goes dead.

So that's it, is it? That's your lot, missy, you've well and truly screwed up so you might as well forget it all. For fuck's sake! How does anyone manage this? One false step and it all falls down around your ears.

I stare at my mute phone, and a sudden plume of anger cuts through the sickly dread. This isn't fair. I try to do the right thing, and I lose Tori. Amy finds out about something that, let's face it, doesn't actually affect her in the slightest, and now she's acting as if I'm some kind of criminal. I mean, come on! So I sat in on a few lectures. I wrote some essays. She even *copied* me—if anything, she should be thanking me! I basically wrote her last assignment for her; didn't she wonder why I wasn't that bothered about us being accused of plagiarism? If anything, I've done her a favor. I've gone to stupid clubs with her, listened to her twitter on about how terrible her charmed life is, done half her coursework for her . . . but no, all of that means the square root of shag-all, simply because I'm not a "proper" student.

In the grand scheme of things, what I did was nothing. Less than nothing. No one died. No one got hurt. Hell, no one but her even knows!

But she does know. And I know. And I also know nothing will ever be the same between us again.

I should have known things would end up like this. Nice things don't happen to Fuglies. This is just the natural order being restored. Our Cosmic Overlords have decided to hit the reset button. I'll just have to go back to living online. Who needs real life, anyway? I could just melt back into the background. It would be easy enough. Amy doesn't know where I live. Block her number. Block her on social media. Pretend that she never existed, that I just made her up, my new imaginary friend. No one would ever need to know.

I blow out a trembling sigh, hoping that might relieve the tension trapped within me, but nope, it's still there. And I know, deep down, that ghosting Amy would be the worst thing I could ever do. Because she's the real deal. A proper friend. And no matter how many excuses I might try and make, my fugliness had nothing to do with this. This one's on me. I lied, and now I'm paying the price. Funny how you only realize how good things are when you're on the edge of losing it all.

51: #THERULEOFTHREE

It's been five days since my fight with Tori, and two since Amy confronted me. I haven't heard from either of them, but then again, I haven't tried contacting them either, so I guess it balances out. I suppose I was hoping that if I gave them some space, they'd eventually cool off and come back to me.

This morning, though, I can't log into Facebook. It's doing that "I'm going to randomly throw you out of your own account and make you log back in" thing again. It pisses me off when websites do that, forcing you to scrabble around your brain to remember which incarnation of your go-to password you're using at that particular moment. For some people, that's a pretty simple task, but that's because they are total muppets who still think *password123* or their date of birth is a good idea. Since I am not one of those muppets, my passwords tend to be jumbles of random letters and numbers, or at least they look random unless you know all the things I like and can figure out the little codes I have for them.

First attempt . . . no. Second . . . dammit! Third . . . what, wrong *again*? A sneaking sense of something not being right steals over me, which is saying something considering my whole life is generally one big suspicion that something isn't right.

Okay. Hammering in more passwords isn't going to help here. I bring up Google and take in a deep breath: *Beth Soames+facebook.* The first hit is my Facebook account, which is both good (don't have to wade through potentially loads of horrible stuff I never knew existed about me) and extremely worrying, as I usually set my privacy setting to "friends only" (although recently I switched to the more optimistic "friends of friends," because I am an utter tool).

I click the link.

The first thing that strikes me is the pictures. The pictures of me. Pictures from my cloud account (fuck you, cloud account—default settings, my big fat ass) which I should have deleted but hadn't. And pictures I had sent Tori, including aaaallllll of the "private" ones she'd coaxed out of me, the ones showing cleavage, the one in my bra.

I stare at it and at the comments it is attracting.

I can't take them down. My hacker (yes, I know, it's obvious, but I don't think I can physically cope with admitting that to myself right now) has changed all my settings to "public" so they have as broad an audience as possible. And that's not all. "Beth Soames" has managed to comment on quite a few profiles, including members of my extended family and complete strangers. She's a vicious bitch who is obviously inviting trouble—in fact, she has loads more "friends" now. Some are asking bewildered questions, such as "Who are you?" and "What have I done to deserve this, B?" and "Do you want me to have a word with your mother, Bethany?" An even smaller cohort are trying to defend me, saying I've obviously been hacked, don't respond, report it. But a disturbingly large amount are ripping into her like she is a prime cut of ribs dripping with delicious BBQ sauce.

I blink. I can't quite take it all in. I can't do anything except scroll, read, and despair.

Of course, there is only one person who could've done this. I've seen her do it before. Hell, I've been involved.

More seconds tick by, and Tori-As-Beth spreads more bile, more spite. She's all over my friends' profiles, calling Amy a stupid bitch, telling Indigo to go fuck herself, telling as many of Indigo's Beautiful People friends as she can get her claws into that they're all sad excuses for human beings and I hope someone rapes them to death—I mean, seriously? Yes, I was awful. Yes, I said terrible things to people who probably didn't deserve it. But even I drew a line at rape and death threats. Although these people don't know that.

At least she hasn't brought Dizzy into it, a thought that starts off in relief and ends up in terror, because Tori isn't the kind of person to forget something like that, which means she's holding it back for later.

My stomach twists painfully. Amy's online, pleading with "me," asking "me" what I am doing. She's probably trying to message me, but since I can't log into that either, Tori must be in control of that too, which is enough to have me running to the bathroom.

I rinse my mouth out and sit, shakily, on the edge of the bathtub. It takes three attempts to bring up my contacts, and I swipe through them, always fumbling past Amy's number, like one of those nightmares when something bad is happening but no matter what you do, nothing works, and no matter how hard you try to stop it, everything you try is doomed to failure. Finally, I manage to catch the squirmy fucker and hit the call button. At least this is one form of communication Tori can't take over.

Of course, it's only effective if the other person picks up, and I'm back in my nightmare as the phone rings and rings, finally dumping me to Amy's voicemail, where she declares that she's super busy but she'll get back asap. Yes, she even says "asap." I hang up and try again. More ringing, super busy, get back asap. Oh, come on! Just pick up! Surely you've realized that this isn't me . . .

Finally, on the fourth try, I leave a message. I tell her it isn't me, that I've been hacked—except that's a lie, isn't it? I haven't been hacked. I invited Tori in. "Circumnavigate the Blue Check Mark," I said. "Sure, babe," she said.

I handed all of this to her on a plate, and there's nothing I can do about it. I hang up, and like a masochist seeking their next flagellation, I flip back to Facebook, watching helplessly as more hate spills out from the screen, from "me," at "me," about "me."

Why would she do this? I mean, yes, she was furious with me. And we all know what happens when Tori is furious with someone. Just ask John Corlen. She decimated his life, and I still don't really know why. I thought it had to be something bad for her to go so nuclear, but now? Now I'm not so sure.

And yet, she said she loved me. Told me I was special to her. How could she do this to someone she said she loved? How could she go this far?

Maybe when she said she loved me, what she meant was that she loved using me. Was I just a tool to her, one she tossed into the "Step in front of a very fast train" bin as soon as I stopped doing her bidding? Nothing is good enough except 100 percent compliance. I think back to her "psychobitch" ex and wonder if maybe it was the other way round after all.

There is nothing lower than this.

52: #LOWESTOFTHELOW

Well, whaddaya know? Turns out, there is something lower! Fun, eh?

According to the email I've just received, I am now the proud owner of a "Fat Bitches Love It Hard" account. Needless to say, I've never been a dick pic recipient before. That cherry has now been not so much popped as savaged to bits, if you'll excuse the pun.

SUK ON THAT U FAT BITCH U NO U WANT TOO!!

I'm not sure what I'm appalled more by—the (what I hope is) deformed member assaulting my eyes or the absolutely atrocious spelling.

I zombie-walk back to my room, my eyes fixed on my phone as I scroll through email after email of misogynistic hate. I suppose this is what they mean by "morbid curiosity." It's almost enough to make me look at Fat Bitches Love It Hard to see what Tori has put on there to incite these men to send me such horrific stuff. Almost, but not quite.

It's not far from the bathroom to my bedroom door, but that doesn't stop me from bashing into Brat, who is coming up the stairs.

"Beth? What the fuck is going on with you?" He thrusts his phone under my nose. "You do know you've been hacked?"

It takes me a moment to digest the fact that my now-public Facebook page is on his phone.

"Everyone's talking about it," he says, as if he's reading my mind. "I got a message from Tankie saying you'd gone mental and it was hilarious, then another one from Jason saying you were giving his sister hassle."

"Yeah, I know, I'm dealing with it," I manage to say. Jason's sister? Who the—oh, yeah, Jason Cross, Hayley Cross's brother. Hayley Cross, who bullied me from year 9 to year 11. Okay, not so bothered about that one; in a roundabout way, Tori's actually ticked something off my bucket list.

He snorts. "Yeah, 'dealing with it.' " He does that irritating air quotes thing that unimaginative people who don't know the subtleties of true sarcasm use when they want to seem clever. "What's up? This crap has been going on for hours now, and it isn't like usual hacking. Whoever this is, they've got a real grudge against you."

What surprises me is that he hasn't mentioned the photos. I mean, it was the first thing I saw—all that flesh. I would have thought Brad would be telling me how disgusting I am, but instead he seems . . . concerned?

"I said I was dealing with it."

"Well, you're not dealing with it very well, because they're going apeshit all over everything. I keep telling people you've been hacked, but not everyone's so sure—"

"You've been telling people to lay off?"

"Yeah. Course I have—"

I crumple inwardly. "Oh, God, no, don't do that. Stay out of it. She'll work out within two seconds that you're my brother, and then you'll become a target too." Especially since I once had her track you via GPS, which I am now very much regretting.

"She? What?"

"Just—stay away. Seriously, it's the best you can do, for me and for yourself. The person doing this—they're dangerous. I thought they were my friend, but you have no idea what they're capable of."

"Okay, so this person is what? A troll? Why didn't you just block them and report them straight away?"

I stare at him, dumbfounded. In my determination to be completely miserable, I hadn't even considered this. "Pardon?"

"Why haven't you blocked and reported them?" He talks slowly, like he's addressing a certified imbecile. "You know, make a new account, tell everyone you've been hacked, report the old account, block it, and then tell everyone to do the same. Jesus, Beth, that's, like, How to Deal with a Hacker 101. You really don't have a clue, do you?"

Funny how common sense often comes from the unlikeliest of sources, isn't it? If he wasn't so gross and my brother, I think I could kiss him right now.

"Fucking hell, you noob. I'm amazed this hasn't happened before if this is how stupid you are." At any other time, I'd be yelling at him for being a condescending little prick and that he'd better watch his back because he was just about to lose all his achievements in CoD, but at the moment, he's pretty much on the money.

A new account. A clean slate. Send out friend requests to Amy and everyone else who matters and tell them it's not me. She might not be picking up her phone, but she's definitely online. I might just be able to salvage this situation after all. Report and believe in the powers that be for once. I know, I'm usually the one kicking them in the ankles and giving them major headaches, but right now, I'm grateful they exist. Sure, it won't erase the pictures and it won't stop the vile messages from those horrible websites that Tori signed me up for, but it's a start. At least the people who count will know the truth, and that's all I care about.

"So who is this dick you think hacked you? This is major grudge territory. What did you do to them?"

I shrug. I don't really want to tell him, but I suppose it's the least I owe him, given he's helped me. "Just someone I met online. Thought we were friends, but . . ."

"Fucking hell, you were catfished?" He laughs. I bristle.

"No, I wasn't fucking . . . cat . . . fished . . ."

Oh God.

No.

You hear about it all the time. Like, literally *all the time*. There's even a TV show about it, for God's sake. And we all watch it, smug in the knowledge that we'd never be that stupid, that we'd see right through it all from the start. I mean, how can you not? Surely this is all staged as you'd have to be a right idiot to fall for that, seriously, how do they tie their shoelaces in the morning, they must be total morons . . .

Until it happens to you.

Maybe this was the aim all along. To draw me in, gain my trust, then tear me down, piece by piece, in the most public way possible. To be the ultimate troll. Trolling the trolls.

Was everything just a game to her? All the late-night flirting, the photos, the *I love you*s? She said she was impressed by me, that I was special, and I fell for it hook, line, and sinker. She may as well have said she was a Nigerian prince with a million dollars, or a chiseled model with a thing for chubby girls.

Brad stops laughing. "Look, I'm sure it'll be fine. Everyone will have forgotten by this time tomorrow. That's, like, a thousand years in internet time. Just report them, make sure everyone knows you've been hacked and get them to report it too, and move on. You know the old saying? Don't feed the trolls?"

Bless him, he thinks he's giving me valuable advice. If only he knew.

53: #CATFISHED

I'm back in my room, and a kind of grim determination has settled over me, which is much preferable to the panicked helplessness of earlier. I may not be able to take Tori on directly, but at least I can do my best to stop her from the sidelines.

First things first: new Facebook profile. Bethany Anne Soames. Big pinned announcement: *As you might have guessed my account has been hacked. Please report and block, thank you.* Then I send out friends requests: to Amy, Indigo, Patrick, Auntie Sandie, Uncle Paul, my cousin Frankie who lives in America, the few people from school who tolerated me . . . everyone I can think of, which rather sadly ends up only being about twenty people.

But it's a start.

With each friendship request, I send out a message, reiterating that this is the real me, that my old account has been hacked, please please *please* report and then block them.

To my surprise, the first person who gets back to me is Patrick, via Messenger.

Hey, BB! WTF?! That's major hackage, chick! Didn't think for a min it was really u, tho. Will defo report this fucker and tell everyone else to do the same. Fuckin arsehole hacker! PS: nice pics.

I no u probs didnt want them to go viral, but hey, u may as well own them now. Not bad for a big bird, BB! Paddy x

Oooookkkaaayyy. I'm pathetically grateful for him believing me but could have done without the mention of the pictures. And what does he mean, viral? No, don't look. Can't get distracted.

Thnx P. U think u could get Amy to msg me? Been trying to get hold of her all day and she's not picking up.
Yeah, course! What's goin on with u 2 anyway? Had a fight?

Oh. Well, I guess Amy was never going to be the type to keep her emotions to herself. Sounds like she didn't tell Patrick what the argument was about, though—thank the lord for small mercies, I guess?

It's a very long story. I just want her to know it's not me, and for her to be careful. This hacker is not to be messed with on any level, k? That goes for u and the others too—DO NOT ENGAGE. Just report and block them.
Righty ho captain—whatever u say!
Thanks for helping, Paddy—totes appreciate it xxx
Hey, what are friends for?
Can't stand by watching u get pummeled.
Off to kick butt now. Speak later Px

A rather complicated emotion wells within me. It's a bit like gratitude, but it's also a bit like . . . being happy? And—I don't know—some kind of affection? Whatever it is, it buoys me.

Patrick has my back. And with any luck, Amy might talk to me and everything will be okay.

If I ignore the whole Dizzy thing, of course.

Whatever emotion Patrick briefly coaxed out of me flees like a deer. Because if this works, and Patrick rallies the troops around me and Amy comes back and we all prevail over Tori, it's going to be a million times worse when they find out about Dizzy.

I bite my knuckles, paralyzed by the realization that, sooner rather than later, I am going to have to tell them. And they are going to hate me for it. And I am totally going to deserve that hate.

But for now, Operation Catfish needs to be kicked up a notch.

There are a couple more replies on my new Facebook page, and even a couple of friend requests. I'm not going to add them, though, not yet—can't run the risk of one of them being Tori in disguise. I have to be completely in control of this or it'll all go wrong.

I open my laptop and bring up the secret folder where I saved pictures of Tori. There are quite a few, some innocent, some not so innocent, and I take a deep breath before selecting one and running an image search.

Three seconds later, I've found her.

Unsurprisingly, her name isn't Tori Heidegger. Her name is Adele Durand, and she's an aspiring plus-size model. She lives in Quebec with her fiancé and fluffy gray cat called Claude.

I scroll through her Instagram account, feeling hollow. Even though I knew this would happen, it still hurts. Adele doesn't have many followers, but she seems nice enough. She posts in both English and French, so I don't always know what she's saying, but it seems to be a lot of the old "love yourself" claptrap these girls like to promote. I wonder if Tori ever trolled her, or if she simply left her alone so she could steal her life? It's hard, seeing what I thought was Tori's face, smiling, laughing, pouting, pictures I had treasured, imagining that this was my girlfriend when it was all a lie.

I take a moment to grab a tissue and blow my nose. All fake. All lies.

Time to find out who Tori Heidegger really is.

I am not surprised when my initial Google search brings up nothing. I go through all the different internet handles she used in my presence, but they all come up blank. Then I try different versions of her supposed name: Victoria Heidegger, Vicky Heidegger, Victor Heidegger, Vic Heidegger . . . a couple of hits, but they're obviously completely different people. Hell, Heidegger alone brings up a fucking Final Fantasy character, and I have to laugh—how the hell did I not put that together? She must have seen me coming a mile off once I fell for that one.

If she's a she, of course. She could be a he. She could be absolutely anyone.

And that's the scariest part of it all.

◆◆◆

I keep scrolling through the names, trying to find something that might hint at "Tori" doing something like this to someone else, but there are so many stories out there of people being conned online, there's no way of telling if it's by the same person. It strikes me, a little too late, how sad all of this is. How sad our lives must be, both the perpetrators and the victims, for us to resort to this kind of contact. It takes a special set of awful circumstances for someone to end up in that headspace, and I can't help but wonder what Tori's are. Was the psycho-bitch-ex part true? It would explain a lot. Or was it something else, something even darker? Or maybe she is simply a first-class asshole, an entitled bitch who thought the world should bow before her—and when it didn't, well, I was just another convenient scratchpost.

Or maybe she was one of my victims. Maybe she found out who I was and decided I needed taking down a peg. That thought makes me shiver. Because unlike the other scenarios, that one's personal and completely of my own construction. Did I make the monster? Is this the universe finally telling me it's fed up with my bullshit, and that it's time to sort out my life?

Beside me, my phone buzzes. I seize it—it's Amy, wonderful, lovely Amy, calling me at last.

"Hello?"

"Hi." Amy sounds subdued. "You all right?"

"Yeah. I think so. I'm so sorry about all of this."

"You don't need to apologize. You were hacked. Totally and utterly out of order. Who would do that? Why do they do it?"

Good question. You got a couple of weeks? I might be able to tell you.

"I think it's the girl I met online. You know, the one I told you about the other day? We had an argument, and a couple of days later—boom. I've been played. I should have known. Good things don't happen to me."

The ferocity in which all of this hits me takes me by complete surprise. Before I know it, I'm sobbing, gulping for air, apologizing to Amy for putting her through it, for putting them all through it. Thankfully, I catch myself before my confession leads to Dizzy. I know I need to tell her at some point, but this just isn't it.

By the end of it all, Amy's also crying; for some reason, she's apologizing too, saying she overreacted the other day, and that it doesn't matter if I'm a student or not, all I did was sit in a few lectures, oh, this is all so messed up . . .

"I feel terrible," she sniffs. "Absolutely terrible. But I've reported everything and have spread the word. People are blocking your old account, and I reckon it'll get pulled soon."

"Oh my God, thank you so much," I say, aware of how pathetic that sounds. "And you have nothing to feel bad about. I brought this on myself." In so, so many ways that I can't admit right now.

"No, you didn't. No one asks for this. Bloody hell, what is wrong with these people? First Dizzy, now you . . ."

I shift uncomfortably. "Yeah."

"Are you sure you're okay?"

"I'm fine. I'm going to trust the powers that be on this. I've done all I can. There's no point dwelling on it."

I'm amazed at how sensible I'm managing to sound, and even more amazed that I actually kind of mean it. Once upon a time, I'd be spitting blood, doing everything I could to troll "Tori" back, even if it meant trolling my own page, but now I realize that's futile. Why bother? Seriously, why? With any luck, I have Amy back. That's about as good an outcome as I could wish for. Sure, there's still the Dizzy issue, but let's just focus on the now. That's what all those Mindfulness morons go on about. Stop worrying about the future, and live in the present. It's healthy. It's productive. It's avoidance of the first order, but we don't talk about that. Everyone, chant after me . . .

"Oh, you're so calm! I'd be all over the place if that was me. Look, I've got a lecture this afternoon, not that I need to tell you that"—she giggles nervously—"so I'm a bit busy today, but do you want to go and have a coffee tomorrow? Kind of start anew?"

Fresh tears well. "Yeah. That would be cool. I'd like that a lot."

54: #NEWBOY

Facebook has taken down my old account for breaching community standards. I'm still getting vile emails from all manner of nasty websites where misogynists demand you suck their dicks, but they're easily blockable. I jump like a nervous horse each time my phone buzzes, expecting Wave Two of Tori's Reign of Terror, but it doesn't materialize: no doxxing, no outing on Instagram, no big statements about how I nearly drove Dizzy to suicide, nothing. Bit of an anticlimax, huh?

You might think I'd be letting out a big sigh of relief, but I'm not. In fact, rather than make me feel better, the fact that she seems to be satisfied worries me, because I know Tori's type. I've *been* Tori's type. You never give up until your opponent is completely crushed. So when I go to meet Amy for a coffee a couple of weeks later, I'm still a little on edge.

She's almost back to being her bouncy self with me. I can feel that she's still holding a little bit back; although we agreed to put all of this behind us, we've not been out socially, not properly, since the whole Fake-Student-Gate scandal broke. I actually kind of miss going out with her. Never thought I'd say that, but here we are.

Today, she's grinning, and there's an undercurrent of excitement that makes me smile. Indigo isn't joining us today, like she did last time—it was nice to see her, if you can believe it—but I'm kind of glad about that. I've come to treasure these Amy-and-Me moments. I'm such a big softie at heart.

"So, how's it going?" I ask, sipping on my very fashionable Flat White. Yeah, I know—I'm a hipster now. Maybe I could carry off the fat in a cool, ironic way. I once suspected that the Beautiful People held the secret to living a happy life, but it's becoming increasingly apparent that everybody is actually just winging it. Which means there might be hope for me yet.

"It's going very well," Amy beams, pouring about eight teaspoons' worth of sugar into her own coffee. "Grindle's set us a bitch of an essay, and they're already going on about end-of-term assessments, but apart from that, everything's really cool."

"You need someone to help you revise?"

Amy's smile turns gentle. "If you want. Although I still think you should reapply, Beth. You're really good at it, and it's obvious you love studying."

I scrunch up my face and shake my head. "Nah. Not at the moment, anyway. I've got a couple of application forms for Tesco and the new Lidl. Hoping I can get a job, earn some money, pay my way, then worry about the rest of it."

"Good on you, but I really do think you should try to get on the course, like, legitimately. You'll be wasted working in a supermarket."

She gives me a wide-eyed look of total innocence that no one but Amy could ever get away with. I shake my head and take another sip of my coffee and try not to wince. Ugh, needs sugar. Turns out, some old habits die very hard indeed.

"So, apart from uni stuff, anything else to report? You've been unusually quiet on Facebook recently."

It's a filler question—Amy's life has never been that interesting, even compared to mine—but to my surprise, Amy blushes deeply and says, "Yeah, there is, actually. I think I might have met someone."

"What? Really? Who? Not that Scruffy Dylan guy again?"

"Who? Oh, that knob from the club—yeah, no, not him. Someone else. I met them online."

I can't help it when a cold little shiver chases its way down my spine. "Online? Where?"

"On this horror site I go to. Been posting there for years, you know, reviews and what's your favorite movie and all that. It's all a bit old school, but it's fun. About a month ago, this guy started talking to me, 'cause we're both big Evil Dead fans. Didn't think much of it, you know, I've talked to lots of people about these things"—yeah, I have no doubt about that—"but recently, I dunno . . . things changed. He's sweet. Turns out, he lived around here when he was a kid. At the moment he's studying in Manchester. His name is Anthony, he's twenty-one, he's really cute, and he's single . . ." She lets the last bit dangle, like an enticing bit of fruit.

"Oh." I don't know what else to say.

Amy flourishes her phone at me. And there he is, in a scruffy Evil Dead shirt, giving the camera the ol' devil horns sign. He has floppy hair and bright blue eyes, with a little pixie nose and only a hint of stubble—exactly the kind of guy you'd expect Amy to fall head over heels for. My stomach drops a notch. A little *too* much like the kind of guy Amy would go for.

"So you met him on a horror site, and now you're talking off-grid?" I ask, just to clarify the situation.

Amy nods, cappuccino foam clinging to her upper lip. "We've messaged each other quite a bit. We're friends on Facebook, but *we keep it on the down low. You know, after what happened* to you."

"Yeah. I know," I say, a little more curtly than I intended. "So, what does he want?"

"Want? Nothing. We just chat. Started off about movies, and books, and music, and then, you know. Other stuff . . ." She blushes a bit at that.

"Oh, please don't tell me you're sending him dodgy photos?"

"They're not dodgy! I've got clothes on. Bikinis count as clothes, right?" She giggles at this, like she can't help it, and if it wasn't for a nasty little doubt wriggling around in my guts, I'd be happy for her, because I know how this feels. There is no way I want to rain on her parade, but all of this seems too convenient.

She keeps nattering on about him, showing me a few more photos, including a shirtless one that really has my spidey-senses tingling, because although he is on the skinny side, he's still pretty ripped for a supposedly normal nerd on the street. And then I hate myself, because Amy is a total nerd and is completely, gobsmackingly beautiful, so of course she is going to attract another Oblivious Beautiful Person. Why wouldn't she? His mates are probably sitting there thinking *she's* too good to be true, that she's going to end up breaking his heart, that she simply can't be who she says she is.

"And the best thing is, he's looking at coming down for the weekend so he can go to the Christmas lights being switched on, like he did when he was a kid, and he's suggested we could meet up and go together!" Amy's voice has gone all breathy.

"He's coming down here?" Okay, spidey-senses not so much tingling now as screaming at the top of their lungs. "You're not going to meet him on your own, are you?"

Amy rolls her eyes. "No, Mum. Of course not. I'm not a

complete idiot. That's why I said we should meet at the switch-on, where there are lots of people, and you'll be there, and Indy, and Patrick, and lots of other people."

"I'll be there?"

"Of course you will! Everyone goes to see the Christmas lights being switched on. Even if Tony wasn't coming down, I'd be going. You're from round here, I thought you'd go every year?"

I used to go when I was small, sitting up on my Dad's shoulders. They light up the town square, complete with a massive Christmas tree. I haven't bothered with it since I've been old enough to stay home alone, and I hadn't considered going this year, but if this is where Amy is going to meet "Anthony," then I don't really have a choice.

"I haven't been for a few years, actually," I say, managing to feign a pretty good facsimile of enthusiasm. "Sure, that sounds cool!"

Amy beams, a big proper Amy Grin. "That's so awesome! Then you can meet Anthony and see if he meets your approval. Oh, I am so excited now. I can't wait to tell him!" She does a shuffly little dance in her seat. My fake-enthusiastic smile turns into a grimace, and I bury it into the remains of my coffee, hoping she doesn't notice.

55: #CATFISHEDPARTTWO

Okay, Evil Dead Anthony, your ass is mine. In a manner of speaking, of course.

What, you thought I'd just wait until Saturday night to see if he turned up? No way, Jose. I'm not going to troll him, but a little bit of cyber-stalking? That's okay. It's just research, after all. It's all for Amy's benefit, even if it does make me feel a little bit grubby.

I only have his first name and the memory of his pictures to go on as I trawl Amy's contact list, which turns out to be a rather laborious undertaking given how many "friends" she has. I finally narrow it down to the four Anthonys on her list.

One looks about fifty. An uncle or a friend of the family, I'm thinking.

Another: childhood friend, going by the photos.

Haven't a clue who the third one is. Random friending, probably.

Fourth one—bingo. There he is, with his floppy hair and his pixie nose and his too-good-to-be-true bright blue eyes.

Anthony Helston.

I hold my breath as I click on his name. I don't want to be right. I want him to be as lovely and as innocent as Amy thinks he is. Please don't be creepy. Please don't be creepy . . .

So far, so good. Normal Facebook stuff. Some photos. Some cat memes. Likes horror films, so lots of links to—

Wait a minute. This page is only a few weeks old. There are hardly any posts before the middle of November. Hmm. He's posted loads, like multiple times a day, to make it look like he's been here for ages, but if you look at the actual dates, it's clear this page is new. He also doesn't have that many friends in the grand scheme of things, and they don't interact with him much beyond liking stuff and giving generic "cool, bro!" comments.

My hackles rise, and something else tugs at my attention. Anthony Helston.

His "friends" call him Tony.

Tony Helston.

That would make his initials T.H.

I feel sick. Surely that's a coincidence. Didn't Amy say she'd been talking to him for a while on the horror site? There are links to one all over his profile, so I click one. I wonder if I can work out who he is.

By the looks of it, he's Freekydeeky. I think Amy is, unsurprisingly, HorrorSparkle02, because they've been interacting a lot over the last month, and I don't think anyone else would choose a username like that unless they were being horribly ironic. They do indeed talk a lot about Evil Dead films. It says he's been a member since September this year.

Okay, take a deep breath. Don't call her just yet. You've got one last test.

I download "Anthony's" photos. Run them through a reverse image search.

I sigh wearily.

World, say hello to Rafael Martinez. He's Argentinian. He has a girlfriend who, rather ironically, looks a little bit like Amy.

I'm not sure of his overall interests, given he writes all his posts in Spanish, but he wears a lot of Evil Dead T-shirts and has a life-size cutout of Bruce Campbell. He likes to pose with it.

A horrible, twitchy sense of déjà vu washes over me. I have absolutely no evidence that "Tori" is behind this, but I know in my gut that she must be. She never liked Amy. Always insulted her. She also knew that I *do* like Amy, and hurting her would hurt me.

But this began well before our argument. By the looks of it, she set up this account within a week or so of her first contacting me, even before we shared Facebook details. Since I keep my Facebook profile under wraps, that's worrying, to say the least. It means she knew about Amy long before I told her about her.

And how the fuck did she know Amy likes horror films? *I* didn't know until a couple of weeks ago.

Was she planning this all along?

This is so twisted. If I weren't sickened by it, I'd probably feel some grudging admiration for its deviousness.

I can't tell Amy about this yet. I have to gather as much evidence as I can and show her. Because I'm about to break her heart.

56: #HONEST

I know Amy will be in lectures for most of the day, so I have to risk an evening visit. Amy is pretty excited about this. I might have been, too, if I weren't planning to trash what she thinks is the love of her life.

I gather up all my evidence. I've got my phone, and I pack my laptop, which has a folder on it with everything I can find. It's dark when I get the bus; I hug my bag close to me, as if it's some kind of shield.

Amy's stop is next. I wonder if the driver would let me off early so I can throw up in the bushes?

From the bus stop, it's only a short walk to Amy's halls. I set off way too fast, and before I know it, I'm a panting, sweating mess. Although that might be the anxiety attack that's threatening to take over me. I take in a huge breath, but rather than ease the tightness in my chest, it makes it worse.

Now at the communal door to her halls. The button is just there. Come on, Beth. You've got loads of evidence that "Anthony" isn't who he says he is—you don't even have to mention your suspicions about Tori. You're just looking out for a friend. You care about her and don't want her to get hurt. For once in your miserable life, you're doing the right thing. Okay, so it's making you feel like you've been shot in the stomach, but sometimes the right thing isn't the easy thing. Etc. etc. etc., yadda yadda yadda.

I press the bell. For a moment, I kind of hope no one answers. But before I can kid myself that I've waited for a socially acceptable amount of time and leave, the intercom crackles.

"Yep?"

It's Patrick. Oh joy.

"Hi Patrick, it's Beth—"

"Big Bird! Wow, it's been ages since you've been here. Hang on, buzzing you up . . ."

The door indeed buzzes and unclicks.

No excuses now.

In the lift, I'm not sure my legs can actually hold me up. How come doing something right feels so fucking wrong? I don't think life will ever make sense to me.

Amy's floor. The door's already open.

"H-hello?" I call out.

A head pokes out from around the corner of the communal kitchen area. "Hey BB! She's in!"

I nod at Patrick as Amy's bedroom door opens. She runs out, all smiles and glitter, and gives me a hug.

"Hey, hun!" She's beaming. Oh, why does she have to be beaming? "Wanna drink?"

"Yes," I say, a little too quickly.

"Voddie and Coke? I would offer something better, but *someone*"—she yells it out—"nicked all the tequila and margarita mix."

Patrick's head pokes back out. "Whoopsie!"

Amy pokes her tongue out at him, and he roars with laughter. "Anyway," she says as she turns back to me, "I took your advice and keep it all in my room now. Means it's room temperature, but at least I get to drink it."

She wanders back into her room. I follow her, stiff and nervy. She gets two plastic tumblers out and pours generous measures. I down mine in one.

"Wow, you really needed that. You okay? You seem . . . weird."

That's an understatement.

I sit on her bed and pull my bag onto my lap. Now that I'm here, I have no idea how to start this, despite having gone over it about a million times in my head. Amy, you know that guy Anthony you told me about? Well, he isn't who he says he is. I'm sorry, Amy, but Anthony isn't real. Amy, hun, you won't want to hear this, but you have to—

"Uh, I, uh, I have something to show you." I pull out my laptop and turn it on. Oh, God, why did I turn it off? It's going to take an age to reboot now, and Amy's going to ask questions—

"What's that? Why have you brought your laptop with you?" Bingo . . . "You could have used mine." She gestures with one hand to her far more expensive model. "What's going on?"

I tap in my password. Hurry up, come on come on come on . . .

"Beth, what is it?"

She sets her drink down and sits next to me. I can feel how tense she is. There's a little crease between her eyes as she frowns. God, she's adorable. Am I really going to do this to her?

Finally, my laptop springs to life. "What's your Wi-Fi password?" I ask.

"Uh, hang on." She gets back up and squints at a sticker stuck to her noticeboard. "47245KLF."

I nod and finally bring up my Facebook. I also find the little folder I've stored all my evidence in, and start selecting images.

"What have you got there? Hey, that's Anthony. Why have you saved his pictures?" There's a hint of annoyance there now. Maybe I should start explaining.

"Because—he's not Anthony," I say. I bring up Raphael Martinez's Instagram page. "*He* is."

Amy grabs my laptop and starts clicking on pictures. The little crease between her eyes deepens. "What is this?"

"You've been catfished, Amy," I say, as gently as I can. "I looked because it happened to me, and I don't want you to go through the same thing—"

"Wait a minute! I told you about Anthony, and the first thing you do is go and authenticate him? Bloody hell, Beth!"

She's angry, and she has every right to be. Now, if I can just get her to look at the other evidence, then she can turn that anger onto "Anthony."

"I know, it's shitty, and if he had been authentic I would never, ever have brought this to you, but he isn't. Look. He's using this guy's image to lure you in. Didn't it strike you as weird that his Facebook account is so new? And that he made it shortly after he met you on the horror site?"

"He was hacked! Like you! He had to make a new account!"

"I guessed he might tell you something like that, but Amy, this could be really bad. Really, really bad. You see, the dates—his name—I think it's the same person who hacked my account—"

"Jesus Christ, now you just sound paranoid."

And I do, I know I do. But I also know I'm right.

"I know how all this sounds, but please, listen to me. It all adds up. I met 'Tori' online. She pretended to like all the things I did, and I thought I loved her and that she loved me. She stole another woman's identity to lure me in, and then burned everything I had to the ground. And now I think she's trying to do the same thing to you."

"And why the hell would she do that?" Amy drains her drink and slams the cup down so hard the plastic cracks. "I don't see the connection."

I take in a deep breath. Here goes nothing. "I think she's doing this to hurt me. She knows that by humiliating you, I'll be upset—"

"Are you kidding me? You think this is about you? I meet a guy online, and all of a sudden, it's about you?" Amy stands up slowly, her face hardening. "Fucking hell, Beth. I guessed the whole student thing might have been a cry for help. It upset me at first, but Christ, we've all been there, so I was willing to give you another chance. But this? This is sick!"

"But the photos—"

"All that proves is he nicked some good-looking guy's photos. Doesn't mean he isn't real."

"Amy, look at it! This is classic! Whoever this is, they're playing us like fools. You have no idea how dangerous this person is, what they are capable of. It goes beyond just hacking your account and posting vile pictures. They will try to take control of every single aspect of your life, to break you down, to destroy you—"

"Oh, for God's sake. Listen to yourself. No one gives enough of a fuck about anyone to do that—"

"Amy, stop being so naive all the time! I know what they're capable of, because I used to do it myself!"

She's now giving me a "cute bird is confused" look, with her head cocked to one side and a whole new frown in place. "Do what yourself?"

I close my eyes, because the time has come. I'd hoped to put it off as much as I could, but there was no way I was going to be able to keep this to myself forever. Wish me luck.

"I was a troll. That's how I know this person. She said her name was Tori. I mean, I dunno if it's a she, but let's assume that for now. She complimented me a lot, and I fell for it. We used to go trolling together. We targeted the pretty girls—you know, the yoga-doing, vegan-eating skinny bitches who everyone adores. It was only when Dizzy hurt herself that I realized it was wrong, and I stopped . . ."

"Hold on, what does this have to do with Dizzy?"

Oh shit. Had kind of meant to hold that bit back.

"I—seeing what happened with Dizzy made me realize I had to stop, because I'd done that to other people and . . ."

The frown clears as the light dawns. "Oh my God. Did you troll Dizzy?" she whispers.

"I didn't mean for anything bad to happen! It only started because she was so mean to you, so stuck up, and so I thought we might teach her a lesson—"

"Jesus Christ, Beth," Amy whispers.

"I know, but then Tori took it to a whole other level, beyond anything I intended, and that's what I'm trying to tell you. If this is the same person, they'll prey on your weaknesses, and before you know it, it's all gone to shit." My throat closes over. I can't say anything else.

Amy's eyes are bright, both with anger and unshed tears. "So there's us, thinking you were a real hero, helping us sort out Dizzy, when in fact—you were responsible for tormenting her in the first place?"

No point in making excuses now. All I can do is nod.

"Get the fuck out," she whispers.

"Amy—"

"No! Get the fuck out of my room. You're fucking toxic,

Bethany. I've given you so many chances, and every single time, you let me down. Fuck you. I am done with you. So get out. Now!"

She's yelling, and I'm cringing. I deserve this.

I grab my laptop and stumble to Amy's door as she continues to shriek at me. In the corridor, Indigo, Richard, and Patrick are staring at me, eyes owl-wide.

"What's going on?" Indigo asks.

I can't answer her, but Amy can. From her room, she calls out: "Beth trolled Dizzy. She's responsible for what happened. I can't fucking believe it!"

Indigo's eyes harden. Patrick and Richard look confused.

"You did *what*?" Indigo snarls.

"Beth, why?" Patrick asks, a little hoarsely. At least he used my real name this time.

"I can't—"

"Fuck off," Indigo says. "Fuck off, and don't come back. You are not welcome here anymore."

Judging by the way her hands are clenched into hard fists, I'm guessing she wants to hurt me. Behind me, Amy is sobbing. There's nothing I can do but bolt out of the door.

57: #DOTHERIGHTHING

I can't think. My usual deal of catastrophizing to the point of panic doesn't go far enough this time, because there is nothing to catastrophize about: the worst has literally happened. I have lost everything.

I wander the streets, not even caring if anyone sees me. My usual tactics for remaining invisible are all but forgotten. I check Facebook on my phone; my "friends" are dropping like flies.

Shame doing the right thing doesn't cancel out all the other shitty stuff I've done.

I try to call Amy. My phone rings once and then goes straight to voicemail. Looks like she's already blocked me. I leave a message anyway.

"Amy, it's Beth. I'm sorry for all of this, but please—listen to me. Don't let this Anthony fool you. The last thing I wanted to do was hurt you. I understand if we can't be friends anymore, I can accept that, I just want to keep you safe. Nothing else."

I'm surprised at how calm I sound. I'm beyond tears, beyond hysteria. There is nothing left for me to do but walk and pray and despair.

I have no idea what time it is when I get home. Everything's dark, so it must be late. I can't hear the TV, so I'm guessing

Mum's gone to bed. I know I should check, but I don't. I don't even raid the fridge or check the biscuit tin. I just trudge upstairs and lie fully clothed on my bed, staring at the ceiling.

Whatever happens next, it is totally out of my hands.

But I still can't help wondering why "Tori" would do this. What do they get out of it? I could kind of understand doing the public internet thing, because you can watch that play out—it's there for everyone to see. But this? This feels pointless. Tori is not here to see this happen. Unless she *is* . . .

I shake my head. No. Don't want to even consider the possibility that Tori is someone I know. Although that would make sense . . .

I curl myself up into a ball, or do as good a job as I can. No knee-hugging here; not with this stomach. Oh, Amy, I've really fucked this up, haven't I? I should have left well enough alone. I thought I was being so clever. Dizzy *was* a bitch to you, and to me. All I wanted to do was to punish her for it. I actually lied when I told Tori I thought she was okay, because deep down, I still think she was nasty. It's funny how everyone has forgotten how prickly she was, how judgmental she could be. No, she's an angel now. All sins forgiven.

I wonder if my sins would be forgiven if I hurt myself, too.

It's a seductive thought. It wouldn't be hard. Lots of knives in the kitchen. You don't even need a big one. Just a sharp one. Run a fruit knife through the sharpener a few times, then slice your skin like it's a good, rare steak—easy-peasy. Instant sympathy. Instant forgiveness. A blood sacrifice to wash away all sins.

I risk a peek at Facebook and instantly regret it.

Two faced bitch.

Ruin her life.

Can't believe I trusted you.

Fat cow

You'll get yours, fat bitch.

Turns out, Tori didn't have to mention Dizzy to destroy me; I've managed to do that all by myself. What makes this even better is that I don't even know who half these people are.

Two Facebook pages in less than a month. Wow. Even MidnightBanshee would have been impressed with that turnover.

◆◆◆

I must have fallen asleep, because it's morning now and I don't remember dawn happening. My phone is out of charge, my laptop unplugged, and I think they're going to remain that way.

I don't get up. Even dragging myself out to use the loo requires a conscious effort. Why not lie here in my own piss? It's what I deserve.

Nothing to do. Nothing to say. Nothing to live for.

Funny, it wasn't that long ago when every day was like this. But I didn't know what I was missing then. I do now.

I'm sorry, Mum. I get it now.

58: #IWIN

In the end, it's hunger that gets the better of me, forcing me out to feed the beast. It's been grumbling away for a while now, making me feel weak and weepy. I grab a packet of biscuits, a couple of bags of crisps, and some mini cheeses from the fridge, along with a couple of cans of Coke: all food I don't have to worry about preparing. I go back upstairs and scarf down the lot without tasting any of it.

Later, I plug in my laptop, simply so I can watch something. Maybe a movie will fill the yawning void inside me, or at least help me ignore it for a couple of hours. As I log into Netflix, in the corner of my screen, a notification pops up: an email.

I almost don't look. Why bother? It's probably just more hate. But I do despise an untidy inbox. And can it really be worse than what I've already seen?

I click on the notification. I don't recognize the email address. The subject line is empty. Weird.

I open the email. It contains two hyperlinked words.

I WIN

My stomach lurches. I know exactly who this is from.

I hover the mouse cursor over the words, revealing a link to a video hosting site I don't recognize. It could be anything.

Well, whatever it is, it's probably loaded with malware, so I'd better leave it be.

Unless . . .

No. Delete it. Don't invite her back in. Get rid of it. Close the book. No more. Do what thou wilt, for I am done with thee.

That works for about an hour. I start watching something suitably trashy, but even that can't smother my curiosity. *I win.* Win at what? She already destroyed my life weeks ago. What else could she do?

Oh God. Amy. I thought setting her up to get her heart broken by an online boyfriend was bad enough, but if there's more—

Screw malware; I have to know what's going on. I click the hyperlink. It takes a couple of seconds for it to load, and even longer for me to work out what is going on, but when I do, my insides turn glacial.

The footage is low res, exactly what you'd expect from a cheap, built-in webcam.

It shows Amy. In her dorm.

She's not doing much, just sitting at her desk. I've got a fantastic shot of her cleavage, because she's wearing a tank top and I am obviously watching her via her laptop webcam. I know she's oblivious to the presence, because she spends a good fifteen seconds delicately excavating her nose with her little finger before wiping it on her knee.

In the corner of the screen are two little red numbers. At first, I don't know what they mean, but when they change, I realize they're a countdown. That can't be good. What is Tori going to do? Arrange a private floorshow? But how would she even do that?

I sit, gnawing on my fingers. I have to tell Amy. Warn her.

But she won't listen to me. I reach out for my phone, fumbling it a couple of times, but before I can find Amy's number, another email pops up. This one is from a different account and is also anonymous. This time, the link says:

GAME OVER

What the ever-living *fuck*?! Tori has obviously scheduled this to send when the other one was opened, which means she's monitoring me. I glance up—the little bit of tape I've put over my webcam is still there, thank God. This time, I don't hesitate clicking the link.

This one is from an image hosting site. When it finally loads, I'm presented with a screenshot, showing a snippet of conversation between two people in a private chatroom.

The man is called Pete.

The woman . . . Amy.

Pete: I'll be in the carpark. U walk past, lookin at ur phone. U dont notice me. Im in the shadows, near my van. I walk behind u and say ur name.

Amy: Omg, this is so hot. I'll answer "yeah" and then u grab me and drag me into the van.

Pete: u gotta fight tho, or it won't work. Won't feel real.

Amy: oh ill scream good. Ud better tape my mouth shut before someone calls the cops. ;)

Pete: I'll be ready, babe. U fight me, and I'll give u the ride of ur life . . .

It carries on like this. I want to say it's just a fantasy, it's okay, some people have those—but this isn't just a conversation. This is two people arranging to live out that fantasy. And one of those people has got to be Tori, pretending to be Amy. Setting Amy up.

It's the sickest thing I've ever seen.

I've also figured out what the red counter on her webcam is for.

It's counting down the hours before Amy meets "Anthony" on Saturday night.

❧ ❧ ❧

Amy's still blocking my number, but I still ring her a million times, leaving increasingly desperate voicemails, begging her to ring me back. I even resort to stalking her on Facebook; she's so naive that her settings are public, so it isn't hard. I don't even have to log in, so I can avoid the torrent of hate. #winning.

She seems to have calmed down. She's sharing a lot of stuff about her Saturday plans, tagging "Anthony" into every post, while he in turn expresses his excitement over finally meeting "his girl." I can see why she's fallen for him—he's as adorable as she is. She deserves someone like him. Or would, if he were real.

By Friday morning, I'm having major panic attacks. I didn't sleep a wink the night before, and no matter how hard I try, I can't get Amy to pick up. So I do the only thing left at my disposal: I go to her halls.

I know there's a very good chance I'm going to get punched. If I had to lay money, I'd put it on Indigo, peace-loving vegan though she is (unless she's drunk, of course). But a black eye is a very small price to pay when it comes to saving your best friend from an orchestrated assault.

There's a little part of me that's still hoping all of this is a hoax. Surely, even Tori can't be this evil. The webcam thing is bad enough, but setting up Amy to unsuspectingly meet someone with a very sick fantasy, who thinks she's consented to

319

acting that fantasy out? That's way beyond anything I'd thought her capable of. Beyond criminal, beyond vile, beyond evil.

I sit near the front of the bus, staring straight ahead. I twist my fingers together, over and over, practicing what I have to say in my head, because I know I'm only going to get one shot at this; no time for umming or ahhing, just straight up "You're in danger. Look at this."

I've saved the screenshot as evidence on my phone, and I have the link to the video hosting already set up. All I have to do is get someone to look at it. It doesn't even have to be Amy, it just has to be someone who knows her, who likes her, who cares.

Amy's stop. I march off despite my legs feeling weak, my chest feeling wobbly, my phone in hand just in case I bump into someone on the way.

I don't. No one is around. I check the time: four o'clock. She should be back from lectures. Unless she's gone to the union. Oh, God, please don't let her be there. It's hard enough doing this here.

Okay. Coming up to her halls now. I dart my head around, looking for any signs of life, but everything's quiet. I reach up to press the buzzer with trembling hands, unsure if I have the strength.

One second. Two. Three. Come on, someone has to be in. Someone's *always* in. Dare I press again? Maybe I should. Just to be su—

"Yep?"

Oh, bollocks. It's Indigo. If there's one person I'm not going to convince, it's her.

"Hi Indigo, I know you don't want to see me, but I really need to talk to Amy, or show something to you, this is not me fucking about, I mean it, she's in real dang—"

"Seriously? I thought we made it clear last time that you're not welcome here, Beth. Fuck off."

"I know, but she's in danger, just please let me up—"

The line goes dead.

Tears of frustration and dread sting the backs of my eyes. Well, screw her. I'm going to wait. They can't stay up there forever. At some point, one of them has to go out, and then I'll pounce.

I don't care what I have to do. I'm going to warn Amy.

59: #PLANB

I sit by the rubbish bins. It feels fitting. Plus, it's a bit hidden and not too far away from the communal entrance, so if someone opens the door, I should be able to dart up and catch it before it closes.

Yeah, stop snickering at the back. I can totally dart when I want to.

I've been here for half an hour now. It's cold, and my bum's gone numb, but I'll stay here all night if I have to.

I hear the unmistakable chatter of other people heading this way. I risk a glance around the bins. No one I know, but they're getting closer. And closer. And . . . yes! They're punching in the code to the door! Wish Amy had given me that. Never thought to ask. If I was in a movie, I'd be squinting purposefully now, memorizing the sequence, but yeah— that ain't gonna happen. Instead I scramble up to a crouch, ignoring the burst of fizzing agony in my buttocks as they come back to life.

I have to time this right. The door is heavy, and so it takes a good few seconds to swing closed. They're heaving the door open . . . and going through . . . and RUN! Or, you know, stagger over as quickly as I can and catch the door handle by my fingertips. Whatever works, right?

I wait for the lift to take me to Amy's floor, praying to every single god I can think of that the door to her floor is open. That would make things so much easier. Won't have to deal with any gatekeepers then—just head directly to Amy's room. Or maybe she'll be in the kitchen.

Up, up, up . . . and relax. The lift comes to a stop, and the door opens, and Prayer #1 is dashed: the door is shut. Bugger. Well, time to pull up my big girl pants and knock.

Now, if I was clever, I might have thought about printing off some screenshots so I could write down what was going on, then slip it under Amy's front door, and yes, I hate myself for not thinking of that a couple of hours ago when I was at home, but oh well, too late now.

I wait. I can hear movement from behind the door, then a shout of "You answer it, you lazy bastard!" followed by some more muffled conversation, and finally a rattle and a click as someone unlocks the door.

Thank the gods, it's Amy.

Her expression goes from benign to shocked in a split second. The clock is ticking.

"I know I'm not supposed to be here, but I need you to listen to me," I manage to garble out. Amy is working her mouth, obviously trying to find her voice, but thankfully, her astonishment at my audacity is stopping her from telling me exactly where I can go. "Just five minutes, then I'll be gone and you'll never have to see me again—"

"Oh, for God's sake!" This comes from behind Amy. "What did I tell you before? Have you been hanging around, waiting to sneak in? Jesus, you're fucking psycho."

"Indigo, I know, I'm sorry, but this is important—"

"Like fuck it is. Amy, just walk away. Beth, I don't know

what you think you're going to achieve by doing this, but I'll lay it out as plainly as I can. I know you fancy her, but she does not fancy you. Whatever it is you have planned, it isn't going to work, okay? Now leave, before I call the police."

Wait—what? My mouth gapes open. I don't fancy Amy! Do I?

I do think she's pretty and sweet and OH MY GOD, this is so not the time to be worrying about these things!

I fumble with my phone, trying to open it so I can show her the screenshot, the webcam footage, everything that proves she's in real danger, but Patrick and Richard have joined Indigo now; Patrick looks a bit sheepish, and Richard just looks scared, but then again, Richard always looks vaguely scared. Amy, on the other hand, is giving me a look that might just, if you squint at it, contain a morsel of curiosity. I need to seize that . . .

I manage to get a "please" out before Indigo drags Amy back and slams the door in my face.

"I mean it!" she yells through the door. "If we see you around here again, we're calling the cops!"

Amy didn't get a word in edgewise. If she was less worried about what other people thought of her, she might have been able to tell Indigo to leave her alone and let her fight her own battles. But she isn't, not that I'm in any position to judge her for that.

I let out a long, furious sigh that wants to be a scream. If only I'd thought of printing off some screenshots!

But that probably wouldn't have worked either, because everyone knows Photoshop exists. They'd probably accuse me of staging it as just another example of how mental I am.

I leave the building and trudge toward the bus stop. No point hanging around halls; it's dark and it's cold and I'm hungry and I really do think Indigo would call the cops if she found me there, and I don't put it past her to check. I'd think she was being a good friend if it wasn't for the fact that she's also being a complete dumb bitch. Does she seriously think I'm only doing this because I fancy Amy?

Of course I don't fancy Amy! I just want to keep her safe.

60: #PLANC

So, on to Plan C.

I know where Amy is going to be: in town, at the Christmas light switch-on, hoping to meet Anthony. But Anthony isn't going to be there. Instead, a creepy dude who fantasizes about raping people will be.

From what I saw, Rapey Pete thinks he is arranging to meet Amy in the car park. The main car park next to the square is an old multistory one, which is exactly the kind of place I'd expect to meet someone like Rapey Pete if I were writing a screenplay.

I'd like to think that Amy's sensible enough not to go meet someone in a multistory car park, or that if she does she'd take her friends with her. But Tori's a master manipulator, and who knows what poison she's been dripping into Amy's ear to get her to do what she wants.

All of this is very scary, but it also makes Plan C quite simple. Keep Amy away from Rapey Pete. I'll just stick as close as I can to Amy, without being caught. If Anthony isn't Tori and all is above board, then how she deals with him is up to her. But if Anthony is Tori and her plan to get Amy to meet Rapey Pete in the car park works—well, I'll be there.

My main problem is how to find Amy in the first place. The square is pretty big, and there will be hundreds, if not thousands, of people here, so it's going to be absolutely packed. Luckily, Amy's still in thrall of The Great Social Media Beast, pinning her locations and posting pics left, right, and center, which means I should be able to keep tabs on her. Plus, it's easy to find someone if you follow them from their initial destination.

The other challenge is making sure she doesn't see me. I'm not exactly nondescript, but I'm trying my best. Black hoodie pulled up, scarf to help cover my lower face (although I'm already regretting that. So hot!), hair tied back; with my head down and my hands in my pockets, I'm just another fat girl in the crowd.

I hover at the end of the road. I know Amy has to walk past here to get to the square. I've checked her Facebook update, and she's already excited, gushing about Anthony, saying she can't wait to meet him. Judging by his responses, he is equally excited, saying he's "on the motorway, not long now!" No location pin for him, though. Funny, that.

She's also told everyone she's walking as it's "such a lovely night, all cold and crisp and clear," and has tagged a few people with her. Indigo is part of that group, along with some other names I recognize from uni. So far, she's sticking with her group. Good.

I wonder how long that will last.

I can hear a group of girls chattering and shrieking in the distance. I step back into the bus shelter and get my phone out. To anyone looking, I'm waiting for a bus. Just have to hope no one from Amy's group recognizes me.

The group draws nearer. My heart thunders in my head. Closer, closer, closer—then past me. No one looks my way. Amy's not with them; it's yet another group of random girls.

How many is that now? Four? I don't know. I'm losing count.

Oh, Jesus. What if she decides not to come this way? To take a taxi or something? If she got the bus (which would be ridiculous, as it's, what, a five minute walk, tops? She'd be sitting at the stop longer than it would take her to walk it) she'd have to get off here, but there's always that chance she's going to throw a massive curveball and I'm going to miss h—

Another group approaches. Head down. Look at phone. Make yourself as small as possible. Come on, Beth, you're good at this. Think invisible thoughts.

I recognize that laugh. I risk a peek. I also recognize that walk and those wings and, yep, she's already bought one of those flashy LED-wand thingies from a dodgy street merchant. It's Amy, with about five others. She's laughing, bouncing down the road opposite me, obviously excited. I send up a little prayer of thanks. This is about as good as I could expect. She's on the other side of the road, so her chances of spotting me are even slimmer than before. And she's carrying a great big flashy beacon that I can follow. Okay, so are half the other people at this godforsaken event, but there doesn't seem to be anyone else wearing fake glittery wings over the top of a purple coat. Thank God for Amy's complete devotion to being an *individual*.

I keep a safe distance. There's no entry fee, so I wander into the square, making sure I'm behind the group at all times. There's a heart-stopping moment when a large group of feral youths barges past me, snarling as they suck on their badly rolled fags, forcing me to stop. When I finally manage to get past them I think I've lost her; I can't see her, can't see that stupid flashing stick, can't see the idiotic wings, I can't see her, oh fuck oh fuck oh f—

Then I hear a familiar shriek, and she runs past me, not five feet away. I cringe back, trying to use the crowds to disguise me as she flings her arms around someone's neck. A hard lump forms in my throat. She used to do that to me.

I swallow. Got to keep my mind on the mission. So far, so good—no sign of "Anthony," and no sign of her leaving her little group. She looks at her phone and frowns, then holds it up so her new friend can read it. The friend shrugs. Amy looks a bit upset. The friend slings an arm around her shoulders, and I have to look away. I wonder if I could risk getting a bag of chips? They smell so good. Maybe a hot dog. With onions. God, those onions smell amazing. I wonder what they do to them? They never smell that good when I cook them up at home—

I glance over to where Amy was.

Amy is no longer there. The friend is, but Amy's gone. My heart lurches as I scan the crowd. I can pick out a few people she was with, including Indigo, but no Amy. Oh no, Amy, no no no no. Please don't go off and meet him on your own.

What do I do? What if she's just gone to get a drink or some food? She could be back in a minute. But she could also be making her way over to the car park, on her own, looking for a boy who doesn't exist. If I stay here, no one will be able to stop it, but if I go and she hasn't left, then I definitely will lose her, and if the car park thing's been changed, I won't be able to follow her and fuck, I need to calm down, come on Beth, just think, think, make a decision.

Ask one of the friends? No, that's creepy, and if Indigo sees you, you can forget finding Amy.

Try your luck and ring her? She won't answer, she's blocked your number, remember?

Look on Facebook, okay, yeah, that's an idea, see if she's written anything . . . yeah, yeah, good, photos of people with LED sticks, lovely, where are you, Amy, where are y—

Another photo, a selfie taken near the library. That's near the car park. And a tag: *He's here!! Off to meet my boi!*

I stuff my phone back into my pocket and half-walk, half-run in the direction of the multistory car park. It looms over the buildings that border the square, black and foreboding against the sky. Behind me, there's the whine of a microphone, and a voice echoes out, telling us it's nearly time to light the tree.

I still can't see Amy. I dart over the road and down an alley, dodging small groups of latecomers. Either she's turned that stupid stick off, or she's gone another way. Crap. Still, there's only one entrance, so she has to be there.

Away from the square, the streetlights flicker and hiss. More people drift out from the car park—families, mainly, all looking a bit hunted, obviously wondering why they bothered parking in such a horrible place. That's good. Good that people are around. If Rapey Pete is in there, then there's a good chance someone will hear.

Closer to the car park and still no sign of her. I hate this place. It stinks of rotten concrete and stale piss. Obscenities crawl up its walls. It's almost too stereotypical; if this was a movie, you'd be yelling "Holy shit, don't go in there!" at the screen. Oh, Amy, where are you?

Suddenly I see it. The faint flash of blue, red, green, then back to blue: that stupid LED stick thing. It has to be her.

I jog across the road. She's farther into the car park than I'm comfortable with—she's not waiting by the entrance at all but is actually inside. I duck under the barrier; the cubicles that flank them have been empty since the payment machines got installed, so I can't even ask a guard if a pretty girl in a purple coat came this way.

The lights have gone again. Where the hell is she? The concrete and piss are now joined by engine oil and exhaust fumes. My footsteps echo around me. Why aren't these places properly lit? It's like they *want* something to happe—

Just up ahead, there's a scream. Not a little one. A proper, big, human-in-distress shriek. Everything inside me leaps, and I run.

And there, I see her. A man has her. He's not very tall but quite stocky. She's struggling. He's trying to clamp his hand over her mouth. For a second, I can't do anything but watch.

I am no longer imagining this; this is real. The man takes a step back, dragging Amy toward his van. He thinks this is a game. He's not going to let her go, because this is what he thinks it's all about.

I tense. Time to put my weight to some good use.

Patrick once told me I'd make a good rugby player, and boy, now is the time to test that theory. Head down, I charge forward, not caring that I sound like a steam train, ignoring the flare of pain in my legs. The man looks up, his eyes wide, just before I barrel into both of them.

If I'd been any smaller, it might not have worked, but the force of my impact knocks them both flying. I grunt as I hit the floor, my hip screaming at it smacks against the concrete.

"What the fuck?" the man cries. He pushes Amy away and tries to scramble to his feet.

"Amy, get away! Find security!" I yell and haul myself upright. She's been knocked on her back and is looking at me like I'm some kind of alien. Next to her is the plastic flashy stick, now broken. The shards left behind look sharp.

I hear Amy whimpering as she finds her own feet. The man, Rapey Pete (I presume), looks both terrified and livid, and it strikes me that knocking over a heavily built guy who actively admits to rape fantasies in car parks is probably one of my stupider ideas.

I grab the broken stick and brandish it in front of me, like a sword.

"What the fuck, bitch?" Rapey Pete snarls.

I don't answer him, just lunge out with the stick, because I am not fucking about.

He dodges easily, calling me insane, and then punches out at me, catching me on my jaw. Pain explodes across my face, and I reel back.

There's a screech and the sound of hissing, followed by a man screaming.

Suddenly, the world is filled with people. People yelling, people running, hands grabbing me, asking me if I'm okay, what's going on, oh my God, she's bleeding—

"I wasn't doing nuffin, that mad bitch just attacked me!"

—Amy sobbing, begging me to be okay while I sit there, my head spinning, my jaw and hip throbbing. Next thing I know, there's the sound of a scuffle as Rapey Pete tries to make a bolt for his van and a deep voice declares, "No you don't, mate."

Amy's crying again: "He grabbed me, he attacked me, he said he was going to rape me!"

And Rapey Pete's calling her a bitch: "This was arranged, it's not what you think it is, fucking hell, get off me . . ."

I feel oddly detached from all of it. Maybe I have a concussion. It's certainly a weird sensation. I can't make out much; I'm still sitting on the floor, and I'm seeing everything strobing through a crowd of legs. My hearing's gone a bit funny, too, like someone put a goldfish bowl over my head. I want to lie back, but someone's holding me upright. Please, just let me lie down. The cold concrete against my hot jaw would be so nice . . .

"Beth. Beth! Stay awake!" My eyes flutter open. It's Amy. I try to smile, but it's too painful. Shit, is that a broken tooth? I probe it with my tongue. I think it is. Oh, fucking hell, as if I don't have enough to contend with. First fat, now toothless.

The car park lights up blue, and a blast from a horn echoes throughout the building. It's so loud, it makes my head pound even more. More running, and someone kneels down beside me.

"You all right, love? What's your name?"

"Beth," I manage, although it sounds more like *Beszh*.

"Beth? Okay, Beth, you're going to be fine. Everything's going to be fine."

61: #HEROINE

My jaw isn't broken, just badly bruised. I don't know what pain-killers they've given me, but they're gooood. When the doctors say I'm up to it, a police officer comes to interview me. I tell him everything: Tori, Anthony, Rapey Pete, the lot. The cop asks if he can take my phone and laptop as evidence, and I agree. I give them everything, because I am as desperate as they are to find out who Tori really is.

One good thing: it gets Mum out of the house. Unfortunately, it also makes her sob like a child when she sees me, and I end up doing most of the reassuring. Even Brad looks shocked and mumbles stuff at me about being stupid, but also being brave.

Mum stays with me for a bit, until Amy turns up. She gives me a weak smile and tells me she's going to find a cup of tea. She turns the smile on Amy, who gives an equally awkward one back as she leaves. Gotta love being British.

Amy has a big scrape across her cheek, and her arm has a massive bandage on it.

"I haven't broken anything, it's just a nasty graze. They just wanted to put this on so it didn't get infected. They've rung Mum and Dad, and they're coming down now, so I'm hanging around here for a bit." She sits in Mum's recently vacated chair. "You were amazing."

"I was an idiot," I say.

"Is your jaw broken?"

"Nah, just bruised. Bastard knocked one of my teeth out, though."

Amy tries to smile, her eyes bright with unshed tears.

"It's not your fault."

"But it is," Amy says. "I should have listened to you. You tried to warn me, but I ignored you. I was so stupid! Going to the car park like that—bloody hell."

"You're not the first, and you won't be last."

She shudders. "He's saying I consented to this. Says he has evidence. In a chatroom. Says we were just acting out a fantasy, and you got the wrong end of the stick and went berserk."

"I know. I could hear him yelling it out when the police arrested him."

"I hope he goes to prison."

"Me too. Although, technically, he's not lying. I saw a screenshot of the conversation you allegedly had with him, arranging all of this. The creep pretending to be Anthony masterminded it all."

"You still think it's the same creep who hacked you?"

"Yeah. The one I should have seen coming a mile off but didn't. I'd show you, if I could, but the police took my phone."

"Bummer. Can't even look at sphynx cats."

I want to smile, but it hurts too much. "I know, right?"

Amy looks at her hands, and then at the ceiling. "So, what now?"

"I dunno. I apologize again, I suppose, and hope we can put this all behind us?"

"Yeah. I think I'd like that. Doesn't mean I've forgotten the shitty thing you did to Dizzy—"

"I wouldn't expect you to."

"But at the same time, I think I can see how this person used you. Manipulated you into doing terrible things. I got caught up in something similar with so-called Anthony, so I guess I get it."

I sigh. "No, it's different. You fell for a scam. I actively pursued her. I wanted to impress her. Them. If I hadn't been trolling . . ." I trail off. How do I even begin to explain this? No matter the outcome, I still started this. "Tori—Tori made me feel wanted. Powerful, even. But then Dizzy . . ." I swallow. "After that, I wanted to blame her, you know? I wanted to make it Tori's fault. But it was mine. I was so wrapped up in my own problems I couldn't admit that what I was doing was wrong. But I can now. I was so, so wrong."

Amy perches next to me, so our shoulders touch. She gives me a small smile. "Like I said, I think it's going to be a while before everyone wraps their head around this, but ultimately, you made a mistake."

I snort. Yeah. A mistake.

"Don't sneer." Amy nudges me gently. "What you did was wrong, but what that Tori person did was, like, a thousand times worse."

"I was on that path, though. In a way, you saved me."

Amy blushes a bit and leans over to hug me. I hiss a bit as her shoulder bumps my jaw, which prompts lots of "Oh my God, I'm sorry!"s, but it's a good hug, a warm hug, and it's definitely the one thing I need.

"I've got to go and wait for Mum and Dad now. Will you be okay?"

"I'll be fine."

And I mean it.

62: #SIXMONTHSLATER

I did it. I have a job. At Lidl's. I applied for it just after Christmas, and I started a couple of months ago. For the first time in my life, I have proper responsibilities. And you know what? It's not too bad. I kind of like sitting in my chair, with my till, chatting with the old dears about their days. Bread, milk, gin—ooo, Doris, planning a party? Sure, I'd give it up in a heartbeat if anything else came along, but for now, I'm enjoying having my own money, my own life.

Shame I still haven't managed to get my tooth fixed, but if I save up a little longer I may manage it. Mum says that she'll help me, give me some cash, but I couldn't do that to her. She's seems to be coping much better now. I think all of this was a bit of a wakeup call for her, too. She's gone to the doctor, had her medication changed. She's still fragile, but I worry less about her these days. She's even managed to get Bratley to go to school—went to an appointment with the Educational Welfare Officer and everything. I'm rather proud of her for that. Although she's not proud of me; she's had to get Brat a new phone, one that Tori hasn't tracked. I'm going to pay her back, of course. Phones aren't cheap.

Amy's fine, too. She's thick in the middle of exams right now, but when they're over, we're going to Magaluf for a week.

We got a cheap deal because we're going before the school holidays. I even went swimsuit shopping with her. She picked a tiny string bikini. I picked out a sturdy one-piece and a massive sarong. Hey, baby steps, right? When we came back from buying them, Patrick joked about how he wants to come with us now, just so he can ogle us. Yeah, he hasn't changed one bit. He's a good guy at heart, though, and it meant a lot that he decided not to hold my trollish past against me.

Tori's identity remains a mystery. No one can work out who they are, or even what they were getting out of this elaborate scheme. It's kind of scary, not knowing. I find myself watching people and wondering: Is it you? Or you? Or maybe you? I don't like being this suspicious, but I can't help it. You never know about people, not really. You never can tell.

The police eventually gave me back my laptop on the condition I gave up my life of trolling. I feel very lucky—they reminded me I could be prosecuted for some of the things I've done. To be honest, they didn't need to say anything. I've learned my lesson, very much the hard way. There's no way I'm going back to that life. I barely go online at all at the moment. Maybe at some point I'll pluck up the courage to post some art again, or at least venture back onto social media. We'll see.

My shift starts in an hour, and I need to get the bus. One of the girls who works there, Ellen, gets the same one, and we're going in together. She's a bit older than me; she has blue hair and a tattoo on her foot that reads *One Fat Bitch*, which I think is pretty awesome. She's big, but she certainly isn't fugly. She's invited me out for a drink this Friday. I might take Amy with me, for moral support.

Another good thing about working in a supermarket is I

can bring home dinner, so the cupboards are rarely empty now. I'm thinking fish pie. They do a good ready-made one, with lots of salmon in it. For me, that's almost healthy.

See? I'm trying. And for now, that's good enough.

TOPICS FOR DISCUSSION

1. What experiences have exacerbated Beth's insecurity about her weight?

2. Why does Beth get a rush out of trolling "the Beautiful People" on social media?

3. How does Amy upend Beth's assumptions about "Beautiful People"? What problems does Amy have in her life that aren't obvious on the surface?

4. In what ways are Beth and Brad similar? How have they responded differently to the stresses of their home life?

5. In what ways are Patrick's comments about Beth's weight harmful, even though Beth recognizes that he doesn't mean them maliciously? How does Beth's view of Patrick, and his of her, evolve over the course of the novel?

6. As she falls for Tori, Beth becomes convinced that the internet can foster genuine connections between people who haven't met. What kinds of online communities and interactions might make this possible? What kinds of online interactions create distance between people? How does Beth walk this line in her relationship with Tori?

7. Beth comes to realize that most people haven't figured out the secret to happy, fulfilled lives and are "just winging it." Aside from Amy, give an example of someone who illustrates this reality for Beth.

8. On some level, Beth has known all along that her trolling is wrong. What else does she realize about her behavior after Dizzy's crisis? What does she realize about Tori?

9. Why did Beth lie about being enrolled in university? How does this compare to her other deceptions? Do you agree or disagree with Beth's reflection that this is "the worst thing" she has done?

10. What does Beth come to understand about her mother's depression? How do you think it is similar to and different from Beth's emotional state after Tori's betrayal?

11. Why do you think "Tori" targeted Beth? Who do you think "Tori" actually is? If you were to write an epilogue from Tori's point of view, what motivations would it reveal?

12. In what ways is Beth changing her life at the end of the novel? How do you think the choices she's making now will affect her future?

ACKNOWLEDGMENTS

So many people shaped this book. Thanks to my Lovely Agent (it warrants the capitals), Sandra Sawicka, who has supported me every step of the way and continues to do so every day. My wonderful editor, Amy Fitzgerald, who "got" Beth straight away. Julie Harmon for copyediting, Parisa Syed for proofreading, and Emily Harris for her wonderful cover and interior designs. Allison Hellegers of Rights People, who helped find *Fugly* a home with Carolrhoda Lab. My most wonderful friend Jane Colebrook, who helped me immeasurably not only by typing up the first draft but also by allowing me to talk out my ideas. The Word Cloud (now called Jericho Writers) members for their help, encouragement, and support, especially Debi Alper and Emma Darwin for their marvelous Self-Edit Your Novel course. And last but not least, my family—my husband, Grant; my daughters, Lucy and Emily; and my mum and dad, who have supported me in this little dream turned big. (See, it was all worth it in the end—I did it!!!) Oh, and Mum? Sorry for the swearing . . .

UNEXPECTED.
ECLECTIC.
ADVENTUROUS.

For more distinctive and award-winning YA titles, reader guides, book excerpts, and more, visit *CarolrhodaLab.com.*

ABOUT THE AUTHOR

Claire Waller is a secondary school English teacher who works with teenagers with mental health issues. She is the author of two adult horror novels, *Predator X* and *Nine Eyes*. *Fugly* is her first YA novel. She lives in Portsmouth, England with her family.